A CONTEMPORARY ROMANCE NOVEL

Until the very end...
Whenever that may be

A STOLEN MELODY DUET #2

K.K. Allen

Books
by K.K. Allen

Sweet & Inspirational Contemporary Romance
Up in the Treehouse
Under the Bleachers
Through the Lens (Coming in 2018)

Sweet & Sexy Contemporary Romance
Dangerous Hearts
Destined Hearts

Romantic Suspense
Untitled, Coming Soon

Young Adult Fantasy
The Summer Solstice Enchanted
The Equinox
The Descendants

Short Stories and Anthologies
Soaring
Echoes of Winter

Copyright

To my readers who took a chance on something new, fun, and different! Lyric & Wolf thank you. <3 Mwah!

destined hearts

Chapter One

Lyric

"What'll it be, Lyric?"

A choice like this shouldn't be hard. Not for me.

Seven weeks ago I stepped on a tour bus with bad boy rock star, Wolf Chapman, and did the one thing I promised myself I wouldn't do. I fell in love. Practically zip lined right into it. I took all the right precautions to prevent the fall. I was strapped in tight, with lessons learned from past relationships weighing down my heart, and so I took off, clueless about what would be waiting for me at the bottom.

It wasn't a gentle landing. No, I stumbled and smacked right into Wolf—literally—in an elevator. And then he said my name.

That was the moment everything changed. Our worlds had officially collided in a whirlwind of false pretenses and good intentions to stay far away from each other despite an immediate and festering attraction. An insufferable feat.

But it didn't take long for Wolf to start breaking down my walls as if they were his to break. It started with just a crack on the surface when he called me out for avoiding living my life. He saw right through me. But that little crack wasn't enough, apparently, because he proceeded to sledgehammer off another chunk when he found my private song lyrics that I'd thrown in the trash. Without knowing they were mine, he holed himself up in a room and turned them into something amazing. He titled the song "Dangerous Heart," wrote a melody for it, and sang it on stage to a crowd of thousands, making it an instant viral sensation.

He loved my lyrics. What's worse, when he found out I was the mystery songwriter … he started to love me.

Our relationship was doomed from the beginning. Both of us were suffering from past regrets and self-imposed rules that we told ourselves would keep us safe from each other, from falling, from ending up right where we are now. We knew we'd only leave disaster in our wake.

I tried to be smarter this time.

Wolf made it impossible to stay away.

He grew persistent. Vulnerable. It took everything in me to resist him, and I failed miserably, letting my walls collapse around me in defeat. Because although he was still a bad boy with layers upon layers of issues, he was *my* bad boy. And I was his Lyric.

It's been forty-eight hours since the morning I woke up to a social media explosion that made me out to be an unfaithful whore. Not unfaithful to Wolf, though. Unfaithful to Tony, the lead singer of Salvation Road and my asshole of an ex-boyfriend.

Tony showed up when I was floating on my cloud of bliss, and he shattered everything Wolf and I had. That night changed everything. It falsely exposed me as a cheater because the media is clueless to the fact that I left Tony months ago when I caught him fucking my best friend. Yet somehow in the public's eye, *I'm* the unfaithful one.

It's all lies. And this… *This* is exactly why I didn't want to date another rock star. Well, it's one of many reasons.

But this is what inevitably happens when I follow my heart. I get hurt. And then I hurt others.

Wolf didn't deserve to get caught in the crossfire. He trusted me with his heart—something he never thought he'd trust another person with after losing his mother to cancer. Yet he trusted me. We managed to build something amazing … and now that it's broken, I'm not sure if or how I can fix it.

I'm sitting in the main conference room of Perform Live, the tour company I've worked for since I was fifteen. A panel of executives sits across from me at the table, multitasking on their phones and laptops. None of them gives a shit about the gravity of this situation for me. To them, I'm not a person. I'm a means to an end. Someone they deliver a paycheck to in return for making them look good. At the moment, they don't look so good.

I've just been given two choices, and they want my decision immediately. Wincing, I release my hand and set it on the table. It's safe to say my anxiety is at an all-time high. I've scratched my poor scalp to shreds over the past two days, and it stings as I anxiously rub the side of my head with my fingers.

"Let's go over the terms again," I say, stalling. I know what the terms are. There are two contracts in front of me. One frees me from all contractual obligations of Wolf's tour, but it also releases me from my employment with Perform Live. The other has me rejoining the tour—but as an assistant to the tour director, Doug. It looks like he'll give up the luxury of his office to take the reins from the road, making my former position as road manager obsolete. I'll become a ride-along. A joke. It's clearly a filler position, halfway between a groupie and a road manager because I'm no longer trusted.

Either option is humiliating. While I wish I could say I did nothing to deserve this, that's not entirely true. Wolf's band manager, Lionel Crawley, may be a prick with a gigantic stick up his ass, but I should have been more careful on the road. It may not be written in my contract, but mixing business with pleasure is an obvious no-no. They hired me to do a job, and that should have been my primary focus. Not falling in love with the lead singer, even if his mind and body are sexier than chocolate covered strawberries.

I never stood a chance.

Wright Stevens, CEO at Perform Live, clears his throat to speak. "Lyric," he begins, "you're like family here at Perform Live, and you're a valuable asset to the company. I hope you'll choose to stay with us."

Wright is normally a kind old man. He's been with the company since its inception in the seventies, and like Doug, he has a soft spot for me because of his history doing business with my parents. It seems, though, in any situation that puts a negative spotlight on his company, that soft spot is replaced with cement. Although his words seem kind, everything about him is hard. Unforgiving. His expression, his posture, even the crease between his graying, bushy eyebrows seems to be stuck in permanent disappointment.

He continues, "Our PR team is working on calming down the rumors, and all will be dissolved soon. You can trust us."

Trust. I scoff. This coming from the company that has no qualms with letting me go if I don't make the decision they want me to make. This is so frustrating.

"But an assistant?" I ask, simmering with dismay. *This has got to be a joke.* "My job wasn't the problem. *Tony* was the problem."

Wright nods carefully, but I can see that he's not entirely convinced. "We understand this isn't what you were hoping for, but it will take time to smooth things over. It's not a permanent decision. If the situation was unsalvageable, we wouldn't be pushing you to go back on that tour at all. Besides, the options were presented by Wolf's team first; you can stay on tour or leave without responsibility to the contract. And we agreed to them, but we had to add our own stipulations. I hope you can understand."

So, Wolf is inviting me back on the tour, but he's also giving me an out. How should I take that? That he doesn't care if I stay or go? And on top of that, even though I've worked at Perform Live for close to a decade, they're okay with letting me go because of a one-time slip-up.

Okay, so maybe it was more than one time. I had to end my contract with Salvation Road prematurely too. Maybe it's true; I'm not as great at my job as I thought. I sink into my chair, letting the shame beat down on me.

"Can't you just put me on another tour? Or maybe I can work here in the office for a while..." I look around, knowing that is the worst idea ever.

Staying stationary has never been my thing, especially when it comes to the music business. But I'm not sure if I have the courage to go back on that tour, assistant or not, if Wolf is done with me. Eventually he'll go back to being the rock star he was before meeting me, happily noncommittal. It's the only life he knows. I'd have to witness things I don't know if I have the heart to see. I'm already broken, but *that* would end me.

"I'm afraid not, Lyric. If you choose to leave the tour, then we will have to let you go. It would be hard to find you another gig after this, no matter who your parents are. And we all know you're not an office worker. Your heart wouldn't be in it."

While he's speaking, the rest of the panel looks anywhere but at me—at their phones, their computers, the lovely view of the bay out the window. They are totally and utterly done with me. As this sinks in, more blood rushes to my head in a boil. I want nothing more than to get their attention. I let Wright's words sink in before I speak, and I'm ready to burst. But I aim for a calm rebuttal first.

"What do my parents have to do with any of this, Wright? You know I work damn hard to stand on my own two feet. Their involvement is null."

He looks beaten and malnourished at the start of new conflict. I almost feel bad. *Almost*. "Of course you do, Lyric. I was just making a point that not everyone has the luxuries that you have had. Your name is well-known. Other road managers work years to get their foot in the door with artists like Wolf and still never get the opportunity you got. Maybe you could afford to remember that the next time."

What the fuck?

I stand, and my chair grates across the porcelain floor. I hope I scratched something. "The next time? What do you think it is I did wrong, exactly? I was dating him; so what? I still did my job, and a damn good one. Is there suddenly a rule against fraternizing with the talent?" I raise my eyebrows.

This is where I should stop, but of course I don't. He lit the match; he just didn't know he tossed it on a pile of dynamite. "What about marrying them? Wasn't your wife one of your *clients*? Yet, you're telling me *my* career is on trial."

Wright stands, his own chair slamming into the wall behind him. He furrows his eyebrows in fury—*I guess they do move*—and crimson colors his face. "Young lady, let's not make this personal."

Thank God there's a large wooden table separating us, or we'd be spitting our words directly into each other's faces. "You, sir, made this personal by mentioning my parents."

There's a flicker in his eyes as he acknowledges I'm right. He gives it two beats and then lowers his voice. "I apologize, Lyric. I shouldn't have mentioned your parents. Your reputation in the industry has been above par until this incident. Even when you left Salvation Road, we overlooked it. Unfortunately, this situation has leaked to the public. The damage is done, and now you must decide. Our response to the matter is final. We approve either of the two options presented. We'll look at your position again when your contract with Wolf is—"

"What about Tony?" I'm fuming. Despite his apology, he's not answering my questions. My own guilt aside, on paper, I did nothing wrong, and he knows it.

"I'm not following," Wright answers dryly.

"Tony physically violated me, and Wolf stood up for me. Tony should be exposed, and Wolf should be cleared of the rumors. It's unfair to his reputation, not to mention mine."

Wright's eyes shift to the rest of the panel. At some point, probably during the screaming match, their focus moved to where it should be: this meeting. Now they're all just looking around at each other, baffled, as if I had no right to bring up Tony's name.

"That will be up to Tony's label to decide. We just book the tours."

"But I'm *your* employee. Have you even talked to the label?"

"Lyric!" he shouts. "How we choose to handle this situation is our business, not yours." The poor old man is shaking. He sucks in oxygen like he's been starved of it.

My heart is hammering as I glance back down at the papers. I'm not going to win this war today, but this isn't over. No fucking way. If Perform Live isn't going to do anything about Tony, I'll find a way. I'll file charges if I have to, and then it will be public knowledge.

"We'll excuse ourselves while you think about it," Wright says. "Would you like anything? Coffee, tea, water?" Wright's polite tone makes me want to carve my name into the hideously expensive conference room table. The other executives are already out of their seats and heading for the door.

"Whiskey," I say dryly and plop back into my seat.

Wright chuckles as if we haven't just been slinging angry words back and forth. "One whiskey coming up."

He's gone before I can tell him I'm kidding, and then I'm reading the contracts again, line-by-line.

I'm definitely going to need that whiskey.

"I should have just quit," I'm telling Terese over drinks a few hours later.

My friend's normally perky eyes scan me sympathetically as she throws her long, blond strands up into a messy bun and then reaches for her beer. We found a hole-in-the-wall bar in town and ordered some cheap drinks and food. Not because we need to save money, but there's just something comforting about eating dive bar food in a dark establishment. Punishing myself with grease and booze seems like the perfect distraction from what about I'm to return to.

Terese and I recently reconnected when I ran into her at Perform Live before Wolf's tour. She works for the local tour team now, but we met a few years ago when Tony booked a three-month gig at a hotel in Vegas.

Salvation Road was given the opportunity of a lifetime when they signed that Vegas contract, one that contributed largely to how quickly they blew up. As soon as the three-month run was complete, their new single debuted at number one, and their new album dropped one month later. It climbed to the Top 10 on the charts almost immediately. Waves were made, egos were riding high—but then just six months ago they hit their crest when their newest release flopped. The wave broke. And they've been drowning ever since—in competition. In booze. In drugs. They're lucky they have a hit single out right now, charting just one spot below Wolf, but that number one album was what they desperately wanted. I'm lucky I got out when I did.

"You're stronger for seeing this out," Terese says, firmly. "The circumstances are shitty, but you're doing the right thing."

I frown. "I guess it's only two more shows, and then I'll have a week off to get my shit together."

Terese laughs and takes a swig of her beer. "You sure you don't want to come to Florida with us?"

I shake my head. The band will be in Miami for the week following the tour to record "Dangerous Heart" and take a short break. Derrick, Wolf's drummer and best friend, invited Terese since they've been having a ridiculous amount of phone sex. She's taking a week off work to be with him. Surprised the hell out of me. I knew they liked each other and had been talking casually, but this seems like a huge step for both of them.

"Definitely not." I shudder, thinking about how awful that experience would be. Wolf has rented a large house for his band. Rumor has it, it will be a nonstop party house. The band's ready-and-willing fan club is already on alert, with girls from all over the country booking trips to Miami in hopes of meeting the guys. It's the perfect opportunity for Wolf to go back to his manwhoring ways on tour. I'm definitely not putting myself in the same house as him to have a front row seat of the action. No, I've already made plans to take that week to regroup, fly to Seattle to tie up some loose ends I left behind when Tony and I broke up, and meet up with Deloris—my live-in nanny from the time I spent living with Destiny.

"Why not? Don't you think you two will get back together?"

Terese is such a sweet person. She has no idea what it's like to date a rock star like Wolf. She's getting a taste of it with Derrick, but she's fresh to the game. She doesn't understand that the minute things get rocky, Derrick will have a slew of distractions and countless other women to dip his stick into.

If I'm being honest, I'm torturing myself thinking about how Wolf has probably already forgotten me. There's no shortage of rock skank to go around, and they literally line up for Wolf. All he has to do is take his pick.

"He was pissed when I left him." I shake my head sadly.

"Then why don't you at least apologize? I don't understand why you're being so stubborn."

"I've tried calling him! Not even an hour after I left, I was texting and calling him like a crazy person. He must have blocked me because my messages and calls stopped going through. If he won't even talk to me, then what kind of chance do we have?"

"Of course he's pissed," she sighs back at me. "The real question is, why aren't you trying harder?"

"Because," I start, trying to find the words. But I'm not even completely sure why I left with so much anger like that back in LA. Of course I was reacting to the situation with Tony and to our fight, but it's more than that. Fixing things with Wolf would mean divulging why I hold so much resentment toward my parents, especially my mother. I just want to forget the past. I don't want to have to explain it to anyone, but it doesn't look like I'll be getting that wish anytime soon.

"It's just … complicated. I've loved the music scene my entire life, but it's also led to all the people closest to me hurting me somehow. I should have never given myself to Wolf like that. Not so fast. It was reckless. As much as I care about him, I can't stray from the path again."

"What if he is your path?"

I stare at her. Something tugs in my chest at her question. Words don't come.

"Lyric, this is coming from someone who wasn't there, so you can completely ignore everything I'm saying. But as your friend, someone who is listening to you now and seeing your pain, I don't think Wolf is someone you should give up on. Whatever your parents and Tony did to you, fuck them. You're letting your past control you. Don't give them the satisfaction. You deserve to be happy, and you deserve to be loved the way it seems like Wolf loves you."

I swallow. Fuck. There's a thickening in my throat and my eyes grow heavy with the weight of an oncoming flood. We sit in silence for a moment before Terese excuses herself to find the bathroom, leaving me alone with my thoughts.

God, I miss him. So much. It hurts to think about. By putting up these walls again, I'm bracing myself for the worst. But what if we *can* fix things? Wolf might be hurt, but I can get him to trust me again. I can make things right with him again. I have to.

With my eyes pressed closed, Wolf invades my mind. His morning kisses that start on my lips and work their way down my body until he has me fully awake and aching with pleasure. His strong arms that wrap around me the moment we're alone because he's missed me. His sweet lovemaking, because "fucking" always seems like such a crude way to put it when each moment together makes a home in my heart and soul.

And then an image of Wolf's caramel eyes invades my reminiscence. A shiver runs down my spine as I remember the eyes that could see through me like no one else's.

The buzzing of my cell phone pulls me from my dreams of Wolf. I sigh and look at the screen. Every muscle in my body locks. I swear I can feel the blood drain from my face as, with one shaky finger, I press a button on the screen to view the message in full.

Terese comes back to the table, and it's clear she's noticed my reaction to the message.

"What's wrong?" she leans over to see my screen. "Shit, is that your mom? Do you seriously call her Destiny?"

"She lost the title of Mom a while ago. I'm not sure she ever wanted it." I'm fully aware of the disdain dripping from my tone.

"What is she saying?" Terese is still trying to catch a glimpse of the words on my screen.

I laugh and pull my phone up. I can trust Terese. After clearing my throat, I read the text aloud in my best Destiny accent—sophisticated arrogance at its best. "Heard you're in town. Did you think of maybe calling? I am still your mother."

Terese rolls her eyes. "Is she for real?"

I smirk and toss my phone on the table. It makes a clattering noise when it connects with the sticky metal, and I groan. Terese snatches it from where it landed and reads the next message out loud in the same affected tone. "Lunch tomorrow. My driver will pick you up from your hotel at noon. Dress appropriately."

Terese laughs. "What does she consider inappropriate?"

I laugh too. "Anything ripped. And leather is completely out of the question. You know, just in case the paparazzi were to snap a picture. It would completely ruin *her* reputation." I roll my eyes. "Oddly enough, the paparazzi always seem to know where she is, and she's never surprised to see them." As I'm saying this, I realize how coincidental it is that she wants to see me just after I've gotten some social media attention.

"She plans it all?"

Without hesitation, I nod and take my phone back. "Of course. As a kid, if there wasn't publicity in it for her, I was on my own. I couldn't wait to escape her when I was eighteen. I barely saw her, but when I did..." I shudder. "She thinks parenting is like playing with Barbie dolls."

"And you haven't seen her since you left her house at eighteen?" I can tell Terese feels for me, but it's clear she also can't believe how much I hate my mother. No one can. But that's only because no one knows the truth.

"I've seen her a few times in passing, but they were never planned meetings." I shrug. "Life is better without Destiny around asking me for favors."

"Are you going to see her?"

I think about it for a second and stare at my phone. With a quick tapping of my fingers I reply, "*See you tomorrow,*" then look back up at Terese. "I guess I am."

She's still my mother. And I'm curious.

The rest of the night is better. We change topics from Wolf and my mother to Terese and Derrick. Turns out they haven't been talking as casually as I'd assumed. They've been talking every single day, and they've been out a few times since the band has been back in the area. He wanted to see her tonight since they're only hitting venues in southern California this week, but she chose to have dinner with me instead.

"It's fine," she reassures me when I find out she cancelled her plans. "I would have had to drive back early in the morning for work anyway. Besides, I'll be at the next two shows, and I'll see him all next week. Just don't be surprised if you don't see me very much."

She looks happy. I'm glad. Terese is a good girl, and Derrick doesn't seem like the stereotypical rocker, anyway. If anything, Hedge, Wolf's bass player, is the ladies' man of the bunch, but even he's pretty harmless.

"I get off at five tomorrow night," she says, "and then we can have a car drive us out to Irvine, unless you wanted to leave earlier than me. I could meet you there?"

The thought of seeing Wolf any sooner than already planned makes me nauseous, so I shake my head. "I'll wait for you. Just call me. I'll be ready."

That's a lie. I'll be anything but ready to see Wolf again.

Chapter Two

Wolf

I'm in my dressing room, taking a moment to get into the zone before making my way down the crowded backstage hallway and toward the crowd already screaming my name. A steady syllable ricochets through the stadium, repeating with a passion I wish I could feel the way I used to.

Wolf. Wolf. Wolf.

I'm trying to use the chanting to rev me up, to feel it again—the electricity passing through my body, the buzzing in my chest. I should be fired up by now. The crowd is eating out of the palm of my hand, and I'm not even on stage yet. What happened to the days when I would pop a boner at the first sound of my fans' affection? When my veins would fill to the brim with adrenaline so powerful I thought I could fly?

Where the fuck are my wings?

I need that feeling back. I need to remember what I first fell in love with. The music. The stage. The rush of it all. If I don't get my shit together, they will notice. I'm sure they've already started to. The past two shows have easily been my worst. Like Derrick reminds me, I'm shit at hiding my emotions. My dial only has two settings: hot and cold. Neither is good. There's only been one person who could balance me out. But she knocked the wind out of me when she left, and I've yet to get back my balance.

Someone bangs at my door. "Wolf, let's go!"

It's Crawley. I grit my teeth and fight back a growl. That fucker's going down. He's already been kicked off my bus. I'm just playing my cards right, biding my time until I figure out what he has on me and why he feels like he owns my ass. I'm done with him, but Crawley isn't someone you want to fuck with without a well-thought-out plan.

I throw the door open and breeze by a rosy-cheeked Crawley like he's nothing. Rex, my bodyguard, is waiting. He walks beside me as venue security flanks me on all sides to get through the growing crowd as quickly as possible. Something has got to be done about this crowd control issue. It gets worse at every show.

A sadness fills me at first as I realize, like I have been every single fucking night since she left, that Lyric isn't pressed up against one of the backstage walls where I can reach for her and taste her lips briefly before letting the crowd own me. She was always there—until she wasn't anymore.

The chanting quickens and I start to feel the vibrations in my chest. It's the energy I've been missing for two days now, and it feels good. It's not as powerful as it once was, but it's something.

"Thank fuck." I say it out loud, but the screams from the crowd drown out the sound of my voice. I embrace the energy as it seeps into me, slowly at first, until it's barreling through me at a speed that feeds my soul.

This is what it's all about.

The second I reach the backstage staircase, someone tosses me a microphone.

I wait for the band's cue, and then…

"Owooooooooooooooo!" I'm howling as I run onto the stage until I hit the spotlight, and then I howl again, throwing my head behind me and arching my back, eliciting the loudest welcome I've heard since Lyric left.

Okay. I can do this.

Wake up. Coffee. Breakfast. Rehearsal. Hotel room check-in. Lunch. Soundcheck. Nap. Work out. Dinner. Concert. Meet and greets. Club. Bed.

Fucking clockwork. It's not always in that exact order, but fuck. It's nonstop. I'm busy. But it's the only way to suffocate my thoughts of Lyric. Every time she pops into my mind, like she has now, I get heated. Angry. On the verge of a fucking meltdown.

That's what she did to me, and I hate her for it. I hate her for everything I love about her. And I *hate* that I want her to come back.

Doug is doing a fine job filling in for Lyric as road manager—not that I expect any less. He's had a lifetime to get this right. He's simply not her. I used to wake up excited to see her every morning, even before we were anything to each other. She was always the one I sought out in the frenzy of a late-night concert crowd. And I could always count on her to be there.

I don't know if Lyric is coming back on tour or if she's quitting the scene altogether. I know what her options are, and while I thought I'd gotten to know her well, I have no clue what she'll decide. Not after how she left.

The wait is agonizing. What if she doesn't come back?

I'm not ready to answer that question. She's supposed to make her decision today. If she decides to come back, she'll be here tomorrow. If she doesn't… *Fuck.*

"Hey, Wolf."

I'm hopping off the bus when I hear the sound of a purring woman call my name. Flipping my shades over my eyes, I turn marginally toward the voice and see a sight that was once the norm. Four scantily clad women lean casually against the bus, giving me that look—the one that tells me they're down for whatever. No-strings-attached fun.

Looks like Rex has already started allowing the girls to line up outside the bus again, probably at the band's prodding. They never could believe I was changing my ways for the long haul. They probably think I need a good fuck to get Lyric out of my head. Maybe they're right.

The woman who called my name starts to walk in my direction, a syrupy smile on her overly made-up face. A panic alarm sounds off in my head, and before she can get any closer, I turn and walk toward Rex, Crawley, and the band, who are all watching and waiting near the hotel entrance.

Most of them look amused by my disinterest, but Hedge throws his head back and howls with laughter. *That little shit.* I punch him in the gut as I walk by, not trying to hold back.

"What the fuck?" he cries as he curls over himself, and the rest of the band laughs. It wouldn't be the first time Hedge got socked by one of us. As the trouble maker of the bunch, he usually deserves it.

Derrick jogs up from behind me, throwing an arm over my shoulder and pulling me toward him. "Hang in there, dude. Everything will work out. Don't let fucking Hedge, or Crawley, or any other one of these dicks mess with you. I'm proud of you, man. Seriously."

I roll my eyes at Derrick's pep talk. He's way too optimistic as always, and while I appreciate it when it comes to music, I could do without it right now.

"Thanks, man," I return, because no matter how I feel about my situation, Derrick is still my best friend, and he means well.

"I'm sorry, Wolf," Hedge cries loudly behind me in a playful plea of desperation. "Forgive me!"

Derrick chuckles, and as annoyed as I am, I can't help but smile just a little. No fucking way I'll let Hedge see it, though, so I flip him the bird over my head instead.

The band is the closest thing to family I have, but when it comes to the feelings I have for Lyric, I keep them to myself. Ever since she stumbled into that elevator at Perform Live, she was it for me. Nothing was going to get in our way while we figured out what was going on between us.

But things have changed drastically since then. And the band knows as much as I do that it's just a matter of time before I let some hot rocker chick ride my cock. It's been three days without sex, and I can already feel the ache. The need. Pleasuring myself to memories of Lyric can only hold me over for so long. I'm unfulfilled. Damaged. Lyric completely ruined me.

"Want to grab a bite?" Doug hands me the keycard for my room, just like Lyric used to do at every hotel stop, and I can't help but frown. Everything reminds me of her, and it feels like someone's punching me in the gut every time. As much as I'd rather hole myself up in my room and drown out the noise in my head with an action flick, I need to eat, and Doug's a good guy.

"Sure, man. Let me shower and shit. Where to?"

As Doug nods to the restaurant on the other side of the lobby, I can't help but focus on the silver of his hair contrasted against California tanned skin. Doug and my father are probably around the same age, somewhere in their fifties, and neither have a wrinkle on them, except for that crinkle around the eyes when they squint or smile. I haven't seen my father's smile in years, but the resemblance is haunting.

"We don't have to stray far. We'll grab something quick before soundcheck," he says.

I head to my room and jump in the shower, wondering what comes next. For the tour, and for Lyric and me.

A lunch invite from Doug isn't unusual. I've known the dude since the first tour we booked with Perform Live, when he accompanied us on the show from hell. Seriously. Everything that could have possibly gone wrong, did. Imagine us showing up to our very first venue for our first-ever show in front of more than a couple hundred people and seeing clouds of smoke and three fire engines rolling up to the joint.

It was a kitchen fire, no one was harmed, but the fire marshal refused to allow anyone inside. So Doug, being the quick thinker that he is, quickly made arrangements for a parking lot show instead. It was badass, and in retrospect, probably one of our best shows ever.

He's always been a great guy, so it's no surprise he and Lyric are so close. Given the timing of this lunch, I wonder if he could be prepping me for Lyric's return ... or permanent exit. The latter radiates an unkind pressure in my chest. I pound on it with my fist a couple times, replacing one pressure for another one that I *can* control. But nothing helps. I take a deep breath and lean against the wall of the shower.

I think about her face. It's not hard. Every time her sweet face comes to mind, I imagine her wrapped up in the white sheets of my tour bus bed, her sage eyes pointed out the window with the morning light streaming down, illuminating the glow of her perfect skin. How can someone so angelic wreck me so completely?

I groan as the image of her transforms to the face of the Lyric that left me. Seething with anger. Too worked up to see what she was doing to me. To *us*. I just watched her as my forever became the end. She walked out and took all the good parts of me with her. My Lyric gutted me.

For the first twenty-four hours after her exit, I couldn't see straight. She called and called, but I ignored every single one. Eventually, I blocked her number, knowing that any conversation we would have in the heat of the moment would end badly. After delivering Lyric's options to Perform Live— coming back on tour or letting her walk without penalty—I unblocked her, but it's only messed with my head. I've spent the past two days with my phone in my hands, waiting for a goddamn call that may never come.

Do I want to see her again? Do I want her to come back on tour?

Yes.

I'm afraid of what I might do if she doesn't. But that doesn't mean I'll forgive her for leaving. My biggest fear is that she won't even ask for forgiveness.

I can't keep doing this to myself.

I turn the shower to cold, and the temperature changes fast. I gasp but take the sting, forcing a breath and letting the icy water drown my thoughts of her.

"You look like shit."

Doug is already sitting at our table in a sectioned off corner of the beach-themed restaurant when I stroll in fifteen minutes later, and he's eyeing me with full-on criticism.

I roll my eyes, then blink against the blinding sun streaming in through the large paned windows. "Thanks. I feel it."

He takes a sip of his tea. At least I assume it's tea. That's all the guy seems to drink, besides alcohol. "Would it help if I told you she made her decision?"

I shake my head, fighting my subconscious. "Nope." *I'm a fucking liar.*

"You're going to be a miserable ass either way, eh?" He laughs, and I can't help but quirk my lips in a smile.

"Most likely."

The waitress comes over and hands me my whiskey water. I raise my chin in thanks, then look at Doug. "Don't give me trouble. I'm doing my best."

He shrugs. "You won't get any judgment from me. You're the tamest rock star I've had the pleasure of accompanying on tour. And that includes Mitch Cassidy."

I chuckle. "Tame, huh? Fuck. I've really lost my touch, haven't I?"

"A little." He smirks. "But it's not a bad thing. As long as it's not affecting your show. And as far as I can tell, it's not."

"Really? Because I feel weak on that stage, man. Like a robot, just going through the motions. All I can think about is her."

Why the fuck did I say that out loud?

"It's not my place to speak for Lyric, but you should know—and maybe you already do—but she's been through a lot of heartbreak in her life. I witnessed the worst of it, and it wasn't pretty. A young girl like that shouldn't have to face what she's faced. But she's strong. And she may have done something you didn't agree with, but I'm sure she was just protecting herself. She had to do a lot of that growing up, and she does it the best way she knows how."

I'm pissed. Of course Doug is on Lyric's side. They're like family. But her past doesn't change her present. A present that includes keeping the truth about what drove her away a secret—even from me. That's an issue I can't just ignore.

"I'm sorry man, but that doesn't change our situation or how I feel right now. I would have stood by that girl for anything, but she wouldn't even talk to me. She just left. Everything before that moment just feels—"

Doug leans forward and pointedly pushes my drink in front of me. His eyes are glued to my face like he's examining me with his professional tour director eyes. I can feel them burning a hole in my fucking forehead. He sees too much. And now he knows too much. I take a swig and let him talk.

"Don't go there," Doug warns, carrying a fatherly tone that both warms and irks me. "You don't know what will happen in the future. Take it from someone who's been in this business far longer than you. The rock star life can be the best thing in the fucking world, but the moment you let someone into that world, that control you once felt is gone. Out the window. You and Lyric, you're both so young, and this thing between you is still new. You're figuring how your worlds work together. Don't let the media destroy everything you've built. And don't let Lyric's past get the better of you two, either. She just needs time to open up is all. She needs to grow up and let go of her past so her hurt no longer defines her."

"She seems to have a good handle on herself," I retort. "She's independent. Determined. What's missing?"

He leans back in his chair and shrugs. "I think I'd be crossing the line if I went into specifics. She's still living in her parents' shadows. But she needs to pave her own way. Working for Perform Live may not necessarily be the best thing for her, but she's not ready to see that."

By the time our food comes, we've thankfully switched topics to the remaining two days of the tour.

"So," Doug starts.

Cringing, I lean back in my chair, readying myself for the news I've been not-so-subtly agonizing over. It's unavoidable, like a damn opened wound that's attached itself to a Band-Aid—it's going to be a bitch to rip off.

Something twists in my chest, but I make no move to stop him when he continues. "Wright called me today, and we had a long talk about the tour and Lyric. She's coming back."

My next breath is heavy, as if I've finally come up for air after days of drowning, and a whoosh of relief fills me. I'm unprepared for the emotions, but I do my best to mask them. "Tomorrow?"

I don't miss the small smile on Doug's lips. Guess I'm shit at hiding things. The bastard knew what I wanted to hear. Of course he did. "Not sure. I know she'll be at the final show, and then she'll be flying with you guys to Florida for the studio record. The company wanted me to take the reins, but things changed today. I'm getting pulled onto another show." He sighs. "I wasn't planning to travel for a good while, but they need someone to babysit Tony after that catastrophe between you guys. Rumor is, he completely lost it after that night. Went rogue on his band, missed a show, and now he's hitting the drugs hard."

I lean forward, raising my brows in intrigue while trying not to reveal my satisfaction. If it weren't for Tony's bitch move that night, showing up at the club and manhandling Lyric like he owned her, none of us would be in this mess. Lyric would be here, with me, in bed. Under me. Full of me. Loving me.

Shaking my head to rid my mind of useless could-have-beens, I focus on Doug. "I don't know how much of it is true, but with Lyric back out on tour with you, the company doesn't want to take any risks."

"Makes sense. So you're taking off at the end of this leg?"

Doug nods. "Looks like it. I'll get Lyric settled back in, and then I'm off."

"I appreciate you telling me. And thanks for filling in this week. You're always welcome on my bus, man."

He smirks. "Thanks. Figured I'd tell you first. I should have told Crawley already, but I can't stand the guy. Sorry."

I shake my head. "Don't be. He's toast, anyway."

"I can't say I'm not happy to hear that. He's definitely got it out for Lyric. You know he tried to alter the terms of her tour contract, right? I probably shouldn't be telling you this because it's a non-issue, but Crawley is a real sleazeball. I don't trust him."

My face flames. "What?" I try not to shout, but I know my voice is raised. I lean forward and grip the table so hard my knuckles turn white. "You've got to be fucking kidding me."

"I wouldn't lie. He added a line about her working for him, not you. Some shit like that. The legal aid from your attorney's office totally missed it and sent it through to the label. The kid should have been fired. You're telling me no one talked to you about this?"

I shake my head, face flaming. "Crawley handles communication between the lawyers and the label. I trusted that he'd pull me in as needed." Shaking my head, I take another swig of my drink. "I'll call Fredrick today. Sounds like I need to be point of contact from now on." Fredrick has been my attorney for years. Crawley talked me into hiring him when the band was beginning to catch the eye of labels.

Doug nods. "Luckily the label caught the new wording, questioned it, and had it fixed immediately. Crawley claimed it was an accident. The legal aid who missed it is a bumbling idiot, if you ask me. Your attorney must be fond of the kid because he got off with a warning. Reprieve for a first time fuck up or something like that."

I don't care about the legal aid. "Crawley's got to go today. Fuck." I pause, wondering how much I should tell Doug. "He says he's got something on me. I wanted to find out what it was before I cut him loose so I wouldn't be blindsided."

Doug leans back, stress lines creasing his forehead. "Do you have any idea what it could be?"

I shake my head, gritting my teeth and still reeling from the legal fuckup. "Not a clue. I think he's full of shit."

Doug nods. "He's probably bluffing. I've known the dipshit too long. It might be better to take your chances at this point and cut him loose."

"Thanks, Doug." I'm grateful for some sanity in all of this. "You wouldn't happen to want to take the job, would you? You'd make a helluva band manager." I flash him a grin.

Doug chuckles. "Thanks for the offer, but I'm quite looking forward to babysitting Tony. Keeping him far away from you and Lyric."

I'm looking forward to that too, actually. "All right, then. Well, if you know any band managers who are up for the job, let me know." I toss my napkin on the table and stand to shake Doug's hand.

"You're a good man, Wolf."

"You too, Doug."

Walking away from lunch, I'm feeling a million different things, but above all, I'm anxious. *She's coming back on tour.* And I have no fucking clue what comes next.

Chapter Three

Lyric

She's thirty minutes late when she finally breezes through Buon Appetito, a quaint Italian restaurant in downtown San Diego. I'm surprised. Although the establishment is high-end, the customers seem laidback, mostly dressed in casual attire. I fit right in, ripped denim and all.

I have to laugh when Destiny takes a look around the room and lifts her nose slightly in distaste. She, unlike the rest of us, is dressed in her finest pressed beige and white suit. Not much of a rock star look, but Destiny has always been a little different. She's more socialite than rock star, anyway. And I have to admit, she looks Botoxed to perfection.

There's no question that Destiny Lane is a world class beauty. Flawless skin, thanks to her premium gold and caviar-laden products and enough smarts to stay out of the sun. Perfect figure, thanks to Frank, her personal trainer, and her Jennifer Lopez-inspired diet of green smoothies and kale salad. And her hair is every woman's dream—thick, long, waves straightened daily, every strand perfectly in place.

Lunch patrons turn to watch her walk through the elegant restaurant. As a little girl, I was in awe of the attention she always drew to her—like a spotlight followed her every move. Not much has changed.

A tight smile settles on her face when she finally sees me. Her eyes sweep over me, and I know she's fighting the criticism already. I'm dressed just as I normally do: tight, dark designer jeans and a ribbed dress shirt. I can tell she wants to pick me apart, but it doesn't bother me the way it used to. I look classy—especially with the Louboutins on my feet, the one concession I'm willing to make to placate my mother.

"Destiny." I stand and kiss her cheek, returning her tight smile with one of my own. It hurts to pull off, then again, my face still has its full range of expressions, free from fillers and enhancements.

It's so strange to hug the woman who gave birth to me but feel like I'm embracing a complete stranger. A twinge of anger surfaces, as it always does when I think of her, at just how much I've missed out on because of her. A reminder of why I don't do this. Why I never respond to her desperate text messages. Because today, she'll ask me for something that will send me over the edge. I already know it. It's just a matter of time…

"Lyric, you look well," she greets. Even after all these years of having this awkward, strained relationship with my mother, her formal tone hurts.

"Thank you."

The waiter comes to take our drink order, and Destiny orders for us. A bottle of their best red. Of course. When another server brings a basket of bread to the table, she shoots him a glare and waves her hand, gesturing for him to remove it. My eyes go wide at her rudeness. Not only that, but I'm starved. I want that bread. I snatch a piece from the bowl before our server retreats.

My mother shoots me a disapproving glare, but I don't care. I pick at the bread while staring back at her blankly. "I don't have much time," I say, careful not to betray my distrust and annoyance with the tone of my voice. "I have to pack for a tour."

She nods and taps a perfectly manicured fingernail on the table. "Yes, I understand you've been off the road for a few days. I can't say I'm surprised you're returning to that tour. But can I ask why? Haven't you embarrassed yourself enough? First Tony, and now this Wolf character?"

My insides immediately boil. There was no warning, but then again, there never has been. I was stupid to think the insults would take a few minutes to roll in.

"Excuse me?" I narrow my eyes back at her, and she takes in a quick breath.

"Lyric, you know how I feel about you touring. People don't understand why you aren't making more of yourself."

Because I don't ever want to be like you.

"People?" I ask before shoving a bigger bite of bread in my mouth. "Or you?" Crumbs fly out of my mouth, and I'm completely satisfied to see a look of disgust cross her face.

"I know what you're doing," she says, her voice low. Then she sighs again. "I'll never understand what you see in that job of yours, but fine. I have no strength to change your mind. However, your personal life, now that it's public knowledge, is bad publicity for me too."

Surprise, surprise. She only cares because of her reputation. Not mine.

"I don't care how this looks for *you*." My voice is low but starts to shake, so I pause a moment to try again. "Tony physically assaulted me. Did you know that part? *He's* in the wrong here. Not me. Not Wolf. Wolf was just trying to protect me. His name has been tossed in the mud more than mine, yet no one seems to care that he's innocent in all of this."

My mom snorts. That's right; Destiny Lane snorts. "Well, I hardly doubt his reputation isn't deserved. Everyone knows about that boy. Why, dear, do you fall for these hopeless rock stars? You should know better than anyone that no good will come of this relationship."

"Stop!" I say, louder than I meant to. Heads turn in our direction, and my face blanches.

"Look." I lower my voice and stare back into her cold, brown eyes, which are wide with surprise at my outburst. I'm glad I got my eyes from my father. Hers are as dark as her soul.

"My love life and my job are of no concerns of yours. If you care about me at all, then please, keep your judgments to yourself. Your words don't affect me anymore, Destiny. Nothing you do does."

She gasps. "I am your mother," she whispers back, but it's dripping with contempt.

"You haven't been a mother to me for as long as I can remember." I push my chair back to stand, but she holds out a hand in a desperate attempt to get me to stay.

Predictable. She wants something.

"Stop," she pleads. "I wanted to have a nice lunch with you. I'm sorry. I didn't mean for things to turn so ugly."

I do stop. Her expression is one of genuine concern, but I can't help but think there's something else beneath the surface. She definitely wants something from me.

I sigh, giving in for the moment. "Can we talk about something else?" I try. "What have you been working on?"

And that does it. There's nothing that does the trick better than allowing Destiny to talk about herself. For the next hour as we drink our wine and eat our food, Destiny tells story after story about what she's been working on, how her label plans to rebrand her and bring her back on the music scene with a splash.

By the time we've finished our food, my eyes are sore from eye roll restraint. I'm about to excuse myself to call for a car when she drops the bombshell.

"So," she says casually, "Soaring Records is looking for some original material. The rebranding part is going great with the photoshoots and the producers we picked out, but the label wants me to emerge with something as fresh as my last album." She takes a sip of her wine. "I can't believe it's been six years since I released *My Forever*."

My Forever. I can't believe she has the nerve to bring that up.

"You want my lyrics."

No need to ask the question. This is what Destiny is after, what she's always been after. At least she's asking this time. I've never meant a thing to her, except for when she can use me. Thank God I'm not seventeen years old anymore.

She's smiling brightly. "Honey, I thought we could work together. You know, collaborate? It would take you off that awful tour and out of the spotlight. Give the rumors some time to die down." She's smiling as if we've been great friends our whole lives. "And we could be closer, like we used to be."

Bullshit. She's delusional if she thinks we've ever been close.

She continues, "Maybe you can make a name for yourself as a songwriter. It's the perfect solution to everything you're going through."

I sit back and assess her bright smile. She's halfway gone on the crazy train. "Destiny, I *am* a songwriter. Just because there's nothing published in my name, that doesn't make me less of what I am. Or did you forget?"

She sighs and slouches in her seat, as if my words are an inconvenience to her plan. "Lyric, not this again."

"Yes, this again, because you brought it up. You disappeared for months, made a record out of *twelve* of *my* songs, and never once mentioned me. Your daughter. And when I confronted you about it, you waved me away like I had no right to expect anything more from you." I'm seething, but I do my best to keep my voice calm. "How could you do that to me? Every single song credited you as the writer and composer. *Just* you.

"Tell me, Destiny, how the hell did you manage to arrange an entire album all by yourself?"

Destiny's eyes dart around the room, but no one is paying attention to us anymore. "Keep your voice down. I thought we settled this long ago. It was a misunderstanding."

My eyes widen. We never settled anything. "A misunderstanding?"

She's not worth the years of pain I've suffered trying to understand how a mother could steal something so significant from her own child. Songwriting was my dream. My everything. And then she just disappeared for months, only to return home with a hit record, and zero acknowledgements to the original artist. Me. Destiny Lane is a thief.

It still breaks my heart. Every single time I think about it. And there's no way I'm ever going to let her hurt me like that again.

I pick up my things without another glance in her direction. "You'll manage on your own, Destiny, just as you've always done. It's been a pleasure."

With that, I gather my purse, slip out of the seat, and exit the restaurant. There will never be closure with Destiny, and I've given up on hoping for it. All I want in life now is to move on and away from the pain and sadness. It's time to get ready for my next challenge.

Tonight, I see Wolf.

Chapter Four

Wolf

"Hello, Irvine! You all ready to rock this shit?"

They scream. I smile. It's like someone ignited a fire in me again, and I'm one with the crowd, letting them feed me. I've been starving, but all it took to get my metabolism back to normal was knowing that I'll be seeing *her* again.

I give Derrick a nod and he's on it, knocking his sticks together and leading the start of "Joke's on You." We kill it. Song after song, we're at the top of our game. And then it's time to introduce "Dangerous Heart," and like they do every night, my eyes search the side stage for Lyric. Of course she's not here yet. It's just habit at this point, but waiting to see her again is driving me crazy, and the crazy feelings fuel an impromptu speech.

"Have you ever had your heart broken, Irvine?"

I hold the microphone out and let the crowd scream back at me.

"Me fucking too, Irvine. Me fucking too. So you know what we're going to do tonight? We're going to do a little cleansing. I'm going to heal your broken hearts, Irvine. Tonight, we're going to dedicate this next song to all the heartbreakers out there. For fucking us up. For getting the best of us. For breaking down our walls and then slipping right in there. Like a snake." I laugh as the crowd roars. "Thanks to them, we know what it's like to live. To feel real pain." I lift my fist in the air like I'm making a toast. "Thanks for reminding us why we're better off alone."

"Marry me, Wolf!" a girl in the front row screams, and I get another brilliant idea. I'm still riding the adrenaline wave as I scan the crowd.

"I need a volunteer."

The loudest fucking roar rains down on me.

"I used to have someone to sing this song to, Irvine, but not anymore. I'm going to need some help with this one."

The guys are trying to get my attention. I can see Hedge inching closer and looking at me with his "Are you crazy?" eyes, but I don't care.

The house lights come on, and the screams grow to frantic volumes as arms wave wildly to grab my attention. I'm scanning the front few rows for a victim, without a clue as to what I'm looking for. And then I spot her. A cute brunette with an amazing rack. I could do her. She looks nothing like Lyric, but I could pretend. If Lyric wasn't on her way back to the tour, I just might consider it.

All I know is that this current of energy running through me has taken days to return, and I want to ride the wave as far as it will take me.

I grin at my possible victim, and her eyes widen in shock. She looks around in question before returning her gaze to mine.

Chuckling, I nod my head in her direction. "Yeah, I'm looking at you, honey. Come on up here."

This time she doesn't hesitate. She has to push and pry her way through a couple rows of elbow throws and shoves, which I wish I could help her avoid. Luckily security is able to reach over the blockade and lift my sweet, innocent victim into the press pit before boosting her onto the stage.

"Hi." I kiss her hand, and I can practically see her heart beating in her chest.

I pull my eyes up to her chocolate-covered ones and notice the strange combination of panic and adoration in her expression. I chuckle lightly, loving the effect I have on her. I'd bet money this girl wouldn't walk away from me like Lyric did. She'd probably drop everything just to step on my tour bus, be my girlfriend, and hang by my side. Something Lyric wouldn't even consider.

"What's your name, sweetheart?"

She nearly melts as she looks into my eyes. "Suzie."

I'm distracted by the sight of Trey, one of our stage crew, setting a chair in the center of the stage. Smiling, my palm meets the small of Suzie's back and I walk her to the chair. When she makes a move to sit, I wrap an arm around her shoulders and face the audience first.

"Irvine, I'd like to introduce you to the beautiful Suzie. Suzie, say hello to Irvine."

I place the microphone against her lips—the microphone that just touched mine. I think she realizes this too, because she shudders under my hold. And now I'm thinking of Lyric again, goddammit.

"H-Hello, Irvine." Suzie giggles.

Goddamn, this chick is good for my ego. After pulling the microphone away, I help Suzie get seated. Despite my impromptu mission to prove a point that Lyric doesn't own every inch of my heart and soul, the guys are good sports about it all. Derrick kicks of the song with a four-count, and the rest of the band follows as if this is the most normal thing in the world.

It's natural by now to sing the words without even thinking about the meaning behind them. While "Dangerous Heart" was originally inspired by Lyric's asswipe of an ex-boyfriend, there's something deeper in her words that connected us before we could stop it. Something that tugged on emotions deep within me that I could never tap into myself.

My mom's death changed a lot of things for me. I turned a blind eye on my future and started living only for my band, syncopated melodies, and charged up crowds. I let music consume me in all ways possible until the darkness I was living in became my norm. Everything was perfect—I thought. Until these fucking words entered my life, bringing me closer to the woman who would ruin me.

Two wrongs don't mend hearts like ours
Two wrongs can never break our fall
I give, you take, it's no mistake
We're in too deep, losing sleep
Trying to forget what started it all

I serenade Suzie's soaked panties off. Not literally, of course. That's not allowed. But she's cute, so I circle her playfully like a shark before grinding on her a little bit. I even let her run her hands over my thighs and arms while I curse the visions of Lyric that are now clouding my thoughts. I try to hide it by giving Suzie flirtatious smiles and suggestive winks, and she eats it up.

I'm sure the guys will give me shit later for giving an innocent girl a lap dance, but what can I say? She's into me, and the need to feel wanted again is strong. Besides, the crowd is going insane as they live their fantasies vicariously through Suzie. It's a win-win for all.

But it's all an act. A show for the fans, the media … and myself. A weak attempt to fill the emptiness Lyric left in my chest when she walked out of our hotel room, leaving me wondering if I'd ever see her again.

The song ends, and I help Suzie up from the chair and swing her around in a bear hug. She giggles and puts her lips on my ear. "Let me return the favor."

My face blanches. *Shit.* Sweet, innocent Suzie just went dirty girl on me. There was a time not long ago that I'd have given in to her advances without hesitation. I'm still playing the game, but the game makes me feel like a piece of shit, like I'm cheating. The feelings are starting to piss me off.

I give Rex the nod to take her from me, so he does, handing her a backstage pass and taking her to the side stage to let her watch the rest of the concert. Unfortunately for me, that also means Suzie-Q has free reign to seek me out after the show.

A vision of my former self pops into my mind as I realize how just a few months ago, I lived for all the girls like Suzie waiting for me backstage. It was so easy. But the last thing I need tonight is sweet and dirty Suzie on my bus when Lyric could return to the tour at any moment.

Not that I want Lyric on my bus either. *Nope.*

Twenty minutes later, we finish our set and run off the stage. While the guys head to our dressing room, I nod at the venue security team, who are helping us navigate the crowd backstage. Meanwhile, I'm searching for Rex. Usually the dude is right on my ass the moment I leave the stage. Where the fuck is he now?

Then everything happens too fast. We're nearing the back exit of the venue when my eyes connect with a familiar pair of green eyes, a fire of pain and anger behind them. She's standing right there under the exit sign as if she's waiting for me. And by the look in her eyes, it's clear she caught the show, including my performance for Suzie. *Shit.*

Just looking at my Lyric wearing all that fury, I can almost forget my own pain. My first instinct is to walk faster. Pick her up and slam my mouth onto hers. Then fuck her full of all my anger. My dick has a lot of pent-up aggression, and after the show tonight, he's ready to go.

I'm with her in seconds, staring back into the eyes of the one who stole every good piece of me when she left. But before I can get a word out, Rex approaches me with a wide-eyed Suzie on his arm. She's fast as she disconnects with him and latches onto my arm.

Fuck. No. No. *No.*

My eyes dart to Rex, who glances at Lyric and then me. His face contorts, registering the mistake, and then he starts to pull Suzie back. He must have gotten my signal completely wrong up on that stage. I haven't nodded for him to bring me a girl in months. I guess with things so messed up between Lyric and me, he assumed wrong.

He struggles a little with Suzie, who's determined to cling to me. Meanwhile, the look on Lyric's face is making my heart sink into the bottomless pit of my stomach. "Well played, Wolf," Lyric says. "Well played." I can almost hear the slow-clap beneath her sarcasm.

What the fuck do I do now? I expect her to run away again, and I'm ready to chase after her. But when she lifts up onto the balls of her feet and takes my face in her palms, my every muscle trembles in response. Then her mouth is on my ear. It takes everything to not grip her waist and fall into her. It's all I want. But I remain frozen and waiting, until her words seep like vapor into my soul. "I came back, Wolf. Don't make me regret it."

With a final look of disappointment and warning, she turns away and pushes through the exit door.

Suzie snuggles up to me, and I shake her off with a muffled apology and a look at Rex to signal for him to keep her back.

I'm on fire when I throw the door open to storm after Lyric. It slams into the exterior wall, and I swear it's about to detach from the hinges. Her back is to me, and I see she's dressed in jeans and a leather jacket. Her ass just as curvy and tight as I remember as it moves briskly toward the bus lot— but now's not the time to stare at her ass.

"What the fuck?" I yell after her.

Lyric swivels around and shakes her head. "You're pissed at me. I get it. But right now, I'm pissed at you too."

I step forward and get in her face, so close that our foreheads are almost touching. I missed this face. So much. It's full of emotion and vulnerability, and it still makes me want to give her the world. But right now, I'm fueled with too much fury at her audacity to give her anything but my anger. She deserves nothing more.

As I'm gearing up to unleash my pent-up rage, I realize that part of me is glad she witnessed my exchange with Suzie. What did she expect when she left with no promise to return?

"You have no right to be pissed off." I growl through my annoyance.

Her eyes flare. "I don't?" she spits.

I shake my head. "Nope. You left. Remember?"

"Were you really going to fuck that girl?" She pushes into my chest with all her strength, but I barely flinch. Her eyes search mine, giving me a chance to answer, but I'm too fired up to be the comfort she needs. "Really, Wolf? Three days and you're already getting your dick wet." She uses my chest as leverage to push away and spin around.

I throw my head back and laugh. This is too good. Too fucking good. Our reunion wasn't going to be pretty, I knew that, but this was not what I expected at all. Does she really think I'd be able to get it up for anyone just days after she left me so cruelly? This isn't something I should have to explain, and right now, I have no desire to.

I stalk after her, not caring who can hear us. "You think you can just walk away and expect everything to be waiting for you when you come back?" I yell. "Think again, Lyric. Things have changed."

She faces me with narrowed her eyes and nods. "I see that. I didn't expect it to happen so soon. I fucked up, but I came back, hoping to work things out. If that's not what you want, then fine." She's shaking now. She points a finger at the backstage door we just walked out of. "That's not love, Wolf."

"I didn't do anything!" I explode. "Not that it matters, Lyric. What the fuck do you know about love, anyway?"

She flinches as if I slapped her. "Then what *was* that back there? Just because we had a fight doesn't mean you go out and screw the first girl that comes along."

My body is vibrating with anger now. "What makes you think she's the first one?"

When Lyric's face drains of color, I want to take it all back. She swallows and I reach for her, but she steps away and shakes her head. "Don't fucking touch me."

I grit my teeth and plant my hands on my hips, lowering my head as I take a deep breath. "I said that to piss you off. Fuck. I'm sorry. I haven't—"

She takes another step back.

I move toward her again, closing the gap, and grip her face in my palms. I'm gentle despite the fact I feel nothing but. "Don't do that. We both know what it meant when you walked away. It was over. It *is* over. You're back for your job, not for me. Perform Live wanted to can your ass, but I didn't want that to happen to you. Or at least I wanted it to be your decision. *That's* love. The fact that I still want to protect you even though you royally screwed my heart over. Maybe you should think about that instead of getting pissed at me for venting on stage."

She's quivering in my hands. She knows I'm right. She's scared. I know my Lyric. My heart still beats for her. My heart still belongs to her, but there's no way I can hand it over again. At least not so soon.

Right now, nothing makes sense. My determination to stay away from her even if she did come back on tour is already failing.

I remove my hands from her cheeks and step away, needing to distance myself from the one person with the power to destroy me. The one person who almost did. Then I head straight for the bus without turning around.

Now I'm the one walking away. Let's see how Lyric likes it.

Chapter Five

Lyric

Wolf has every right to hate me, but he still loves me. I feel it in his touch. I see it in his eyes. He missed me as much as I missed him.

But he's pissed. Hurt. And I don't blame him. I need to find a way to make this better, except it's not happening tonight. That's for sure.

Terese is driving to the hotel with Derrick, so I walk to bus number two alone. My things have already been loaded, and a bottom bunk has been reserved for me, so I crawl into it and sigh. I don't want to be antisocial with the crew, but I need to be alone right now. I need to calm down.

I expected a confrontation of some kind with Wolf, but I didn't expect to find him straddling some girl on stage and serenading her with our song. He may not have fucked her, but the fact that he could have and probably even wanted to hurts like hell.

My alone time is over seconds later when Melanie rips my curtain open and beams. "Hey sexy." She crawls onto my bed, sits beside me, and nudges my shoulder gently. My eyes fall to her high waisted plaid skirt first, and then her black and gold Wolf tank beneath a checkered leather jacket. That's when I notice the strand of hair that's resting over her shoulder. She's dyed it in a red, pink, and purple ombre, and it's fucking brilliant. On her. I'm not sure I could ever pull that off.

She eyes me, warily. "You okay?"

Before I know what's happening, I feel a tear running down my cheek. I wipe it away and force the rest of my emotions back into my stomach. Melanie pouts but doesn't say a word.

"I'll be fine," I say. "Things will be weird for a while, but I'll deal."

"Probably," she agrees sympathetically. "That was quite the argument you two just had."

I groan. Everyone must have seen that, or at the very least heard it. "He's so mad. He's already moving on."

She nods slowly as if she's deep in thought. "Between you and me," she says quietly, "Wolf has been off his game since the moment you left. I don't know what that was about back there, but he hasn't touched another girl. Trust me. We've all been waiting, wondering when it was going to happen. Because he's Wolf, and it will eventually happen." She throws me a frown. "Sorry, Lyric. Just being honest."

"It's okay."

"We weren't sure if you were coming back, though, and he's been a total wreck. The guys have been pushing girls on him like a candy factory."

That feels like a low blow. When I was touring with the band, I spent so much time with Wolf that I didn't make much time for rest of the guys. We didn't exactly forge the strongest of bonds, so when I left, they probably didn't care less. They were probably happy to have Wolf back to themselves.

"You must not have seen Suzie then," I say, "because he was all about it."

"Oh, I saw Suzie." She snorts. "Wolf wasn't going to touch her."

I narrow my eyes. "He all but stuck his dick in her on stage, and they were on their way to his tour bus after the show."

Melanie rolls her eyes. "I'm not convinced. We were out last night, and the hottest chick any of us had ever seen straddled him in the club. I swear, I even got a boner watching her."

"I do not want to hear this, Mel." The knots in my stomach twist and tighten.

She laughs gently. "Let me finish. He couldn't get her off him fast enough. And then he left. Alone."

"Really?" It's been my worst fear, the fact that Wolf would move on so soon. I've been hoping I would make it back in time before anything did happen, but after seeing him with Suzie, my hopes definitely faltered.

"Really." She says, her eyes wide to convince me. "The band is calling him Broke Dick." She giggles. "Hedge tried to pick the chick up after Wolf dumped her off his lap, but she was so pissed." There are tears from laughter in Melanie's eyes, and I must admit it helps a little.

I smile. Not because of Wolf's new nickname, but because I feel even more confident that we can fix what I broke if he hasn't touched anyone else. We can get back to what we were. We have to. I just need to get him alone first.

"C'mon," Melanie says. "Come hang out with us. We all missed you, and it's the last night we can hang out before Florida."

"Will you be in Florida too?" I ask, surprised. I thought it was a band-only thing.

Melanie's eyes widen. "Oh my God. Wolf rented the biggest house. You know about it, right? We're all going. You have to stay with us. We can be roomies!"

"In the house?" I ask, then shake my head. Perform Live called me before I got to the concert and told me they needed me in Miami with the band, so I'll be in Florida against my wishes, but there's no way I'm going near that house. "No. I'm staying in a hotel. I wasn't going to go at all, but the tour company would rather me be close to the band while we prep for Europe."

Her eyes sparkle with mischief. "We'll see about that."

I lean back to study her. "What do you mean?"

She shrugs. "Just that I highly doubt you and Wolf can be in the same city and not find your way to each other. Anyway, come hang out tonight. We always do an all-nighter on the last night of tour. It's tradition, and you're a part of our dysfunctional family now, whether you like it or not."

I give her my best sideways glance, already giving in.

Melanie laughs knowingly. "We'll be at the hotel in an hour, and then it's party time. You're coming, even if I have to tell everyone the party is at your place."

"Jesus, fine," I groan, burying my face in my hair to hide my smile. I like Melanie. I like this crew. And I'm part of this group now, whether Wolf forgives me or not. My time spent with them will be much more enjoyable if I step out of my Lyric and Wolf bubble to enjoy them.

When we arrive at the hotel, Doug's already there waiting with our hotel room keycards. I linger behind, letting everyone else get theirs first so I can have some time alone with him. It's nice to see a friendly face.

"Good to see you, darlin'," Doug says as he scoops me up in his arms.

His hug is long, strong, and comforting, an embrace that almost brings me to tears. "Good to see you too," I say into his shoulder.

He pulls away, smiles, and gestures for me to follow him to the elevator. He presses the button for our floor and waits for the door to close to speak. When he does, it's with an upward curl of his lips and sideways glance. "Glad to see you and Wolf were able to speak civilly to one another."

I cringe. "Don't start."

He chuckles. "I'm just giving you shit. It was pure entertainment on the bus with Crawley after that. Wolf kicked him off his bus days ago, but Crawley couldn't wait to give Wolf a piece of his mind. Wish you could have been there to see it."

Groaning, I lean against the wall and fold my arms. "I'm surprised Crawley's still here after everything."

"Well, rumor has it he won't be around for long. But I'd stay clear of him if you can."

"Ha. That won't be a problem. I'm just a ride along now." After everything that went down, I have no intention of getting anywhere near Crawley.

Doug looks like he's bracing for impact, taking a deep breath and tensing up, like he's about to drop a bombshell on me. "Looks like I'll be headed out after tomorrow's show.

They need me on Tony's tour. And Wright thought it would make you happy to have your job back."

"What?" Why wouldn't Wright call to tell me that? After the shouting match between us the other day, I was certain the last thing he'd ever do was give me what I wanted. And as grateful as I am to have my job back, I'm a little sad to know Doug won't be around. I was looking forward to spending time with him again. He's always been like a second father to me. Someone that had my back when I wouldn't let my father help me. Someone who kept his eye on me when I was sixteen, working odd jobs around the tour company to experience everything I possibly could.

"Job's all yours again," Doug confirms. "There's something I should tell you, though." His warning tone hits my gut. I'm so over bad news.

"Out with it."

He gives me a sympathetic look. "Your father will be in Miami."

"No way." My jaw drops and I shake my head. "Is this a coincidence?"

Doug shrugs. "Kind of."

I narrow my eyes, pissed because I know Doug way too well to accept that answer. "Kind of?"

"He asked about you. I told him where you're going to be, and he made arrangements. I just didn't want you to be surprised. He wants to see you."

I shake my head in disbelief. "Doug. Seriously? I already have too much drama to deal with right now. I can't spend this time mending my relationship with my father, too. That one goes way too deep. What's up with everyone lately, anyway?" I uncross my arms and toss my hands in the air. "First Destiny and now Mitch. I just can't deal with this."

Doug tilts his head. "What about Destiny?"

With a half-sigh, half-groan, I bite my lip. "She basically harassed me until I agreed to meet her for lunch, so I saw her earlier today. She's still a bitch."

He throws his head back and laughs. Doug only has loyalty to my father. He dislikes Destiny just like everyone else who's gotten close enough to see past her bullshit exterior. "Let me guess. She asked you for a favor."

I smirk. "Turns out the label is relaunching her career. Rebranding or some shit. She's looking for new material, and guess who she thought would make the perfect songwriting partner?"

"That woman has some steel balls, doesn't she?"

"I told her no, of course. I don't even know how she found out I was in town."

We exit the elevator on the ninth floor, and Doug hands me the folder in his hands. Inside is all the room information for tonight's hotel stay. It occurs to me that I could find Wolf's room and go to him. But it might be less destructive if I happen to run into him at the party instead.

"All yours now," Doug says with an encouraging nod.

I smile. "Thanks. So, Mitch will be in Miami. You sure?"

Doug walks me to my room and pauses outside my door. "He'll be at the studio. But you know him, Lyric. He's not going to push, but he will try to see you. Make time for him. He's your father, and he misses you like crazy. Your silence is killing him. I get why you hate Destiny, but your father doesn't deserve the silent treatment."

"You don't understand, Doug. It's all just one big ball of pain. The only way I could cope with it over the years is by cutting off ties with them both. The moment I let my father in, I inadvertently let my mother in too. I need to stand on my own two feet right now, and I can't do that with them hovering over me, constantly telling me what I'm doing wrong."

"But your father would never tell you what to do. He'd never steal from you, Lyric. He's only ever wanted the best for you, but he would never try to control what that meant to you. That's all your mother."

"No, he wouldn't steal from me, but he's the one who sent me off to live with the witch. He was too selfish to see how wrong it was."

Doug nods. "Now that I'll agree with. He was being selfish to an extent, but he also wanted what was best for you. And you touring with him while you should have been in a real school, making normal friends... It wasn't the life for you. He knew that. He didn't realize what would happen when he sent you to live with her."

I push my door open, ending the conversation. "I know. Thanks for the warning. I'm going to get cleaned up and over to Melanie's. You going to the party?"

He makes a face and shakes his head. "No, thank you. Those days are over for me. I'm all about the bathrobes and overpriced, late-night room service."

I smile. "Okay, see you tomorrow."

He smiles one last time before turning to walk down the hall. "You're the boss."

Chapter Six

Wolf

It's midnight and I'm stepping out of the shower when my phone rings. I haven't attempted sleep. As soon as we arrived at the hotel, I ran to my room, changed, and went to the gym. I knew there would be a party, and I also knew Lyric would probably be there, so I decided not to go. I just need to stay busy. Knowing she's here is enough for me right now. Building up the courage to actually talk to her is a whole other story.

I ignore the call and immediately get a notification, so I check the text.

Derrick: Where are you? Hedge is trying to shove his tongue down Lyric's throat. At party. Room 912. Come now.

What the fuck?
All my calm instantly goes out the window, and I'm forced to throw on a pair of shorts and a shirt. That didn't take Hedge very long. I know he has the hots for Lyric, and let's be honest; there isn't really a girl he doesn't try to bone if given the opportunity.

I fly down the hall and pound on the door of Room 912 until someone opens it. I'm too blinded by my rage to notice who. I push my way through the crowd and through two adjoining rooms to find her. She's there, leaning against the bed's backboard, knees up, a red cup in her hand, and a smile on her face.

Our eyes connect, and I'm unable to pull away. Her smile fades and her eyes bore into mine with hope. My chest burns from the look she's feeding me, and I want to reciprocate.

Lyric always looks amazing, but I have a hard time controlling my dick when she removes her makeup and throws on sweats. And that's exactly how she looks right now. Natural and perfect.

And then I remember the feeling she left me with when she got in that car, and all thoughts of stripping her down and ravaging her dissipate.

She's shoulder to shoulder with Terese on one side, Melanie on the other. Hedge, Derrick, and Lorraine are on the bed too, facing them.

Everyone seems to glance at me at the same time. I realize I must look like a freak with my hair still wet and eyes as wide as a tarsier. Derrick raises his eyebrows, and the corners of his lips turn up in a smirk. And suddenly it becomes clear he was fucking with me. Dipshit.

The laughter starts. Derrick and Hedge are rolling all over the bed, holding onto each other and losing their shit. Melanie and Terese have their heads bowed together with giggles, and even Lorraine is smirking. By the look on Lyric's face, I can tell she has no clue what's going on.

"You asswipes are dead," I growl. But I don't pummel them now. I'll get them later. Right now, I need a fucking drink.

"Where's the alcohol?"

Lorraine hops off the bed and tugs me into the bathroom, her high, blonde, ponytail bouncing with each step. She mixes me some colorful shit that appears to be all alcohol, thank God, and hands it to me. She's a good friend.

"You okay, buddy?"

Instead of answering, I knock my cup against hers, then take a drink. I wince as the liquid fire burns my throat. "Ah, shit. What is this?"

She chokes back a laugh. "I have no fucking clue. It's potent though, ain't it?"

I shake my head and take another drink, opening my throat and gulping down the liquid without tasting it. "Perfect."

Lorraine smirks and walks out of the bathroom, leaving me to myself. Looking back in the mirror, I catch a glimpse of my fucked up hair and untidy stubble. I run a hand through my hair to make it presentable, but I know there's nothing I can do about my face now. I take a deep breath, trying to calm my nerves.

There's a reason I've declined every party invite since Lyric left: the fear of drinking too much and doing something stupid when my heart still belongs to her.

Unlike me, Lyric's not a big partier. She likes to go out and have drinks on occasion, but to get plastered in a hotel room with the band, the entire crew, and a bunch of random groupies is not her style. She would much rather curl up in my arms and watch a movie in bed. I loved those times with her. When the rest of the world would fade away. Our bubble was safe. Perfect.

I know how these douchebags get when they see a pretty girl. And Lyric is beyond pretty; she's stunning. I should have gotten here sooner, just in case any of these douchebags really did get the wrong idea and start hitting on her. I might be angry as hell at her, but Lyric's still mine.

Now that we're both here, I'm not sure what to do. Leaving is out of the question, but after our last interaction, being in the same room is probably not the best thing for us.

I slam the rest of my drink and pour myself another. When I walk out of the bathroom, Derrick and Terese are making out on the bed with a yawning Lyric still sitting beside them, slouching awkwardly against the headboard. Hedge has disappeared, probably afraid of my fist—as he should be.

Melanie bounces up to me, liquid splashing from her cup. "Hey, Wolfman," she says, slurring slightly. "See your girl over there? I think she needs a cuddle." She giggles, and I roll my eyes. They must have started partying hours ago.

"I think I'll pass," I say, loud enough for Lyric to hear me. My words don't really fire her up the way I want them to because the moment I look over at her, I can see her eyes drawing shut and her head tipping to the side.

"Shit!" I cross the room in three strides, catching her before she falls off the edge of the bed. "How much have you had to drink?" I ask as her eyes flicker open.

Her glazed eyes search mine, and the most beautiful, sleepy smile lights up her face. "I'm back, baby," she says, reaching for my face and caressing it with the lightest touch.

Even in my pissed-off state, I can feel the tingles crawl over my body. For a moment, I imagine we're back to our happy place, when I would take that beautiful mouth in mine and swallow her moans. And then her eyes stutter closed again, and she relaxes into my arms.

"Whose room is this?" I ask Melanie over my shoulder, but she's nowhere to be seen. Fuck. I turn to Terese and shake her foot to get her mouth off Derrick's. "Terese, whose room are we in?"

She shrugs, clearly annoyed that I interrupted. "Mel's, I think."

"Do you know where Lyric's room is?"

Terese shakes her head and leans back into Derrick. "Not sure." He pulls her beneath him and shoves his tongue down her throat.

I think I'm going to be sick.

Looking back at Lyric, I know I'm fucked. There's no way I can leave her here, but I can't exactly take her back to her room if I don't know where she's staying.

I curse under my breath. Lyric is weightless in my arms as I carry her out the nearest door and into the hall. As I'm walking toward my room, I steal a glance at her, and my heart thumps erratically in my chest. Her breathing is steady and there's the smallest smile on her face. I'm not going to lie to myself right now; it feels damn good to be holding her in my arms again. No matter the circumstances, I'm crazy about this girl.

Her eyelashes hover over her cheeks. Her skin is as light and flawless as I remember. I could caress her soft skin for hours. There was a time, not too long ago, when I did just that. The feel of her in my arms is as familiar as the memories of me pressing her against the rooftop wall at the Aragon.

Damn, that was a good night.

I push my door open and carefully carry her to my bed. I lie her down on the sheet so her head is on the pillow. Then I kneel down beside the bed and just stare. Her breathing is deep and even. There's no way she's waking up anytime soon.

What the fuck am I supposed to do now?

I scan her body and see her slippers dangling halfway off her feet, so I remove them and set them by the bed. Lyric always gets hot at night and prefers sleeping in her underwear—or in the nude, which was always my vote, so I remove her pants next, careful not to check out her panties. As much as I want to take a gander, I know it's not healthy for my dick right now. He's already getting excited. I leave her tank top and bra alone because there's no way I can deal with that, and then I tuck her body in under the covers.

After peeling off my own clothes and brushing my teeth, I curl up beside her and wrap my arms around her sleeping body. Before I can stop myself, I'm pressing my lips to the soft skin of her shoulder. Then I'm running them across her back, breathing her in and remembering how she would shake beneath me as I made her come. Every single time.

I groan into her hair, my balls already aching to the point that I think I might wake her up and make her beg for forgiveness, just to make her come again.

Why am I so pissed again?

Running my hands over my face and through my hair, I let out a frustrated groan. "Fuck." There's no way I can sleep next to her tonight.

I slip out of the bed, grab a pillow and blanket from the closet, and throw them on the couch at full force. Tossing one more longing glance over my shoulder at Lyric, there's only one thing I know.

I'm in hell. Right now. This is hell.

Chapter Seven

Lyric

It's been two hours since I woke up in Wolf's bed, confused and nursing a hangover, and Wolf is still dead asleep. I don't dare wake him. Right now, I'll take what I can get. If that means being as still as a board so that I can watch him sleep for the rest of the day, then so be it. I'll watch him forever.

He's usually a restless sleeper, kicking off the covers and reaching for something to hold onto. That something used to be me. Now, he snuggles with his pillow, squishing it so hard the seams just may come undone. One muscular leg hangs over the edge of the couch, and his mouth falls slightly ajar.

He's totally adorable.

Impatience breaks me a few minutes later after memorizing every detail of his sleeping form. I rip the covers off me, wondering for the hundredth time how I ended up in his hotel room wearing nothing but my underwear and tank top. I climb out of bed, and my toes land on my pants, which are lying on the floor next to the bed. I frown. Wolf must have removed my clothes. Well, not all of them. My top and panties haven't been touched.

I tip-toe to the couch and pull the pillow from his grasp, careful not to wake him. When I snuggle up beside him, his familiar skin warms mine. I didn't even realize I was cold before now. He's quick to wrap me in his arms like it's the most natural thing in the world. Like we were never apart and this is just another normal morning together.

And when I feel him grow thick and hard against my stomach, my heart starts to beat fast. I know I'm fully taking advantage of this moment, but I don't care. Wolf can yell at me later. It's worth it. He smells so good, comforting, like warmed oak and melon.

Pressing my lips to his chest, I shiver. Just one simple touch and I feel it all. Fear and hope crash like waves inside my rib cage. Fear that he'll awaken and push me away. Hope that he'll eventually forgive me.

As if Wolf can hear my thoughts, his hold strengthens around me. I've always loved the way I feel in his arms. Safe and secure. I've missed everything about him so much, but it's these arms wrapped around me that I've been yearning for every lonely night.

"Lyric," he says in a sleepy, whispered breath. It's enough to send my heart into overdrive.

My kisses create a trail from his chest to his neck and chin until I'm hovering over his mouth, just breathing. Sometimes I would wake him like this, searching his exposed skin with my mouth, exploring and treasuring the man that continued to surprise me. And then when I reached his lips, they would part for me, just marginally … just as they are doing now.

So I take it as my invitation, this time feathering my lips across his, sweeping it with my tongue in a silent plea to let me in. I think I might faint when his mouth parts for me. Our kiss deepens, and then a hand splays across my lower back, crushing my body against his hard one.

61

I moan into Wolf's mouth, our energy recharging and sparking the air. His fingers dig into my hip as I snake a leg over him and press down so he's hard against my entrance, our underwear the only thing between us—well, physically. In reality, there are a million things between us now, but I refuse to acknowledge anything except this.

His hands are on my ass. Mine are in his hair. We're frantic and panting, clawing at each other to taste more of what we've been missing. I shift my body again so I'm no longer straddling him, and I slip a hand into the waistband of his briefs. I'm not surprised to find him hard in my grasp.

"Fuck, baby," he moans, pushing his hips up so I'm fully gripping him. The fact that he's responding so eagerly fills me with entirely too much hope. I can't imagine he's already forgiven me, but maybe he missed me just as much as I missed him. Right now, nothing else matters.

Within seconds, I slide his briefs off and start to stroke him. His lids flutter open, revealing dark, desperate need. There's also confusion in his eyes, and I worry that he's going to change his mind. He doesn't want this—me—at all.

When he pulls away and sits up, I want to cry. But then he reaches for me, guiding me onto his lap, legs on either side of him, until I'm just inches away from his throbbing erection.

Wolf's palms rub up and down the top of my thighs as he looks at me darkly beneath hooded lids. "What the fuck are you doing, Lyric?" His voice is low and gravely, filled with hurt and desire. Such a dangerous combination. But isn't that what we've always been together? Two dangerous hearts that happened to find solace in each other's arms?

Although his voice questions what's happening, it doesn't look like he's going to do anything to stop it. But I give him time to decide.

"I missed you." I try softly, my voice breaking with each syllable as I roll my hips and inch up his lap. "And I want you inside me."

His eyes glide from my legs to the thin, black lace of my panties and linger there for a second before rocking his hips upward slowly. Wolf's jaw is hard, naturally built to intimidate anyone who crosses his path. While the furious look he's giving me now should send me running, it does the opposite. I feel myself quiver from the inside out as my abdomen clenches in response.

I anticipate him sinking into me and shudder while his finger moves along the edge of my underwear. His careful movements tell me he's considering his options. Should we, or shouldn't we? So I beg with a whimper for him to stay with me. I need this. I need him. And I think he needs me too.

He slips one finger beneath the fabric and gently strokes my opening, growling deep in his throat at the feel of me. His eyes close as if he's in pain. "Fuck, you're so wet."

His eyes open again, and he glowers at my shirt before giving it a tug. "Off." His voice is deep. Commanding. I pull the fabric over my head, and before it's even hit the ground, Wolf has unfastened my bra. I slip the material away from my body, letting it fall to the floor before looking back at him.

He's momentarily frozen, drinking me in and admiring my breasts. He's always been especially enamored by them. A hand runs the length of my side as his tongue slides along his bottom lip. His eyes darken before they flicker back up to connect with mine.

The connection sparks like dynamite in my chest, and I don't even realize I'm mimicking his movements until I bite down on my bottom lip and grind against his lap. I'm aching to ride him until he remembers how well we fit. How not just our bodies connect, but our souls.

My movement seems to have the desired effect because he takes both hands and rips my underwear down the center, leaving just enough room for his cock to slide into me. I gasp at the sound of the fabric shredding, and a fiery sensation fills my center, aching as raw desire pulses through me.

Wolf cups my breasts with both hands and squeezes gently. I moan, not bothering to be quiet. My heart races as his thumbs circle my nipples before rolling them between two fingers. I cry out from pleasure or pain … maybe both. Wolf could do anything to me right now, and as long as his hands are on me, I'm good with it.

He brings me forward until my breast meets his mouth, licking and then biting down harder than expected. I cry out, and he soothes the ache with another taste before pulling me fully into his mouth, torturing me as he devours both breasts like the hungry beast he is. God, I've missed this man. The way my body responds to him. The way he worships me with each touch.

I roll my hips again, trying to find friction against his hardness, but it's not good enough. I need to ride him. I move more aggressively so he'll get the hint, but a hand presses into my thighs to stop me. "What do you think you're doing?" The anger in his eyes is unmistakable.

My breath comes in pants as my frustration grows. "Don't you want this?"

He growls again, this time louder than the first. He removes his hand from my breast, and a rush of dread fills me.

"You don't make the rules this time around."

I open my mouth to ask what he means, but he's not ready to listen. His eyes are glazed and his finger is slowly rolling over my clit, dangerously close to entering me. "How does this feel?"

It takes a second to find my voice. "G-good."

"You want more?"

I nod eagerly, then swallow as his thick finger pushes into me, but only up to a knuckle. "That better, baby?"

The evil quirk of his lips tells me just how much he enjoys torturing me. I swallow over my erratic heart and move to push down on him, but he holds my waist steady to stop me.

"More," I plead.

He pushes in a little further, this time not trying to hide his smile. "Better?"

I glare at him now. He's toying with me more than usual. "No." With a swift move, I lift myself from his finger, grab his thickened length and place it at my opening, working my way down. I gasp as I remember with each inch how his girth stretches and fills me until I'm barely breathing.

Wolf chuckles knowingly as he squeezes my ass and presses me down toward his base.

Really? He's laughing at me now? I'll wipe the smile from his face soon.

As my muscles adjust to him on the descent, I know I'll be sore tomorrow, but it will be totally worth it. Being a few days out of practice makes everything feel like our first time, and I know he's feeling it too. That cocky look in his eyes is fading fast as my tightness moves firmly around him. There's no escaping now.

Once I'm fully seated, we both let out a sigh and hold each other's gaze. In this moment, all anger has subsided. We're together again, the way we're meant to be. I'm still made for him, and he's still made for me. No matter what happened, no matter what will happen, this is right.

Before I give into the eager drive inside of me, I lean forward, planting my lips on his. My heart is pounding as he weaves his fingers through my hair and grips the back of my neck before pressing my mouth harder against his. He's ravenous as he kisses me, his tongue filling my mouth in desperate strokes as he keeps me locked in place.

I didn't forget how good Wolf tastes. He gives and takes, gentle yet demanding. Kissing him is everything. *He* is everything.

I'm not even sure when I start riding him. I stay close, my movements small, but I press down with all my weight. We've had plenty of intense, quiet sex while on tour. We mastered it when we were trying to keep our relationship a secret from the band and Crawley. It was a lot like this. Slow and careful. Torturous and mind-blowing. Every time our bodies joined, my heart rate accelerated a little more. Just like it's doing now.

When I begin to feel dizzy from my racing heart, I lift my mouth from his and gulp in air. Wolf's mouth falls to my neck. I already know what's coming next, so I arch my back, allowing room for his bared teeth to drag down my sensitive skin until he's at the crest of my breast. At the same time, his hands grip my ass, shifting his pelvis to rock into me.

It's not until his mouth latches onto my breast again that I begin to completely lose myself. I feel the match light within me. Not much longer now.

Recognizing that I'm getting close, he plants both hands on my ass and pulls me away from him before slamming me back down. We both groan at the impact, and he does it again, wasting no time in between. He smiles and leans back so he can watch me lift and sink above him. I'm watching him right back, feeling weightless and free as his hooded eyes take me in.

He's at his breaking point. I can see it in the hardening of his jaw. I'm close to the edge too, but still trying to hold on, never wanting to lose this feeling again.

My mind fogs over, whirling at the feel of him, craving more of his kisses, more of his touches. The buildup is happening so fast. I fight and chase my orgasm at the same time, but all I really want is to live in this moment forever. The deep ache is spreading, and there's nothing I can do but let go.

"Wolf." I gasp in anticipation, throwing my head back and pressing my chest into him wildly.

My pace quickens, and each time he fills me I know I'm close to unraveling. I focus on steadying my breathing as sweat drips between us. Just as I'm about to come, he pulls his mouth away and meets my eyes with an upward curve on one side of his lips.

"I'm going to come," I sigh, and even as I'm saying this, my head starts spinning and the raging fire in me grows. It's no longer in my control.

His hands move up my slick stomach until he grips my breasts in both hands. I move again. "So fucking tight. C'mon baby. I'm right there with you."

A warm buzz is released over my entire body as I crash down on him again, my orgasm sending me spiraling into an abyss. I'm lightheaded, somewhere between heaven and hell. I'm flying. And then I'm falling. The fall is endless as I ride it out, screaming his name and letting him take control of my movements until he's releasing his own buildup inside of me.

I might black out for a minute. All I know is that I'm opening my eyes, and my arms are wrapped around a heavy-breathing Wolf. He's still inside me, and his arms are locked around my waist. We're breathing together, completely sedated. My body already feels sore, fresh from a crazy, sex-driven workout. Probably the best workout I've had in years.

"I missed you so much," I whisper, praying he doesn't pull away.

His silence crushes me, but I still don't remove myself from him. I'm not letting him give up on us that easily. "I know this was just sex." I hate my own words. "I know you're still pissed at me. But I love you. You're why I'm here. I'm going to figure my shit out, I promise. Whatever I have to do, I'll do it."

He sighs and kisses my shoulder, filling me with an ounce of hope. "I am pissed. And hurt. And fucking confused. I tell you I love you, and then you run away. I get that you have some big secret, but you didn't even give me a chance to understand it." He takes a breath. "I've respected your privacy, because I know whatever it is, it's hard for you. But, Lyric, I can't keep doing this knowing you're holding onto a secret big enough to tear us apart. Next time, you might not come back."

"Wolf," I plead. "I'm not leaving you again. I swear. It's you and me, babe."

He shakes his head. "No, Lyric. It's not that simple. You scared the shit out of me, and you broke me when you left. That's not something I ever want to go through again." He sighs again. "I don't know what the fuck to do."

"Can't we just start over?" I ask, my voice filled to the brim with emotion. "We're so good together. You can't deny that."

He looks at me as if I haven't heard him at all. But I have. I know what he wants, and I'm ready to let Wolf in on my story. The one where my future was stolen. The one that left me pathless because there never was a plan B.

So I'll give him what he deserves. My truth. My pain. But this isn't something I can just say. I need to show him.

He sighs. "I'm not denying anything, but I don't think starting over is the answer."

His words all but break me, but at least he's honest.

I take this moment to lift myself from him. Once standing, I look around the room for my clothes and start dressing. I can hear him behind me, doing the same. Then I remember I have no clue why I'm in his room.

"Wolf, why did I wake up in your bed?"

"You were drunk and passed out at the party last night. No one knew where your room was so I brought you back here."

"And you slept on the couch?" I shouldn't be hurt right now, but there's a pang in my chest at the thought of him unable to be near enough to sleep beside me.

I meet his eyes and he lifts his arms in defeat. "What do you want me to say, Lyric? I'm fucked up over you leaving. You're the only one in my life who's ever gotten me to open up, and I'm trying to not regret doing it. I don't know. Maybe we just need more time. We went full throttle ahead, and that probably wasn't smart. We obviously don't know each other very well, and you clearly don't trust me enough to let me in. To be completely honest, right now, I don't have much trust in you either."

"Wolf—" I plead.

"Lyric." He sounds exasperated. "You can't just hop on my dick and make everything better."

My mouth falls open. "You weren't complaining a few minutes ago." I can't stop the burn in my tone.

He walks past me, his jaw hardening by the second. It's like all his anger from last night is coming back. When his hand reaches the door and he opens it, I realize what he's doing.

He's kicking me out. What the fuck? Embarrassment and rage swirl within me. I step up to him, making no move to leave, then place my hand on the door and slam it shut.

"We're going to talk about this, and you don't get to cut me off. You don't get to kick me out of your room, either."

He leans into me so his nose is just inches from mine. "And you don't get to walk away from me and show up four days later acting like you didn't completely fucking ruin me."

A tear slips from my eye, and I can't help it; I throw my arms around his waist and meet his fierce gaze with a soft, fearful one of my own. "You know I didn't have a choice, but

I am sorry for the way I left. You need to trust me. There's nowhere else I'd rather be than with you."

He glares down at me. "Does that mean you're ready to talk? Tell me what the big secret is, Lyric. What's worth more to you than us?"

I'm lost for words. *Nothing* is the simple answer. Nothing is worth more than being with Wolf. Do I want to tell him everything? Yes. Am I ready to reveal my every insecurity and all the resentment I have for my parents so he can understand the effect it's had on my life? Yes. At least, I think I am.

I open my mouth, a weak attempt to respond to his question, but he holds up a hand and shakes his head. "No. I deserve more than this from you." He opens the door again, a sad look darkening his features. "We'll talk later, Lyric. We've both got work to do. Until you're ready, I think that's all this should be. Work."

Stunned into silence, I release my grip from his waist and move through the door. "Sure," I respond without turning around. I won't let him see the pain that I feel. "Business as usual. I can do that."

Chapter Eight

Wolf

Why am I the one standing here, feeling like the biggest asshole in the world when I'm just protecting my heart?

Lyric is long gone, and I'm still standing half in the hallway, half in my room. Wanting to go after her but making myself wait for her to come around. We can't just jump back into what we were before. Things have changed. If we're going to do this, we need to trust each other.

Maybe I shouldn't have let her fuck my brains out, but I needed it just as much as she did. And I still love her. I may not have said those words, but if she was paying any attention at all, my mouth, my hands, my eyes—they all spoke to her.

Lyric has always been a rock star in the sack. She loves the control. But I've never seen her like that. Unbridled. Ravenous. Completely lost in the feel of me. I loved every second of it, and just thinking about this morning will make it difficult for me to stay away from her. But I need to try.

I can't just give in to her. How do I know she won't pull the same shit and leave again? I don't. Not until she knows she can trust me with whatever she's keeping hidden. So that's what needs to happen because there's no denying what we have is incredible. At least, it will be when she's ready.

"Wolf!" Derrick's voice blares from my phone. "Hurry your lazy ass up, man. We've got rehearsal in five minutes, and Crawley's got not one, but a few sticks up his ass today."

As I walk down the stairs to the lobby, I see Derrick pacing back and forth. I hang up on my end of the line and chuckle as I watch him get pissed, thinking I'm ignoring him. Then he sees me crossing the lobby and glares.

I roll my eyes, following him through the sliding glass door to the sidewalk. "When does he not have a stick up his ass?" I laugh.

"Hey, sugar," Derrick greets a smiling Terese, who's standing just outside the doors. He swoops her up and kisses her before letting her catch a ride on his back for the rest of the walk to our waiting van. He turns back to me. "I think Lyric's got Crawley all riled up. She's already confirming bookings for Europe and emailed him some stuff, but he's still giving her shit. And you know her. She's not taking it."

Terese giggles. "Lyric's a badass. When's Crawley going to learn not to mess with her?"

I smirk, agreeing with Terese. "I've got plans for that douchebag. Don't let him get to you. Where's Lyric?"

"I'm covering for her," Doug replies as he comes up behind me.

"What? Why?" I'm surprised by my anger, and it takes me a second to realize I'm upset because I was looking forward to seeing her. "She just got back on tour and she's already bailing?"

Doug chuckles and holds the van door open for me. He eyes Crawley and then leans in. "Dickhead over there has her working on some things for Europe. They went at it this morning in the lobby, so I figured I'd help keep them apart since it's my last day, anyway."

I nod. "Fine. Tell me about it later. I'd like to know what he's got her doing."

"Sure thing."

We spend less than an hour at rehearsal, just going through the motions. I think I'm the only one not painfully hungover after last night's party, but I'm still as distracted as everyone else. I'm preoccupied with thoughts of Lyric's return and our fight this morning. She's had this effect on me since the day we met. She's like a branding iron, scalding and raw upon first kiss, then permanently engrained where it hurts the most: my fucking heart. And nothing I do can make it go away.

Everyone's still in zombie mode when we get back to the hotel, so we head straight for the restaurant on the first floor and have the waitstaff pull four tables together for us near the back of the restaurant. The crew is loud and boisterous as always, even after a late night of drinking. Until Lyric walks in, that is, and all eyes turn to her. I couldn't pull mine away if I fucking tried.

She smiles sweetly at Melanie and pulls out the empty chair next to her. I shift, feeling the anger from earlier bubble up within me. If this were a week ago, there would be no question about who Lyric was going to sit next to.

Hedge, who's chugging a mimosa next to me, must notice my discomfort, because he coughs mid-sip and then stands. "Switch with me, Lyric," he says. "I need to talk to Stryder."

Lyric looks panicked for a second as she looks from me to Hedge, but then she stands and comes around the table without arguing—and without making eye contact with me. I haven't taken my eyes off her since she walked through the door, and the fact that she's avoiding my gaze pisses me off. But of course, Lyric walks toward me. Always the professional. It doesn't matter that I kicked her out of my room this morning or that Crawley's apparently been up her ass.

She sits down beside me and immediately turns toward Terese. What is this shit? She can't even acknowledge me now? She should be trying harder to earn my forgiveness after leaving me with no promise of return. I shift in my chair noisily, hoping to catch her attention somehow. Like a fucking toddler.

I can feel the eyes of my crew as they wait for my next move. Everyone's witness to our tension, probably wondering what happened after our fight last night. There's not much time to dwell on it. I'm distracted by the giggles coming from Terese and Lyric as they chat about something, and then Lyric's phone starts vibrating.

At this point, I'm the only one paying attention to Lyric besides Terese. Everyone else has gone back to their loud chatter, but I can't stop looking at her. Her phone vibrates again, and she glances at it. The name Destiny lights up her screen, but the message is hidden. Lyric ignores it and turns back to Terese.

Interesting. I wonder what's going on there. When it goes off again, I lean in casually to ask Lyric about it, but she swipes her phone from the table and shoves it in her pocket. I frown. More secrets.

Lunch is awkward. Lyric and I don't speak at all, and when the meal is over, she's the first one to get up and head back to her room. In typical Wolf fashion, I follow her to the elevator. There are a few crew members readying to get in next, but I silently gesture to them to take another elevator. Rex included. This is one of those times I have to pull the asshole rock star card. I'll apologize later. When the doors close and we're alone, I breathe a sigh of relief.

"Is this a coincidence, or are you following me?" Lyric asks flatly.

I look at her, wondering if she's flirting or angry. Definitely angry. "Following you."

She turns to face me. "Why?"

I mirror her, crossing my arms across my chest. "Because I can't stop asking myself why Destiny's been blowing up your phone and why you aren't responding to her."

Lyric narrows her eyes and a flush spreads on her cheeks. "I … I don't know. She wants something from me, so I'm ignoring her."

"What does she want from you?"

This is it. The moment of truth. Lyric is either about to change the subject or divulge something she'd rather keep hidden. When she takes a deep breath and releases it slowly, I know she's about to let me in.

"My mom wants me to work with her. To write for her. Soaring is rebranding her image, and they need fresh songs. She thinks I can help, but I don't want to. So, I'm avoiding her."

I know better than to take Lyric's explanation as the entire story. What she says doesn't sound so bad, but there's anger behind her calm exterior.

"Well, I'm sure your mom will get her songs elsewhere. Or maybe she can write her own. She is Destiny Lane, after all. She'll figure it out."

Lyric snorts. I'm surprised to hear the sound come from her, and my look of shock doesn't get past her. She chuckles at my reaction and wipes a tear from her eye. "Destiny's sure resourceful, but not in the way you would imagine. She's not the most ethical person when it comes to getting what she wants."

What the hell is that supposed to mean?

The ding of the elevator brings us to our floor, and I step back to let her out first. Like always, a feeling of yearning tugs at me, and I want to pull Lyric into my room and make love to her. We had our sexcapades down pat before she left. Every moment we could steal to be alone, we were rolling around naked together. I miss it. Even after our argument this morning, I want her.

"This is me," she says flatly when we reach her door. "I'll see you tonight, Wolf."

She inserts her keycard into the slot, and a dull ache hits my chest as she pushes open the door and steps inside her room.

"Lyric."

She swivels around, her face lighting up with hope.

I'm not ready to give her hope, so my expression remains blank. "Thank you for telling me that."

She swallows and nods, the hope fading from her eyes first, smile last. "It's not easy, you know? I've kept it all locked up for as long as I can remember. Just give me time, Wolf. It's not that I don't trust you. It's just…" She swallows. "There's a lot of shit I need to let go of, and don't know how."

I can't respond. She's not giving me a choice. She's not giving me a chance to be someone she can trust. And I'm not sure how long I can settle for the mystery that is Lyric Cassidy.

Chapter Nine

Lyric

I'm exhausted by the time the show ends and Wolf is escorted from the stage to his dressing room. The band still has a meet and greet with the fans, and then we head to the airport to catch the private plane that will take us to Miami. The guys have to be in the recording studio tomorrow afternoon, so leaving tonight is a must.

I groan as I make my way to the bus. Terese catches up to me and slings an arm around my shoulders. "Ready for Florida, sexy?"

I smile at her, loving that she'll be in Florida with us, even though she will undoubtedly spend the time constantly sucking face with Derrick.

"I guess." Then I frown. "I wish I was more excited, but with things so awkward between Wolf and me, I'm just not sure. I have a hotel booked, but now that seems kind of weird."

Terese gives me a sympathetic expression and links my arm with hers. "You and Wolf will be okay. He's looking for something you're not ready to give, but you'll get there. He's crazy about you, Lyric. And no arguments, you're staying in that house with us. Don't leave me stranded."

I want to laugh and keep the conversation light, but my heart has been so heavy since I left Wolf's room this morning.

Even after our short talk this afternoon, not being with him feels wrong. And I'm afraid that every second we're apart only widens the divide between us.

Instead, I change the subject. "C'mon, let's get our bags transferred. I can't wait to pass out on the plane."

Terese groans. "Me too. But I think Derrick has other ideas in mind. That boy is constantly trying to get in my pants."

I can't hold back my laughter. "You two are ridiculously cute. It kind of makes me jealous." I pause, turning serious. "Wolf and I need to get back together fast. I miss him."

"Then get over your shit and talk to him about whatever's bothering you. You know you can trust him."

She's right.

"I know I can," I resolve. "I'm telling him everything."

"Good." She smiles. "And then maybe you'll tell me." She winks and then tugs on my arm. "C'mon, let's go get our bags."

Once our bags are loaded into the van, we wait for the boys to finish up with the signing. It occurs to me that when I left for San Diego a few days ago, I was in such a rush I didn't grab my things from Wolf's room. I should probably get whatever's left before we take off.

As I walk toward bus number one, I'm surprised to see Rex standing near the entrance in a heated exchange with Rory, the band's bus driver. They don't look like they're fighting, just talking, but I've never seen Rex so angry. He's a huge guy, capable of taking down an entire football team if given the opportunity, but I've never seen him show anger. He just *looks* threatening.

A voice catches my attention, and I turn to see Derrick approaching Terese, a wide smile on his face.

"The signing's over?" I call out to him. "Where's Wolf?"

He's already pulling Terese in for a kiss, but he stops to respond. "Said he had to grab his shit from the bus."

That's all I get before he devours Terese's mouth. My stomach rolls as it hits me that Wolf must already be inside.

I rush the last few steps and reach for the door. Rory calls for me to stop, but fuck that. This used to be my bus too, and my things are still on it. I quicken my pace down the narrow aisle and past the main living area, my heart pounding like crazy in my chest.

Something feels wrong.

I stalk toward Wolf's bedroom at the back of the bus. Behind me, Rex is now the one calling for me to stop, but I can barely hear him over my raging heartbeat. I'm at Wolf's door. It's closed, but that's not unusual. That's not what makes my stomach churn to the point I think I might lose my lunch all over the floor.

It's the moaning. The moaning is loud. The screaming is louder, a woman's voice pleading, "Fuck me harder."

Rage swirls through me as I pound on the door twice before deciding that I don't actually want to see what's on the other side. I just want him to stop. But the sounds keep getting louder. I clasp a hand over my mouth, stifling the sob quickly building in my throat. Without energy to fight, I allow a pair of strong arms to lead me off the bus.

The pressure in my chest is too much and my vision is blurry. I think I might fall if not for the arms around my shoulders. Even when we step off the bus, the arms keep me steady. Maybe so I don't make another run for Wolf's room; I don't know. All I want to do is run back on that bus. Find Wolf and rip his heart out of his chest the way he just did to mine.

When the arms release me, I swivel to find a sympathetic Rex in front of me. He opens his mouth to speak when a voice from behind him cuts in.

"Lyric." The voice sounds like Wolf's, but that must be my imagination. Wolf is fucking some rocker slut in his room. Tears sting the backs of my eyes, and I try to breathe through the pain. It doesn't work. The first tear slips from my eye and rolls down my cheek ... and then another. I'm not sure I could have stopped them if I tried.

Strong, familiar arms wrap around me. "Lyric, what's wrong?"

I look up, but I have to blink the tears away to see clearly. Wolf wipes a finger across my eyes, drying them tenderly. He must be a mirage.

But no, he's here, standing before me, concern etched into every line on his face. And then he gently moves the strand of hair from my face and hooks it over my ears. "What the hell is going on? Are you okay?"

He grips my face with his palms, pleading for me to speak, but I'm still reeling from the sight of him.

"It wasn't you?"

"Who?"

I inhale sharply and look up at the bus. "On your bus."

He shakes his head, clearly confused. "What? No. I was backstage with some VIPs. Why would you think I was on the bus?"

I pull away from him and dry the rest of my face with the back of my hand and stare back up at the bus. Confused, I turn to Rory and Rex, shaking with adrenaline. "Who's on the bus?"

The men exchange worried glances, but neither says a word.

Wolf faces them fully, narrows his eyes, and puffs out his chest. "Who the fuck is on the bus?"

Just then, the door to the bus opens, and out stumbles none other than Destiny Lane. Crawley's behind her, zipping up his jeans. Both look wasted and are cackling with laughter as if sharing an inside joke. Destiny looks completely strung out, a large Chanel handbag weighing down her arm. Destiny and her fucking purses.

And her eyes... I've seen that look before, as she snorted lines off the bathroom counter right in front of me when I was eight years old. Coke was always her weakness, but I thought rehab fixed her the last time. It's been years since I've heard any rumors of her addiction resurfacing, but here it is, in the flesh.

My eyes are fixed on Destiny's bugged-out eyes, her jittery body flying high—but then a loud, gravelly shuffle catches my attention. Wolf is moving quickly, his hand gripping the collar of Crawley's black button up shirt and slamming him against the bus. Everything seems to shake.

Wolf's expression is as ferocious as the beast he was named after as he uses his grip on Crawley's shirt to lift him just enough so that his toes have to fight to feel the ground.

"What the fuck are you doing, you shit stick? Were you just fucking her on my bus?" He slams Crawley into the bus once more.

Crawley already has blood running down his face, but the prick is laughing like a madman, spinning me further into a spindle of rage.

"You piece of shit," Wolf spits. Then he looks over and sees Destiny in Rex's arms. She looks like she's about to topple over without him.

"Is that Destiny?"

Wolf doesn't wait for a response before his fist slams into Crawley's face, and I hear a loud crunch as blood sprays from his nose.

Oh my God. I run to Wolf, but Hedge leaps toward me and holds me back, hugging tightly me from behind. "You don't want to go over there, Lyric."

"He's going to kill him!" I say, desperate to free myself.

Chaos becomes charged with more chaos as screams and shouts wake the night. Security pushes their way through the crowd, rushing to reach Wolf and Crawley.

"Let him go, Wolf!" I shout. "He's not worth it."

I'm not sure if he hears me or if he knows he's done enough damage to the old prick, but Wolf slams a dazed Crawley into the bus again and then throws him onto the ground before backing up until he's by my side.

"You're fired, asshole. We'll mail you your shit."

Concert security rushes forward, wasting no time to haul Crawley away.

"What is that dick doing with your mother?" The question is directed at me, but his heated eyes are still on

Crawley as security hauls him off the ground and toward one of the vans.

I shake my head, overcome with embarrassment. I'm just as bewildered as Wolf at the sight of Destiny and Crawley. The woman is desperate to get to me. It doesn't completely surprise me that she showed up here. When she wants something, she goes after it. That form of perseverance worked well for her early in her career, in her teens, when she was competing for the spotlight against the Cyndis and Madonnas of her generation. That competitive edge, paired with perfect timing and well-produced, catchy pop songs catapulted her into fame.

But over time, all her music started to sound the same. Autotune can only get you so far in this industry, and her clock was running down. Another big artist began to outshine her efforts, and then another, and then another … and then, when I was seventeen, she released her best album ever.

Wolf lets out a huff, distracting me from my thoughts, and then he walks away without another word. I watch as he approaches Doug and security while the van holding Destiny and Crawley pulls away from the lot. I didn't even have a chance to talk to her to find out what she wanted. Not that she'd register much in her state. But maybe I could have tried. My expression hardens in response to my hopeful thoughts. Always hopeful, even when I know better.

I reach for my phone and scroll through the text messages she sent me today. Nothing gives any hint that she was going to show up. And definitely nothing about Crawley. Just "Call me, Lyric," and "Pick up the phone, Lyric," and "I'd like to talk."

Wolf's rising volume catches my attention. He's only a couple yards away, but his chest heaves like he's working himself up again. Or maybe he never calmed down. It's instinct to walk toward him and reach for him, but I hesitate the moment my hand begins to wrap around his arm. I'm not sure if soothing him is what he needs, or if I'm the person he needs it from.

The moment I touch him, I feel the flinch I feared, but he doesn't pull away. That's something, right? He's too busy talking to Doug to react, so I'm not sure.

"I've been waiting to fire his ass. And now it's done." I feel the heat of his words as they rumble from his shaking body, and it's all too familiar. Not the anger, but the adrenaline. It reminds me of our sex after his shows. How amped he'd get. How ready he was to fill me with every ounce of his need. But I know this isn't that kind of energy.

I'm surprised when his eyes lock on mine. "You don't know what your mother was doing here with Crawley?" He's repeating his question from earlier as if expecting a different answer. What's worse, he's searching my eyes like he's waiting to confirm that I'm telling him the truth.

My chest grows heavy as my throat tightens. Is this how it will be now? He'll forever question everything I say?

"I have no idea. She's been texting me, but she didn't say she was coming to the show, and I had no clue those two even knew each other."

Wolf lets out an exasperated breath and addresses Rory and Rex over my shoulder. "Can you clean out my room? Just throw everything into bags and get it to the plane." He turns to Doug, who's on his phone with someone from the label. "I'm getting Lyric out of here."

Doug shakes his hand. "Take care of my girl, Wolf," he says, his tone carrying a hint of warning. I wonder if they've talked about me. Would Doug tell him anything? No. He wouldn't.

Doug hugs me with one arm and then gestures to his phone as his focus turns back to Wolf. "I'm giving your label a heads-up. They want you to call as soon as you can."

Wolf nods and tugs on my hand, but I halt in my tracks. "Wait. I have stuff on your bus."

Wolf looks at Rory and Rex again. "Grab everything out of the drawers. Don't miss anything."

"You got it, sir," Rex agrees. He and Rory start to jog off, but Wolf stops them again.

"Wait," Wolf calls. The guys look back expectantly.

"Why didn't you stop Crawley from getting on the bus? He hasn't been sleeping there for a week."

Rory and Rex look at each other, their faces red with guilt. "He said he had to grab something, so I unlocked it for him," Rory explains. "I didn't think anything of it. Figured he left stuff in his old bunk. I didn't see the lady with him until I'd already opened the door."

"That's when I walked up," Rex adds. "We were deciding how to handle it when Lyric jumped on the bus. I'm sorry, boss. We didn't realize what was going on."

I watch the expressions on Wolf's face morph from anger to confusion and then exhaustion. His shoulders slump. "Fine." He's not happy, but he takes my hand and leads me to a car. Everyone else is taking a coach bus to the airport.

Derrick and Terese are standing by the row of vehicles, just as confused as most of the onlookers—myself included.

"We'll catch up with you guys on the plane," Wolf says to Derrick. "Tell the guys."

Derrick nods, and Terese squeezes my hand as I pass by.

As soon as we're alone in the car, I look at Wolf with a silent plea. I just want him to pull me close so I can relax under the crook of his arm. One week ago, that's exactly what he would have done.

But things have changed. Wolf doesn't even look at me, just shakes his head angrily. "So what's going on, Lyric? You come back on tour and your mom shows up on my fucking bus with Crawley? And don't tell me you don't know. She's your fucking mom, for Christ's sake."

My jaw drops, and I can feel heat rapidly climbing my chest. "Excuse me?"

I lean back to get a good look at Wolf's expression. Stern jaw, eyes pointed forward. He's dead serious. He thinks I had something to do with what just happened back there. *Fuck no.*

"No," I snap, feeling my body begin to quiver. I'm so tired of answering the same goddamn question. He can be pissed at me for leaving all he wants, but to put me in the same category as Crawley and Destiny is too much. "I found out when you did, Wolf. You were standing right there with me."

He rolls his eyes and stares ahead. "Jesus," he breathes. "I'm just trying to figure out what the fuck is going on. That was a shitshow back there, Lyric, and somehow your mother is involved."

My face heats with embarrassment. "What can I say, Wolf? I've answered you every time you've asked the question and the answer remains the same. I have no idea. Not a single clue why Destiny was with Crawley. You're just going to have to trust me. You think I *wanted* to walk in on that?"

"Well, forgive me for asking more than once, but you have a funny habit of keeping things from me. Pretty fucking significant things, apparently. Tell me, Lyric. Why *should* I trust you?"

His words hit me like shrapnel to my heart, and he couldn't take them back even if he wanted to. My body trembles with anger and so much hurt. I shouldn't have come back on tour. I shouldn't be here. Not if Wolf is set on twisting my silence into something it's not. Haven't we been through enough this week?

Shaking my head, I face front and lock my arms in place by my sides protectively. "You shouldn't. Keep telling yourself I'm this awful person you never really knew. Keep pushing me away, Wolf. Your heart is safer that way, right? If you really think the worst of me."

He reaches for my hand but I tug it away, scooting closer to my door and facing the window. Inside, I'm crying, but I won't shed one single tear for him. Instead, I let my chest fill with emotion. I let the influx of pain and confusion swarm within the confines of my ribcage, building to an excruciating level. But I won't let it go. Not now.

I'm not sure how else to handle these arguments with Wolf. They seem to begin with only good intentions as we cling to what we once had together. So if we're still fighting to understand each other—if we're still fighting to hold on— then why do we continue to unravel as if there is nothing to save?

Out of everyone in my life, Wolf has been the only one who has been patient with me. Who's never pushed me. Who, even through my silence, has understood me. Seen the best in me. Why can't he do that now?

We're silent the entire way to the private runway where Wolf's jet awaits. We're the first ones there aside from the captain and the crew. They stand at the foot of the staircase that leads to the jet door.

I exit the van before Wolf can stop me, and I dart for the stairs. It's going to be a long way to Miami. A five-hour flight. With the amount of sleep I've missed out on lately, I'll be out in no time and wake for nothing.

When I enter the jet, I'm too upset to appreciate much of it. Normally I would luxuriate in the creamy leather seats, built-in televisions, and crisp air. But tonight, I take the first seat I see and pack the seat next to it with my small handbag. Wolf walks in after me. I avoid eye contact, and out of my periphery I see that he does too. My heart grows heavier as he steps past me and continues down the aisle. His footsteps grow faint long after I've realized we're done fighting tonight. That should probably be a good thing; I don't know. Maybe not. Because that means we're done trying, too.

Chapter Ten

Wolf

"So, what are we going to do about Crawley?"

Lyric, Terese, Melanie, and Stryder's girlfriend, Misty, fell asleep as soon as the plane took off, so the guys and I decide to have a huddle session to discuss recent events while I ice my throbbing hand. We're in a section of seats that face each other, and Derrick's asking all the questions.

We call Derrick the dad of the group for this very reason. He's the first person that wants to get to the bottom of what went down back there, resolve it, and restore peace in our lives.

The one thing that sets Wolf, the band, apart from most other rock groups out there is the fact that we actually get along. We're family that respects each other. And we all play our own roles.

I know Derrick's worried. Hell, we all are. Not that we particularly liked Crawley, but he did serve a purpose, even when he was being an asshole.

"Not sure." I remove the burning ice from my hand and peer down at it. My skin is a palette of blues, red, and greens. A memento of a well-executed beatdown. "I have a call with the label in the morning. I sent Presley a text and gave her the short version of the story."

Presley is our label rep at Wicked Records and yet another person who can't stand Crawley's ass. She was more than happy at the news that the dick was on a one-way trip back to the label. There, he'll have to answer to the higher-ups who have already promised me he's out of a job.

Stryder leans in to check out my hand, his long, blond hair a wild and tangled mess falling over his shoulder. Stryder is our California beach bum. Always chill. Never argumentative. And completely obsessed with his girlfriend. His life revolves around music, Misty, and the beach. Traveling with the band keeps him away from the ocean more than he'd like, but the sacrifice is worth it. Besides, he's able to steal enough beach time when we travel—enough to satisfy him, at least.

"Those were some mean throws, dude," he says. "I thought you were aiming to kill him."

"I should have. That fucker had it coming. Crawley got his warning, and he continued to fuck with Lyric. I wasn't putting up with it. I'm more than happy to deal with the consequences."

"You could have just fired him," Hedge cuts in, surprising me. Hedge is normally the first one to have my back in a fight. The reckless one who'd rather ask for forgiveness than ask permission. And his bad behavior is almost always accompanied by a bottle of booze.

"Hopefully you don't get stuck with more PR drama," he warns.

I turn away, knowing he's right but too pissed off to care. "So what if I do? It'll do wonders for my badass image."

Hedge snorts. "Good plan. Everyone knows you've gone soft with Lyric around."

I shoot him a glare, although his words don't actually make me angry. I used to like that Lyric made me soft. She made me hard when it mattered. Mostly, she just made me happy. I hate what our relationship has become. The tension, the anger, the fighting. That's not us.

But she left me with no choice. I'll keep her close because I'm still hoping she decides to come clean, but until she does, things won't be the same. Whatever is eating her up is affecting more than just her. And while I've never been one to push Lyric, this problem with her mom isn't just about her anymore. Not after she showed up on my bus with Crawley.

"What was Destiny Lane doing on our bus, anyway? Does Lyric know?" Lorraine asks as she takes the ice from me and wraps a napkin around it. "Here. Keep icing it. We need your hand to work."

I give her a tight smile and lean back in my seat. Her question reminds me why Lyric and I are miles apart right now.

"Nah, Lyric doesn't know. Destiny's a piece of work, though. They don't get along very well, but I don't know the whole story. I'm sure she was there to see Lyric. Maybe I should have made Crawley talk before I fed him my fist for dinner. I wasn't exactly thinking clearly."

Stryder chuckles. "You realize he's going to retaliate, right? With whatever dickhead scheme he can come up with."

I shrug. "There's nothing he can do to hurt me worse than when he fucks with Lyric. I don't know why, but he's got a problem with her. Had a problem with her before she even joined the tour. Who knows; maybe he and her mom go way back."

Lorraine is deep in thought. "You think Destiny is planning some shit with Crawley? She wouldn't do anything to hurt Lyric, though, right? She's her daughter."

I'm stumped. It doesn't seem like Destiny has any respect for Lyric at all, and Lyric clearly just wants to stay away from her. I guess I won't understand completely until Lyric decides to tell me.

"I hope not," is all I can say in response. "It's all good, guys. I'll talk to the label tomorrow. They'll have a backup on hand if we can't find a manager right away. We've done this without a manager before. We'll be fine."

I stand up, ignoring their rebuttals about us being a bigger deal now, stretch, and make my way back down the aisle until I reach Lyric. She's sprawled out across a few seats, sleeping peacefully. I take a seat across the aisle and watch her.

Her wavy brown hair is knotted, a tousled lock drooping over one eye. Her mouth is parted, her soft breaths blowing on the strands of hair that aren't stuck to her lips. I chuckle. I know I'm supposed to be pissed at her right now, but Lyric has always owned every bit of my heart. No matter what happens, she always will.

It's five in the morning when we step off the plane in Miami and load into a group of vans to head to the house. When I awoke from my catnap and couldn't find Lyric, Derrick told me she'd already deplaned and stuffed herself into a loaded van with Melanie. The next time I'll see her will be at the house. That doesn't sit right with me at all, but there's nothing I can do about it now.

I'm watching her van drive off when Hedge slaps a hand on my back and nudges me toward our ride. "Get in, Romeo. You two will work it out."

Shaking him off with a huff, I climb into the van and take a seat in the back row to stew. I didn't think this far in advance when I was angry as hell last night. One entire week of pushing Lyric away is going to get old fast.

Then again, so will her secrets.

Thirty minutes later, our driver pulls through the gold-accented wrought iron gate of our vacation home, I take in the badass setup. The Mediterranean mansion is insane. Tucked away in a high-end residential neighborhood of Coral Gables in Miami-Dade County, every inch of it is secure and private. The pad is big enough to house the entire 30-person crew. Not everyone decided to come, but the core group is here or arriving soon: the band, my merch team, and some of the techs and roadies.

Just the sight of the place gives everyone a second wind. It's chaos as everyone explores the house and calls dibs on their rooms. Derrick and I have already claimed ours—a master bedroom and guest bedroom on the main floor.

The kitchen has been stocked with food and drinks, and the guys waste no time distributing shots as everyone funnels back downstairs. I join in for a couple of drinks but then sneak away the first opportunity I get to find Lyric. I haven't seen her since before I fell asleep on the plane, and now I'm beginning to worry. Not that I think she's in trouble, but because maybe I played the asshole card a little too strong.

After searching every floor of the damn house, I stop in the kitchen where Melanie is cutting limes. She looks up, recognizes my frustrations, and then looks back down with an expectant half-smile on her face. Suddenly, I have a sick feeling in my stomach.

"Where is she?"

Her eyebrows raise. "Come again?"

My jaw tenses and I can feel my face flinching with annoyance as heat bubbles in my chest. "Tell me, Mel, or you'll find yourself without a fucking bed tonight."

Melanie rolls her eyes. "Calm down, Wolfman. Lyric's a big girl. I'm sure you'll see her later."

"Where is she?" I try again, somehow containing the pending explosion that's brewing in my chest. Time stretches, and when she's silent for a second too long, my eyes search the room for Terese. My last hope. I step around the island and close the distance between us.

Derrick is on my tail and steps between Terese and me like he's afraid I'm going to lunge at her or something. "Dude," he says before I can speak, "it's been a long night. You'll see Lyric later. Just get some rest."

Fuck that. I let out a breath through my nose and twist my neck until it releases a satisfying crack. Maybe I should just let this go tonight, but I can't. I need her, and I know I'm not going to get what I want by throwing around my rage. "Just tell me where she is. Is she okay?"

Terese frowns, her brows bent toward the center. I know she can see the plea in my eyes, as if the desperation in my voice wasn't enough. "I can't. But she's okay, Wolf."

Everyone in the room is silent, staring at me like I couldn't fire them all. The pit in my stomach widens, and I realize I'm all alone in this. How did this happen? How the fuck did I become the bad guy?

With a flippant wave of my hand, I turn from my crew. I'm already walking out the door when Terese calls after me, but I don't stop to listen. I fly outside and stomp toward the minivan that held Lyric earlier. We've hired a company to have transportation on standby at the mansion for our use. I wanted everyone to be comfortable and free to roam about safely. There are sedans, vans, and SUVs at the ready.

"Where to, sir?" asks the driver.

Rex climbs in beside me, shutting the door while I reach for my phone. "You tell me."

Chapter Eleven

Lyric

The Bellmonte is a completely renovated 1920's hotel in downtown Miami. It's quaint with its ivory pillars and miniature gardens placed strategically around the indoor-outdoor lobby. I'm staying in a standard room with a queen size bed on the sixth floor. Nothing too fancy, but I can't complain. I chose it because it's walking distance from the recording studio and far enough away from Wolf to avoid any distractions.

I've done my best to convince myself that this isn't me being overly dramatic or a ploy to get Wolf's attention. But the truth is, it's both. Wolf is the one set on being angry with me, so I'm more than willing to give him the space he says he wants. But it's not just that.

When he rented out the mansion, he did it without saying a word to me about it. I can't exactly invite myself to live with him and the band. Maybe he assumed I would just show up. That I would take a guest room and endure another week of torture, suffering in the silence that has become our new normal.

No. I'd rather keep my dignity. And since the hotel room was already booked in my name … why not?

I toss my duffel bag on the bed and dig through it to find my shower kit. After stripping down to nothing, I step into the bathroom and turn on the water, catching a glimpse of myself in the mirror. I've got a tangled knot of wavy brown hair on top of my head, and my makeup is smudged in black halos around my eyes, making me look like I haven't slept in days.

Sighing, I grab a wipe to remove the residue of foundation, eyeliner, and mascara from my face. By the time I'm done, the bathroom feels like a sauna. I let down my hair and step into the steady stream of hot water.

Being alone isn't as horrible as people make it seem. It has its benefits. I've never been one to let myself be alone with my thoughts for long, but tonight, it's necessary. I feel like the shitstorm that's been my life has only been building to whatever waits on the horizon. How do I weather this storm? Do I plant my feet and endure what comes? Or do I make like a bird and head for safety?

I've never had to make that choice before. Living on the road has provided me the luxury of constant change and zero time for analyzing. I'm not scared of change like most people. I embrace it and always make the most of whatever comes my way. It's planting my feet that scares me. It's standing in one place, being forced to deal with the tornado as it encircles me, throwing my life into disarray.

After my shower, I towel dry my hair, brush out the tangles, and let it fall in loose waves around my head. My body lotion is still in my duffel bag, so I wrap myself in a towel and walk out of the bathroom.

Just as I'm covering the last inch of my legs with moisturizer, three steady knocks pound my door.

My heart jumps. There's no doubt in my mind those knocks belong to Wolf. But how? Why? Melanie and Terese are the only two who know where I'm staying, and when the van dropped them off at the mansion, they swore to me they wouldn't say a word to Wolf. No matter what.

I swallow and take hesitant steps forward, my heart now beating into my throat. "Lyric, I know you're in there," Wolf's voice booms through the walls.

"Jesus," I mutter under my breath as I peek through the hole in the door. Wolf stands there with his hands in fists by his sides, his eyes fierce, and a slight twitch in his jaw.

I sigh and send a silent prayer to up above for whatever is about to happen. It looks like distance won't work. He's coming for a fight.

With a flick of the lock and a turn of the knob, I'm facing a heated Wolf. My stomach muscles clench at the sight of him, so angry and so damn hot.

"You found me." My voice is low, but confident. I don't know why he's here, but I'm glad he is. Whether it's to argue or make amends. I'll take either option as long as it means we're moving forward.

He shakes his head, nose flaring, and then steps into my room. As the door shuts behind him, he doesn't make a move right away. Neither of us speaks.

The energy between us is just as intense as it's ever been. I can feel it compounding around us like a dynamite stick before it's triggered at the base.

He steps forward, his forehead only an inch from mine. I swallow. "Let's get one thing straight, Lyric," flicking my name off his tongue like a curse word, all while magically maintaining a hard jaw and his hold on my heart. "Where the band goes, you go. No detours, no private hotel rooms. Not while you're on my dime. Got it?" He lowers his voice for the last part, the words sending a rush of chills down my spine.

My eyes narrow, knowing exactly where this is going. I roll my shoulders back, raising myself an inch to combat his warning. "I'm not your property, Wolf."

His nose flares and he pulls me forward with a tug, drawing my body closer to his. My feet shuffle forward to keep up. Looking down, I find his good hand tightly gripping my towel where it's folded together.

"Really?" he challenges, his voice a whirlwind of husk and desire. His upper lip curls at the corner, and I swear the only reason I'm still standing is because he's got a good grip on my towel. His eyes scan my face, drawing an invisible line down my neck to the space between his hand and my heaving breasts. "Your body says different."

I whimper as he leans in, his nose skating along my jawline in one smooth stroke. It's impossible to ignore the dampness between my thighs. It's painfully obvious just how much I *want* to be his property right now. How much I need it.

Teeth find my neck and drag down slowly, digging in at the base. "I think you wanted me to find you," he murmurs against sensitive skin. I shiver at the truth of his words, and I can feel his lips curl in satisfaction. "But Lyric," he starts, his voice low, "you have no fucking clue how angry I am right now."

He licks where he just bit and then presses his mouth into the spot just below my ear. My eyes roll into the back of my head.

"Show me," I say, trying to keep my voice even but failing miserably. I would sell my soul for this man.

Wolf's tongue freezes on my skin, and he pulls away slightly. "What?"

I let out another breath through my nose and move my head so our eyes connect. My eyes narrow. "Show me how angry you are, Wolf. You think you own me?" I raise my eyebrows. "Then shut the hell up and *show me*."

I can see it in his eyes. A switch flips and Wolf's entire body goes from warning to full-on threat in less than a second.

A rush of adrenaline thrills through me as Wolf uses his grip on my towel to move me against the wall. He's not trying to be gentle. He's got something to prove. I feel the impact of my back meeting the wall, but it barely registers compared to the desire that's raging in Wolf's eyes.

The hand on my towel loosens, and with a single finger he unknots it, letting it fall to the floor. My nipples are already hard and very much the focus of his attention. He smiles wickedly and bites his bottom lip. "Oh, Lyric. I bet you hate that you can't control the way your body reacts to me." He brushes a thumb across one nipple and then he sinks to his knees. He nips the inside of my thighs, and I cry out from the delicious pinch of pain that lights up my core.

When his hand runs up the length of my leg, I'm already shaking. His mouth is so close, but his finger is inside me first, dipping and then reaching my depths in one effortless movement.

Three months with Wolf, and he's gotten to know me pretty well. Not just the way I come for him best, but the things that tug at my heart. It was the little things that made me fall hard and fast for him. It was his attentiveness and his generosity and the way he always ensures those around him are taken care of before he is. Even now, when he's mad as hell, he's tending to me first when it could have easily been the other way around. That's how I know this is more than just an angry fuck. This is Wolf telling me that he still cares. But he's going to make me pay first.

With a smirk, he releases his finger and places one of my legs over his shoulder, easing up to me and examining me like I'm fine wine that needs to be inhaled, then appreciated in just the right away. He pulls in my scent through his nose. My entire body shakes as I watch his relax. He tastes me—I gasp—swirling his tongue—I swallow—and then he completely devours me.

His tongue laps relentlessly before pushing flat against my center. I let out another cry, this time all pleasure just as his finger sinks back into my core. He flicks and sucks on my clit, sending me full throttle into the quickest orgasm of my life.

My legs feel like Jell-O, but I know Wolf, and he's not done. When his hooded eyes find mine, I might start to fall, but I wouldn't know because he'd never let me. His hold is firm under my leg and on my waist. "Turn around," he demands.

He unhooks my leg, setting it on the floor beside him. His other hand moves to my waist, and he spins me before I can do as he says. "Wait for me."

This time I listen, my palms firmly pressed against the wall, happy for something to support me as I'm still reeling from my orgasm. I hear the sound of a zipper, followed by the shuffle of clothing getting tossed to the side. And then I feel him pressed against my back, length hard between my ass cheeks. God, I've missed him.

Wolf runs his injured hand down the length of my arm, onto the dip of my waist, and then down my hip. He slides around to my front and doesn't waste a second before he's massaging my wet opening.

"Your hand," I moan, praying he's miraculously healed.

"I don't give a damn about my hand right now, Lyric. I've always been gentle with you," he warns.

His fingers at my head move through my hair, twisting and gripping so hard I almost cry out. The thrill of adrenaline races through me, and I swallow before he tugs at the ponytail he's made with his fist.

"Don't be gentle," I beg, just above a whisper.

He chuckles behind me, low and raspy, sending a flair of heat between my legs. He didn't need my permission. "I don't plan on it."

His mouth finds the back of my neck again and he sucks, marking me as his. The finger on my clit moves away to my hip, tugging slightly while tilting my ass out and spreading my legs with his knees. His thickness fills me quickly until I'm dizzy with him, clenching around him in ecstasy.

He grunts in response and pushes deeper while pressing my cheek flat against the wall. Every movement is rough but controlled, like he's a man on a mission. A mission to show me just how much I fucked up. And with each drive of his hips, I'm inching closer to the edge.

I try to press my ass into him, to meet him halfway, but my muscles submitted a long time ago. His hips stop thrusting, and he slowly slides out until his tip is all that's left inside me. So I try to move again, but he holds me down with a firm grip on my waist.

Oh, fuck.

I brace myself, breath held, mouth open, and that's when he charges forward, slamming his entire length into me, hard and deep. I scream out in pleasure at the impact as everything inside me coils.

Before I can manage the shock, he's doing it again, each thrust driving into me with such force I'm glad there's a wall to stand against. Without it, I'd be flying.

The air is filled with his grunts, my screams, and the slapping of skin on skin in the most erotic sexual experience of my life.

Why hasn't Wolf ever fucked me like this before? It's like he's trying to tear me apart to reach the deepest parts of me. Like he *needs* me to feel every inch of him deep in every inch of me. He's demanding in the sexiest way. Hungry as he tastes the sweat rolling down my back. Punishing as he brings us both to the brink of pleasure, as if I wasn't already ruined for all other men. He ruined me a long time ago, but this ... this is pure dominance.

And I love it.

Maybe I'll never admit it out loud, but Wolf was right. He does own me—every inch. Every beat of my heart is his.

He releases my hair and moves both hands to my breasts, kneading and using them as leverage as he rocks himself into me. And then he's pulling out and spinning me, lifting my leg up, pushing it against me and driving into me again and again without a beat lost.

His eyes connect with mine for a second, and in that moment I see everything his body is trying to tell me. Nothing is lost. He's still a badass with a heart that beats only for me, and I'm still his in every way.

His mouth slams against mine and I bite against his bottom lip. He grunts and pushes himself deeper into me. My head is spinning.

He growls, gripping my ass with his good hand and lifting me off the floor. I wrap my legs around his waist and kiss him back as he takes me to bed. It's like we've practiced this dance a hundred times before. Hands gripping and scratching, legs tightening and squeezing, mouths tasting and biting. Neither of us misses a beat, every chord right on tune.

The only gentle moment between us is when he places me on the bed and hovers above me, breathing heavily. I'm certain Wolf will have scratch marks by the time this is all over—bite marks, too—but I don't care. I nip his lip and he howls.

He sits up slightly, disconnecting our mouths and reaching past me to the pillow. He's up to something, but I'm not sure what. While he busies himself emptying a pillowcase, I wrap my hands around the many inches of his cock, stroking it and loving the way his stomach muscles clench under his perfect skin.

Suddenly, Wolf grips my wrists and lifts them above my head. I feel soft fabric wrapping around one hand, and then I feel a tug as my wrists clamp together. He's tied me up, and now he's pressing my hands into the sheets. "Keep them there," he commands as he uncases another pillow and ties my feet together.

It's like I weigh nothing when he flips me onto my knees, presses them together, and pushes my chest flat into the bed, my hands straight above me.

He nips at my ass before licking my core and moaning with pleasure. "I'll leave your ass for another day. Right now, I just want you to take all of me." His fingers sink in deep, and then he removes them with a chuckle. "Tight and soaking. Perfect." He runs a palm on my backside, and I feel his body shift. "Get ready, baby."

But he doesn't give me time to get ready. Wolf inserts his length, this time slowly, letting my tightness wrap him firmly until I'm so full of him I gasp for air. There's a growl of satisfaction behind me as Wolf's hands run the length of my hips, waist, and back. And then he's curling over me. I can feel his weight and the sticky heat of his breath as it floats across my back before he begins to move.

Well, move might be the wrong word. No, he's ramming me like it's punishment, which only intensifies the pleasure. He's gripping the sides of my breasts as if they're his last chance of survival in rocky waters. And he's groaning like he's fighting to hold onto his release, because letting go could mean the end.

My insides clench on his next plow and everything starts to build quickly after that. I have no chance to stop it or slow it down since he's tied me up. I can't control a thing. I'm just here to take his anger, inch by angry inch.

"Wolf," I warn, but it's the guttural sound of my insides uncoiling that tells him he's won.

His hands slide up to my mouth to muffle my screams as he continues to slam into me, never relenting his pressure or speed. So I bite down on his ring finger.

Wolf growls in response and pushes into my center harder, and then faster.

My eyes tear when his next thrust sizzles through me, catching fire and blasting through me like an inferno. I'm convulsing around him, and he's filling me, every drop surging into me like the rush of a wild river, and I'm crashing … falling …

And when I fall, I can only hope that he's right there to catch me.

Chapter Twelve

Wolf

She must sense me after a few minutes because she stirs as she moans, and then she opens her eyes. They land on mine, fluttering as she registers that I'm with her.

Not even an hour has passed since the fucking best sex in the world. We've always been good together. Always knowing what the other needs. But this … Lyric gave me a gift tonight—all the pieces she's willing to give. Physically, she didn't hold back. Emotionally, we still have work to do.

"Hi," she says softly.

"Hey," I respond, matching her tone.

She blinks. The room is dim, lit only by the lamp on my side of the bed. Her hair is pooled in waves around her face like a sexy halo. Her expression, peaceful. I didn't want to turn the light off because then I wouldn't have been able to see her.

"You going to sleep?" she asks.

"I'm not sure if I can. Still worked up."

She moans as she tries to adjust her body. "Holy shit, Wolf. I think you did some damage."

I can't help my smile. I absolutely know I did some damage. There's a bruise on her neck where I sucked her raw, and I'm sure there are aches where I gave her the no-mercy sex she asked for. She didn't leave me unscathed, either.

There's a harsh sting on my upper back where she clawed me like a fucking cat.

I reach for her small waist and pull her to me, letting my face fall into the crook of her neck. "I'd say I'm sorry, but I'm not. Not at all."

She sighs. "Nothing to be sorry for. Except ... how did you know where to find me?"

I can feel my brows pull together as I remember my panic attack when I searched for her at the mansion. "I have my methods." She starts to pull away, but I tighten my hold. "Who do you think paid the driver you had bring you here?"

Her expression registers embarrassment, and I just sigh. "You can't disappear like that, Lyric. I don't think I can handle you leaving again." I let out a breath.

There, I said it. As mad at her as I am, I don't want her to walk away from this. Nothing in my life has been worth fighting for as much as what we have together. Nothing.

Her voice is small when she speaks. "You think we'll have time to ourselves this week?" I can see her swallow. "To talk?"

My heart beats faster, hoping this means she's finally going to let me in. "I'm yours whenever you want, babe."

She brushes her finger along the length of my bottom lip. Her smile fades and her head drops as she sighs. "I don't deserve you."

Heat spreads in my chest. "Stop it. We'll make time this week to talk as little or as much as you want." My nose brushes against her soft skin, pacing the length of her neck. Lyric has always been so confident. I'm not sure what's making her lose that confidence now, but it only makes me want to protect her even more. "Nothing's changed. This week will be awesome. Miami for a week! The house is enormous, and we have the best room." I wink at her. "We can sneak off anytime we want."

The smile she gives me is big, and slightly mischievous. "Guess I can cancel the hotel room."

I shake my head. "Yeah, Lyric. What the fuck were you thinking?"

She sighs. "I asked the company to book it when you hated me. And after what happened earlier, I just figured it was best to keep our distance from each other."

Sometimes Lyric's logic drives me up the wall. "I never hated you."

"Good."

But now that we're on this subject, I'm reminded of the moment the night took a bizarre turn. "Why were you so upset when I found you by my bus tonight? If you didn't know your mom was in there with Crawley until I got there…"

She looks at me, fear dancing in her eyes as she takes a deep breath. "Rex and Rory were trying to keep me out of the bus, and I just got this strange feeling. So I walked back to your room, and the door was closed. And then I heard them … having sex … and I thought it was you." Moisture forms in her eyes, and I pull her to me tighter.

Jesus. I can feel my face crumbling. "No fucking way, Lyric. Never. It's you and me, okay? No matter what."

She's got to know I'm not giving up on this. On us. Not even close. But just the possibility of it being over … the thought of me fucking around with someone else. It feels wrong to consider. If roles were reversed and I had walked into what she did, I would have lost my shit. I kiss her cheek, and then her forehead, and then her neck again.

"I know the way I left was awful," she says. "It was like panic completely took over, and I couldn't think straight. My childhood was fucked up, Wolf. Everything was stolen from me, and when I think about it, I just get angry. That morning, that situation, it triggered feelings I've suppressed for so long. I may have left that day, but I wasn't leaving *you*. I get now that it felt that way, and I'm so sorry. But I don't want to wake up another day without you. Ever."

She wipes a tear from her face and searches my eyes. She's looking for me to believe her. I move above her, straddling her legs and holding her face delicately in my palms in stark contrast to the hold I had on her just one hour ago. I drop my head and touch my lips to hers before kissing her, delicately but deeply.

Her lips are a little burst of heaven, and when her tongue dips into my mouth, I can feel the pending explosion of my heart. It's like our first kiss all over again, but this time, I don't hold back. I let her feel me, rock hard and ready for seconds. I always want her. But right now I just want to focus on kissing her. I slip my tongue in between her lips while her hands weave through my just-fucked hair.

When her mouth moves to my neck, I groan and pull away for just a second to speak. "For the record, I'm glad you came back on tour." She sucks in a tiny breath. I swallow. "I just needed it to be your decision."

Her eyes fall shut and then she kisses me. "There was ever only one viable option, Wolf."

And I believe her.

"What are you going to do now that Crawley's out of the picture?" Lyric frowns, and I can see there's some guilt there, like she feels responsible for the band's loss.

I stroke her hair, wanting to comfort her. "The label's going to find us a new manager and fire Crawley's ass. It's going to be hard for him to find work after this, which is a good thing."

Lyric nods, then furrows her brow. "I don't understand how he knows Destiny. I mean, I guess everyone in the business knows each other to some extent. I suppose they've run into each other before." She looks up at me with confused eyes. "Maybe she was trying to get backstage to see me and ran into him."

I shrug. That's the first thing I thought too, but it doesn't add up. "Why my tour bus, though? Why my room? He obviously lied to Rory and Rex about why he needed to get on the bus... But why?"

Lyric sighs. "Your bus is the only one with a big bed and a door. It's the best place to fuck, if that's what you're saying."

All goes quiet. What she just said completely changes the direction of my thoughts. It wasn't long ago that we were hiding out in the bedroom of my tour bus to fuck like sex-crazed teenagers. I loved our stolen moments, our borrowed ones, and eventually the ones that she let me own.

"Yeah, I remember that," I say softly, unsure if now is the time to start that conversation again. My eyes drift over her silky skin, her taut stomach, and her luscious curves before I finally drag them to Lyric's, holding her gaze intently.

As much as I want to hold on to my anger to show Lyric just how wrong she was for leaving the way she did, I also just want to forgive her and move on.

She inches closer to me, running two fingers lightly up my arm and over my shoulder until she's rubbing the scruff on my cheek. Something twists in my chest, and I have the strong desire to lean in and capture her mouth with mine. If forgiving her for leaving is what I need to do to move on, then it might be easier than I thought.

Her forehead wrinkles with her frown. "You have my word, Wolf. You'll never feel like that again."

I kiss her wrinkles away, finding the need to believe her stronger than the fear that I shouldn't. She's still holding back from me. But for her, and to savor this moment, I'm going to let this go.

I run the tip of my nose along her jaw and then to her ear, nipping and sucking on her sensitive skin. "I'll never get enough of you. You know that? And I don't just mean the sex."

She moans and nuzzles her chin into me as she slips her hand down to my throbbing cock. "Are you sure? Because I want you again."

Lyric

"We're here," I say quietly, wishing for just a few more minutes alone with Wolf.

We're sitting in the back of the van as our driver pulls through the gate of Wolf's vacation home—*our* vacation home. The moment we sat down in the car, Wolf pulled me onto his lap and we've been in this position ever since, talking and kissing.

I lean in, pressing my nose to his while searching his eyes. "It's never been like this for me before, you know? No one has ever made me feel the way you do." I kiss him again.

He swallows and nods before holding me closer. Then he nuzzles my neck with his facial scruff, making me giggle. "This is my new favorite position," he says with a tilt of his lips. "I've always liked it with you on top, but this is nice. Just holding you." He kisses me again, firm but sweet. "I don't want to work this week. I just want you, in our bed."

The sound of the van's engine shutting off interrupts our moment. I have a feeling there will be a lot of interrupted moments over the next week. We ignore it and kiss again, dragging out our time together for as long as possible.

When we finally exit the van, I hear Wolf grunt. I turn. He's shaking his right fist. "Damn, it really hurts."

"We need to get you some more ice." I frown.

"I'll be fine." He shakes his hand again and then clamps down on it with his other one. "I should probably be careful who I punch. I kind of need this hand."

I frown. "Will you be able to play?"

"I've got a week of recovery time. That's not what I'm worried about. I just can't finger fuck you as good with my left hand."

I tilt my head and glare through my smile. Wolf's idea of romance always involves fucking of some kind—not that I'm complaining. "Let's go inside, rock star. If your hand still hurts, I'll let you watch me finger fuck myself later tonight."

Wolf's narrowed lids bring a smile to my face as we approach the front door of the mansion. "You can't say shit like that to me when I can't keep you honest right away. I've got a full day at the studio."

I shrug flirtatiously. "Sorry."

He wraps an arm around my shoulders as we approach the house. Terese and Derrick must have heard us coming, because they step out through the front door just as we make it up the stairs. "You two back together or what?" Derrick asks.

Wolf moves me so that I'm in front of him going up the stairs. "We were never apart, dickhead."

Derrick laughs while my insides grow warm with happiness and the boulder of unease is lifted from my stomach. I should have never doubted us. I never will again.

Chapter Thirteen

Lyric

I can hardly walk today. My muscles are screaming at me after my all-morning sexfest with Wolf. As soon as we got back to the house, we went straight to our bedroom to "take a nap." He's never pounded me so hard, which is surprising with his injury, but I wasn't about to stop him. We were both sex-starved. Making up for lost time, I guess. I smile, remembering all the sweet words that came out of his mouth, along with some dirty ones, as I fill the last plate with food.

"Brunch is ready!" Terese calls into the intercom. I laughed at it when I first saw it, but the house is so big that it's proved to be necessary. We decided to help Alice, the house cook, make a late breakfast for everyone before leaving for the studio at two this afternoon. I can't remember the last time any of us has had a homecooked meal.

One by one, members of the band and the crew come out from their bedrooms. Apparently, everyone started partying as soon as they arrived at the house this morning. No surprise there. They deserved the downtime to just let loose, even if they will have to pay for it this afternoon.

Wolf shuffles over to me, shirtless and fresh out of the shower. He's growling as he wraps his arms around my waist. "Don't think I forgot how to punish you when you leave me with morning wood. We should go back to bed."

I laugh and flip around to face him. "Are you going for a world record? Don't you need a break?"

"Fuck no," he growls playfully, but the intensity behind his words makes me hot. "My dick can't behave around you. He *lives* for you."

I melt a little, even though he's talking about the stick between his legs and not him. I know Wolf loves me. "Tell your friend down there he's confusing afternoon for morning. Honest mistake," I tease. "And he can have me all he wants later. You guys need to eat and get to the studio."

Wolf's eyes light up. "You coming with us? It's our song, babe."

I smile as I remember the part "Dangerous Heart" played in getting us to this point. "Yes, I'll come for a little bit, but I can't stay. I really do have a shitload to do for Europe."

The European tour technically doesn't start for another two weeks, but we fly to London on Monday to rehearse the new set list. There aren't too many changes, other the stage arrangement and some restructuring of their song order, but we need to get the jet lag out of the way before the tour. I have so much to do before we go, including confirming the bookings and making sure everyone has the right international travel documents before we fly out.

Wolf nods. "Fair enough."

With a quick kiss, he heads to the dining room to dig into his food. Everyone has a plate at this point, so I start cleaning the counters and loading the dishwasher while Alice tries to shoo me away.

"Lyric!" Wolf yells from the other room. "Get your ass in here and eat."

I roll my eyes, start the dishwasher, and then join everyone at the table. Wolf motions for me to join him since all the seats are taken. He pulls me to his lap and feeds me scrambled eggs while kissing my arm.

I'm laughing as I chew my first bite. "Stop," I wave away another bite. "I can feed myself."

"Oh, shit," Hedge calls from the other side of the room. "Not only are they back together, but they're going to make us all sick with it."

I laugh as Wolf tosses a piece of bread at Hedge's head. "Don't be a dick. We don't need a replacement for Crawley. Well, we do, but you know what I mean. You should work on getting yourself a girl this week."

Hedge lets out a loud laugh. "I can have a girl whenever I want, shitface. You remember what that's like?" He winks at Wolf, making my stomach unfurl. "I'm not looking to settle down anytime soon like you, chumps."

Lorraine stands up with her plate. "I'm with Hedge. Nothing wrong with being single. We're still young. And sexy as hell." She grins, then tosses Wolf a look. "It wasn't that long ago we were all single." She looks at me and winks. "No offense."

I turn to catch Wolf's hard expression. I'm not oblivious of his past, but I don't want to imagine Wolf as the ladies' man everyone talks about. He's never given me any reason to believe he's anything but devoted to me.

Wolf's eyes catch mine, and his expression softens. I lean in to kiss his cheek, and then I move to his ear. "I love you," I whisper.

His skin bristles beneath my mouth. He doesn't return my words, but before I know it, Wolf has me in his arms and is carrying me out of the dining room.

"You can eat later," he growls.

I giggle the entire way as he carries me to the bedroom and throws me onto the bed.

The moment we enter the recording studio, I feel the same sense of familiarity as when we walked into the Aragon in Chicago last month. The rich, dark brown walls and sleek wood floors that lead to the reception desk scream money and class. This studio is one I frequented a lot as a child, and although the décor has changed since then, the feeling of importance remains. The feeling that any artist who walks through these doors has *made it.*

A dark-skinned woman with light brown eyes and long, black braids greets us from the other side of the room. I don't recognize her, but I'm not sure there are many people I would recognize here anymore. "Ah! Right on time," she says warmly. "Great to see you all again."

Handshakes and warm hugs are exchanged energetically before Wolf brings me forward to introduce us. "Vana, this is my girlfriend, Lyric. Lyric, meet our sound engineer, Ivana. But you can call her Vana. We all do."

Vana's kind eyes twinkle with familiarity. It's clear she knows who I am, but she doesn't say anything about it. "Very pleased to meet you, Lyric. We've got a great setup in the studio, so you girls will be plenty comfortable." She glances between Terese, Misty, and me. "And help yourself to anything in the green room. Drinks, snacks, a game of ping pong."

Terese latches onto me and nudges my side at the words ping pong. "You and me, Lyric. What do you say?"

I grin at her. "You are *so* on."

Excitement rushes through me as Vana leads us down the wide halls of the studios. Gold and platinum records decorate the walls alongside signed photos of the high-profile names that have recorded in this space. I know exactly where to find the photos and platinum records of Mitch Cassidy—next to Studio Blue, his favorite to record in.

To my surprise, it's same one Vana is taking us to.

The layout of the room is exactly as I remember, but just like the lobby, everything else has changed. A large, white leather couch takes up the entire back wall, and a curved window separates us from the audio booth where the boys will spend the rest of their day. Instruments and microphones are set up in the center of the room on a burgundy and black rug.

Wolf's stage crew is already taking charge, switching out the studio equipment for the band's guitars and microphones. The drum kit remains, but Derrick's sticks get placed on his stool.

As the guys begin to strategize their day, memories of great times with my father flood my mind in an unstoppable rush. It's overwhelming, and all of it is exacerbated by what Doug told me. My father is in town, and he'll be at the studio. He wants to see me.

As a kid, the studio was my favorite place to visit. My dad would sit smack in the center of the room, lost in his music, but somehow he would always catch my eye through the heavy glass and wink at me before each take. All I did was sit and listen, but it was enough to feel as if I was part of every creation. Besides, he used to call me his muse.

With acoustics streaming from all angles of the room, the sound always had a magical effect on me, as if the sound bounced off the walls and hit me directly in the chest. It was one of the many reasons that made it so easy for me to fall in love with music.

This is how all music should be heard. There's nothing like tuning out the whole world, leaving nothing but the music humming through your body and soul. I swallow back the emotion in my throat. The memories of this place are so vivid, and it's like that same little girl who would squeal with pride for her father has come alive within me and is ready to experience it all over again.

Wolf must notice something in my expression because he pulls me into his arms and searches my eyes with his. "You okay?"

I nod quickly, not wanting to make this day about me. It's hard not to be anxious, though. "I'm perfect." I lift up onto my toes and give him a peck on the lips. "Kill it, baby."

He winks and pats my ass. "You know I will."

The guys enter the large, soundproof room and take their places, ready to go to work. I smile when Wolf removes his shoes. My dad used to do the exact same thing, and of course as a kid I always followed his lead. On the occasions he would let me join him in the *music box*, as I used to call it, I would toss off my flip flops and adjust the mic, like it was something I did every day. Like I was pop star going to work, ready to record my next hit.

Giggling, I sink into the couch with the girls, all of our attention on our boys, ready for what we know will be an epic session.

"How long have you and Stryder been together?" Terese asks Misty while we wait.

"Since high school," she responds in her usual bubbly tone.

Wait, what? My head snaps to the right to join the conversation. "I didn't know that." I knew they'd been together a while, but high school? That means they've been together for at least six years now. That's incredible.

"You're like an old married couple by now," Terese teases.

Misty giggles. "Not exactly. We broke up for a couple years when the guys started touring. We'd see each other still, but the long distance thing doesn't work for us." Her eyes move to the studio glass where Stryder is placing a guitar strap around his shoulders. "I prefer traveling with him."

Terese has a thoughtful expression on her face, and I wonder if she's thinking about her future with Derrick. They haven't been together very long, but I've seen the way they are around each other, so I don't think she's getting ahead of herself. She has one week with him, and then what happens? Will *they* try to make the long distance thing work out?

A sound through the speakers steals our attention. It's time. I take in deep breath, bracing myself for the familiar sounds of the studio.

And it's so much better than I was ready for.

The moment the guys start to play, the sound fills my body. Fills my soul. It's like I'm hovering above it all, soaking it in. The emotions are heavy, especially when Wolf's voice filters through the speakers. But almost as soon as it began, the tranquility of the sound is broken up by Wolf's cussing.

"Shit. I'm sorry," he apologizes while removing his guitar. "I need more rest on this hand. Can we get a backup to play guitar on this, Vana?"

I cringe. He should have been icing his hand all morning instead of trying to set yet another record for most orgasms in a row.

The engineer calls someone on the phone, and in minutes they have a guitarist standing in for Wolf. The guys immediately go back to work, deep in the zone.

My phone buzzes the entire morning, but I ignore it for the sake of the band. Nothing could take me away from this sound. Not even ping pong—not that Terese requests a game. She might be more glued to her spot on the couch than I am.

I let myself stay until the band takes a longer break to go over some takes with Vana. It doesn't look like the guys are going anywhere soon, and I need to work. Not wanting to disturb them, I shoot Wolf a quick text message telling him I'm going back to the house, say bye to the girls, and then sneak out the door.

When I'm in the quiet hallway, I finally look at my phone. All numbers I've never seen before, and one new voicemail. I press play and cautiously place the phone to my ear.

"Hey, sweet pea." My stomach lurches into my throat at Tony's familiar, gravely tone that grates on my ears.

Isn't Doug supposed to be babysitting him? Why is he calling me?

"Jesus," he says with a frustrated breath. "I got a new number. Wanted you to have it—in case you wanted to talk." There's silence between heavy breaths. "Look, I'm sorry for being a dick the other night. I fucked up hard. But dammit, Lyric. Two years together. I was going to marry you. Joanna was... Shit, Joanna was a mistake, and you know that. I'm not even sure how it happened. But it's over, and we can fix this. I know we can. You can't just throw it all away—and for Wolf, of all people? Just—just call me back."

The voicemail ends, and my blood runs cold. He has no right to call me. There's nothing he can do to take back what he did. And if I'm being honest with myself, our relationship was over long before Joanna happened. Seeing them together just gave me the excuse I needed to walk away.

He was convenience. He was familiarity. Sure, I guess I loved him at one point. Maybe. I don't know. But it was nothing like how I feel for Wolf. Not even close.

Instead of continuing down the hallway to the main lobby, I head in the other direction and peer into the familiar sound studios. All are set up in their unique way—some for instrumentals, some for acoustics, and some just for vocals. There's even a theater on the other side of the building where I first learned to play piano. Well, the basics. "Hot Cross Buns" was about all I could manage at the age of four.

The theater still looks the same, but smaller. Funny how that happens. The same abstract oil paintings representing different eras of music still decorate the walls. Even the grand piano in the center of the stage appears to be the same. Amazing. What's it been—ten years since I've been in this room? Since I've sat in this audience to watch private performances? Since I've been on that stage myself?

I smile and walk toward the stage, running my fingers along the edges of the seats as I pass them. *This room.* The room that fueled so many of my hopes and dreams starting from the time I was four years old. And the more time I spent here watching my father, making friends with the producers and artists that came through … the more my dreams started to feel like reality.

As much as I loved the studio, I could never sit in it for too long. The neverending arguments over creative control became too much at times, so I would wander around the building, almost always finding myself here in this room. I would sit at the piano and dream of playing music for a crowded room. My own original music.

I climb the steps of the stage and sit in front of the beautiful keys, letting my fingers slide across them silently. White, black, white, black, white. I test a few notes. And then a chord. I close my eyes as I feel the rush of adrenaline starting at my fingertips and working its way through my body.

The music owned me back then. This was my home for so long, just the piano and me. We could be anything. Create anything. And it was magic.

At least it felt like magic.

Expressing myself was never difficult, but finding someone to listen was always a challenge. The piano listened. It took my beatings; it embraced my pain. And most importantly, it spit out my truth, conjuring the most beautiful melodies.

I'm not sure when it happens, but at some point, I start playing. *Really* playing. It's as natural as it ever was as my fingers dance over the keys, and it feels... *Damn.* My lids squeeze together tighter, and I remember how long it's been since I last gave myself over to the music.

It's not a hard moment to pinpoint because it was the same moment I realized my dreams were for nothing.

I was eighteen the last time I played piano, living with Destiny. My mom walked into the house and I froze at the keys, the hum of the instrument still ringing in the air. I remember begging silently for the reverberations to stop, to eliminate any proof that I'd been playing at all. Destiny didn't deserve to hear my music, my innermost thoughts expressed in the best way I knew how. Six years later that damn humming still hasn't gone away.

But now ... it's like riding a bike. My fingers effortlessly play a familiar melody, though I can barely remember where it came from.

The tune radiates throughout my entire body, and I'm right back to my happy place. I forget the Destiny and Crawley drama for a moment. Forget the reason I abandoned my intimacy with the music. It's safe to feel it again. But to *create* music—that's where the scary begins.

For the first time in years, I feel the release that lit me up from within as a teenager. When anything felt possible. When dreaming was just the first step to an entire world of possibilities—

"Now that's a sound I didn't think I'd ever hear again. Beautiful, pumpkin. Just beautiful."

My fingers fade to a stop as my heart picks up the pounding melody in my chest. I twist my neck to face the source of the voice, not sure if I'll be able to handle the flood of emotions already building within me. Our eyes connect.

"Dad."

He's smiling. A bright, familiar smile that starts with his eyes—always—and follows his heightened cheekbones to the crinkle in his nose, and finally down to his mouth. It's that full smile that fills me with comfort. Aside from some new creases across his brow and around his eyes, he looks exactly the same. Styled casually in dark denim and a vintage Bulls t-shirt, he's still as charismatic as ever. Strong. Confident. Tired.

Even his strides are just as I remember them. Long and determined as he approaches, his eyes never leaving mine. I realize I've just been staring at him, so I step away from the piano and hop off the short stage to greet him.

My dad hugs me, and I breathe him in. He smells the same, too. His aftershave is cool and sharp, familiar and comforting. The tears are filling my eyes before I can stop them.

It's been almost two years since I've seen him, but I know the distance has been more my fault than his. The pain and suffering I went through with my mother somehow made me cold toward my father, too. In a way, I blamed him for how she treated me. If he hadn't sent me away to live with Destiny, none of the betrayal and pain would have ever happened.

She never would have stolen my childhood. My trust. Thank God she never stole my love for music. But she did steal my dream of sharing my music with the world, and that's almost as bad. She gave me a dose of reality I would never wish on anyone.

"It's so good to see you, pumpkin."

His words squeeze at my heart, and I finally pull away to get a closer look at him. I smile. It's a small smile, but he reacts with a smile of his own.

"It's good to see you, Dad. What are you doing here?"

He cocks his head. "Didn't Doug tell you? I'm here to see you. I'm taking some time off between tours and writing. You know, I think this is the first real break I've taken since we lived together." He smiles at the thought. "I've been doing this for a long time, pumpkin. Time off was overdue, and I hoped we could spend some of it together. Only if you want to, of course." He sighs and looks around the room. "Other than that, I have no clue what to do with myself."

I know my father, even after all the time apart. He's scared of the time off. Mitch has always been a workhorse. Whether he's on tour, or in the studio recording a new album, or mentoring newer bands to help them get an edge in the industry, he's always moving. Always busy.

"It will be good for you."

"I hope so. You look good, Lyric. Sound good, too. Better than I remember."

I blush. He doesn't know how many beatings my piano took after I left Chicago. He also doesn't know it's the first time I've played in years.

"So. Europe, huh?"

I move to sit at the edge of the stage and he follows. "Yup. Next week. The guys have some insanely obsessed fans over there, so things should be interesting."

He nods, but I can tell he has something else on his mind. "Things okay working with the band? I heard about all the trouble with Tony. Hopefully the company took care of you."

I make a face, suddenly uncomfortable. This conversation will lead to my relationship with Wolf, and I'm not sure what to talk about that with him, although it sounds like he already knows most of it.

"I'm okay. Hoping things return to normal, but what Tony did…" I scrunch my nose in fury. "He's repulsive."

My dad nods. "I'd say so. The story is already dying, though. He's scum, and everyone knows his career will be over before it really begins. He doesn't have what it takes to last in this business. Not many do."

He looks at me as his brow lifts. "I'd say that Wolf character has a better chance."

"Wolf has what it takes," I confirm confidently. "He's a good guy. Passionate about his music. Makes smart decisions—most of the time. He cares about his fans, his band. He treats the people close to him like family. He reminds me a lot of you." I smile because I never thought about that before now.

"Doug tells me he cares a great deal for you."

"Dad," I moan.

He chuckles. "C'mon, pumpkin. I never got to be the father that kept boys away with my shotgun. Let me have some fun."

I laugh. "He does care about me, okay? Happy?" I nudge his shoulder with mine. "I almost messed things up pretty good, but we're working it out."

"You still writing?"

My laughter ceases, and I immediately retreat into my shell. The walls that Wolf broke through were built because of my parents, mostly my mother. "I haven't written in the past week, but I'm writing some."

"'Dangerous Heart.' That's yours, isn't it?"

My jaw drops, and I throw my arms up in the air. "How does everyone know about that? I turned it over to Wolf. No one should have ever known that I wrote it."

My dad smiles. "Pumpkin, I would know your writing anywhere. You didn't arrange it, though, did you?"

I shake my head, amazed at how well my father knows me even after our time apart. "I don't arrange anymore. Wolf found the song after I trashed it, and he loved it so much he put it to music." I smile at the memory. "I was enraged at first, but then we made a deal. He promised me his silence, and I gave him my song. He'd rather tell the world I'm the one who wrote it, but he respects my privacy."

"He respects *you*. I like him more than Tony already."

"You didn't even know Tony, dad."

His eyes grow wide. "I met the asshat. Twice, if I remember correctly. Pumpkin, you may have been mad at me for the past nine years, but I tried to stay in your life as much as you'd let me.

"He opened for me before you met him, you know. Hated him then. And then I came out to Vegas once and had dinner with you two. He was a real charmer," he smirks, revealing his sarcasm. "Knew I couldn't trust him for shit."

I laugh incredulously. "Why didn't you ever say anything to me?"

He glares at me, his lips curved up in amusement. "You already hated me. I wasn't about to fuck things up more than they already were. Besides, you're an adult, and I've always trusted you to make your own decisions. I knew that eventually you would realize the error of your ways."

"Ha! Says the forever bachelor."

He groans and rolls his eyes. "No, you did not just bring up *Forever Bachelor*. I could have killed my career with that show. Damn near did."

"I still tuned in every Sunday night. You were a real ladies' man; that's for sure. Did you really have to kiss every single female contestant, though?"

"Yes," he responds with mock confidence. "I didn't want to play favorites."

"What was the point of that show, anyway? I watched it every week and never quite understood."

"They wanted me to ride off into the sunset with one of the women, and that was supposed to be the big twist. That a rock legend like me would go on a show claiming to be a forever bachelor and then wind up falling in love. It didn't exactly turn out the way they wanted."

There are tears in my eyes from laughing. "You picked a winner at the end, though. Even said you were in love with her."

"Lies!" he shouts dramatically. "All lies. We broke up a minute after the director yelled 'cut.' She despised me by the end of the show."

"Gee, I wonder why," I tease.

My dad shakes his head. "I didn't claim to be the perfect male specimen. I just know that my daughter should never date a man like me."

"Daddy, you're a good man."

"Not good enough for my daughter to speak to me."

My heart hurts at his words. "Things just got . . . difficult. I don't know. I felt like Mom stole a huge part of me, you know? I had big dreams. Not to follow in my parents' footsteps exactly, but I was determined to collaborate with the hottest artists and work in a studio just like this one. After I found out what she did, I hated her.

"You know, it's funny," I continue. "Even when I moved in with her and she was never around, I couldn't bring myself to hate her—not until she really gave me a reason to."

It's true. I always made excuses for her when my friends would come over and ask me where she was, or when she wasn't in the audience to watch me perform at my high school's talent night.

It's not like I was alone when my mother wasn't around. There was a full-time house cleaner and a hired tutor to help me with schoolwork. I had a chauffeur to get me to and from school and appointments. And then there was Deloris, my nanny, who took care of everything else. Deloris was my rock through those years, but still, I hoped Destiny would come around.

"You don't hate your mother, Lyric," my dad says. "You'll probably be mad at her forever, and you have every right to be, but your heart doesn't hold hate. That's not you."

I turn my head toward him and frown. "It sure feels like hate. She had zero remorse for what she did, even after she saw how much it broke me. I'd never felt more alone than I did in that moment."

"You weren't alone. Not at all." His face softens. "I would have fought Soaring for you if you'd have let me, but you told me to stay out of it. I just figured there was more to the story I wasn't privy to. Pumpkin, I would have done anything for you. Still would. Your mother..." He trails off. "I should have never sent you to live with her."

I do not want to cry right now, but the tears are pricking the backs of my eyes and my throat feels swollen.

I'm twenty-four years old, and I'm still crying over shit my parents did when I was a teenager. It's time I move on from this. I just don't want to be angry anymore.

My father slips a hand into mine, and my heart expands with love for this man. God, I've missed him. I give up trying to hide the buildup of tears. The expression on his face mirrors mine.

"Let's do something together," he suggests, his voice thick with emotion. "Like old times."

At first I'm not sure what he means, but then I realize his eyes have moved from my blotchy face to the piano. I shake my head. "No, I can't."

"You were just playing. Come on. Play something with me."

I take a deep breath. That hopeful smile on his face and pleading eyes... I can never say no to my father. And anyway, if I'm going to move past all this shit that's been holding me back for so long, I might as well start right now.

He helps me to my feet, and we sit next to each other on the piano bench. He smiles as his fingers play around the keys, toying with melodies for us to play together.

"You ready?"

"What are we playing?"

He winks at me. "You'll know in three keys."

He plays the first line of the verse and my eyes immediately go wide. "'Gravity.' I still love that song."

Without another word, my father places his fingers on the keys and starts the haunting melody from the beginning. His eyes are closed, waiting. I laugh, knowing what he wants me to do. I thought we were just going to play together, but no.

He wants me to sing.

I take deep breath, feeling somewhat shaky. I haven't sung in years, except for in the shower. He starts the verse from the beginning again, and this time I'm ready. I close my eyes, prepared to feel the impact of the music as I let the words lift from my diaphragm and out into the surrounding space. Once again, I'm overwhelmed with emotion and filled with the buzzing from the room's acoustics. This feeling … I forgot what this feels like.

Then something takes over me, a passion I haven't felt in far too long. When the first lyrics escape my mouth, I feel free. This song was made for me. It may be about a relationship with a lover, but to me, it's always been about the music. About my dreams of feeling grounded in my space when my world was filled with constant chaos, something only music could do for me.

"Baby girl, you've still got it," my dad says after he hits the last note.

My chest is so full, it feels like it's going to combust. I'm breathing hard, still reeling from the energy in the room. I'm trying to manage my way through my riptide of emotions when my dad rubs circles on my back with a strong palm.

I needed this. Him. The song. The reminder that I can still do this.

A slow clap starts from the back of the room, and I don't need to look up to know who it belongs to. My heart races. It's like Wolf's soul is tethered to mine and he could sense something big was happening.

When I finally look up, I'm met with an expression of surprise and pride. He tries to hide the hurt, but I know it's there. Another secret, exposed. I'm sure he has no idea why I would hide this from him.

Great. The last thing I need is another reason for Wolf to lose trust in me.

"Looks like we have an audience," my dad says, standing and jumping from the stage.

And then I watch in horror as the two most important men in my life walk toward each other and shake hands.

Chapter Fourteen

Wolf

Mitch Cassidy extends his hand to me. I take it without hesitation as I meet the eyes of my idol—and more importantly, Lyric's father. I'm standing in front the man who I looked up to growing up more than I did my own father.

Mitch is one of the most respected, talented musicians in the industry. I feel like I'm in the company of rock royalty. Normally I would be excited, but all I can think about is how the mountain of Lyric's secrets and lies continues to grow.

I'm trying to keep the hurt from seeping through, but it's not easy. I'm not even sure this is significant enough to be upset over. Still, I'm pissed. And fucking confused.

"Wolf, I presume." I can tell from the way Mitch is searching my face that he's already caught on to my befuddled expression.

"Yes, sir. Mitch Cassidy. I'm a huge fan of yours—and your daughter."

Mitch laughs, relieving some of the tension I brought into the room. "You didn't know my daughter could sing."

I shake my head. "We're still getting to know each other, sir."

He makes a face. "None of that 'sir' crap. Mitch is fine." He smiles. "I hear your tour is going well. And your chart rankings are phenomenal. Congratulations. I'm a fan of the latest album, but I'm hoping for more of that 'Dangerous Heart' sound on the next one." He winks, and it's clear he knows who wrote that song.

Hearing Mitch Cassidy compliment me might just be the highlight of my career. "Wow, thank you. It's been quite the ride. And I agree. We've been working with a talented writer who's chosen to stay anonymous."

Mitch's eyes crinkle, and I can see where Lyric gets her heart. She carries it in her eyes, just like her father. "Hopefully not forever."

Lyric approaches us in that moment, and I almost forget that I'm mad at her. Her eyes are already pleading with me to not be upset. I'm not about to have this conversation here in front of her father, so I wrap an arm around her shoulder.

"Are you guys on break?" she asks.

I nod. "Yup. Someone said Mitch was here, and I wanted to introduce myself. I thought you left."

She looks to her father and smiles. "I was caught up in old memories, and then we ran into each other. I really should get going, though. I have a million things to do for Europe." When her eyes turn up to meet mine I want to ask her so many questions. "Walk me out?"

I nod and turn back to Mitch. "It was great to meet you."

"Likewise." He smiles, then looks at Lyric. "Will you be here tomorrow?"

Lyric hesitates, and I can feel her body stiffen. I'm so confused by her right now, and I have no idea how to interpret her reactions. "I think so. Maybe for a couple hours."

"How about lunch? Can you make time for your old man?"

"Um, yeah. Okay. Let's do lunch tomorrow."

We wave goodbye, and I lead Lyric out to the front door. Once I'm sure we're alone, I turn to face her. "What the hell was that?"

I don't mean to sound angry, but what the fuck? Lyric blanches and steps away from me. Shit. I hate when she pulls away like this.

I pull her back and tilt her chin so her eyes meet mine. "You sing? You play? What else are you keeping from me?"

Her eyes turn down and then back up into mine. "I haven't done that in years. My dad asked me to, and I couldn't say no. It's all in my past, though."

"But why?" I demand. "Baby, you're *so* good. Honestly, your voice is fucking amazing."

She groans. "It's just an old dream. It's not what I want anymore." Her eyes dart around us and I sigh, knowing she's not about to divulge any more to me now.

"All right. I'll see you tonight, then?"

She looks shocked, as if she's expecting me to put up a fight. But I'm tired of fighting.

"Okay." She wraps her arms around my waist and lifts up on her toes to kiss me. I can't help it. I hesitate a little, still consumed with all the secrets. I don't know what to expect from her. This girl that I love more than life scares the shit out of me.

"Wolf?"

I look down and close the gap between our lips. It's a hurried kiss, one I know will leave us both unfulfilled, but I've got other things on my mind right now. She gives me another backward glance when she gets into the car, and then the driver takes off. It all feels wrong.

The same questions that tormented me when Lyric left impale me now. If it wasn't for the entrance door to the studio crashing open against the brick exterior, I might just be stuck in my thoughts for hours.

"Fuckface! Get in here. You have five minutes to piss or whatever, and then we need to work." Derrick is holding the door open for me, Terese by his side.

"Was that Lyric?" Terese asks. "Does she know her dad's here?"

I walk through the door and give her a nod. "Yeah, she knows. She went back to the house to work."

Everything about me is tense for the rest of the day. Luckily, today is mostly about the instrumentals, not the vocals. That's probably not a good thing, actually. It gives me too much time to sit back and stew when I should be listening to the cuts. Usually Crawley would be heavily involved in this part, jumping in to give his two cents. I hate to admit it, but with him gone, I'm a bit lost.

When it comes time to listen to a rough playback of the chorus, I have a hard time focusing. Nothing sounds right. The pacing seems off, the guitar cut in too soon, and it's just … missing something.

"What do you think, Wolf? We need to at least lock down the chorus today. I know you want to beat this thing to death, but we're losing time."

Our sound engineer is the shit. Vana's been doing this for years and knows how to keep things moving in the studio. I respect her, but her push isn't helping my attitude.

"Wait a sec." I stand up and walk out of the room, hoping Mitch is still around.

Lucky for me, I find him right outside the studio door with his cell phone to his ear. When he sees me, he tells whoever it is he'll call them back.

"Wolf. Everything okay?"

I take a deep breath and run a hand through my hair. I don't know why I'm suddenly so nervous. Is it because I'm standing in front of *the* Mitch Cassidy? Or because Mitch is Lyric's father? Or because of what I'm about to ask him?

"It's kind of a long story, but our band manager, Crawley—"

He grimaces. "I'm aware of the prick. Go on."

I laugh. "Okay, well we're kind of between band managers right now, and usually I'd count on Crawley for his input."

"What do you need. An ear?"

I stare at Mitch. I can't believe I'm asking him this. "Could you? I mean, I don't want to tell the guys, but I'm a little lost right now without him. He was a prick and I don't regret letting him go, but he had a good ear."

Mitch groans. "Crawley's an ass. Never forget that. I'll take a listen as long as you never admit to another soul what you just told me."

I grin. Wow. This is really going to happen.

"Deal."

The rest of the session goes much smoother, and my stress levels decrease as time goes on. Everyone in the room has mad respect for Mitch. He's a fucking brilliant artist, and his feedback is on point. We can't help but gravitate toward him after every take, asking him for approval. He never demands a thing, just lets us play and provides pointers on what to do to make everything better. And when he loves something, it's like fireworks are going off with all the excitement in the room.

What are the odds? Lyric writes the song. I compose it. And Mitch fucking Cassidy is practically producing.

Unreal.

"Lyric," I call out.

I'm the first one back at the house. Everyone else went out to dinner, but Lyric wasn't answering her phone, so I decided to check on her.

"Babe?"

No response.

I walk down the long hallways and peer into every room of the main floor, but she's nowhere to be found.

Panic sets in when I make it to the top of the staircase. This is stupid. I'm not going to check every single room in the house until I find her. She probably went for a walk. Or a run. We haven't been on a run in a while, and there are plenty of scenic views to take in around here. And after seeing her father again, it would be very much like Lyric to go for a run to clear her mind.

Suddenly I feel like the shittiest boyfriend for being upset at her. She's going through a lot, and I promised her patience. I groan, reaching for my phone to call her again.

I press the call button and wait. An acoustic song I recorded for her ringtone plays from somewhere downstairs, so I take the stairs two at a time as I track it. The sound is muffled, as if it's buried in something, and once I reach the foyer I know it's got to be in the kitchen.

Lyric's purse is sitting on the stool under the island, so I grab it and shuffle through it. There it is, right at the end of the melody I created just for her. But as soon as my call ends, another call rings in, this ring tone a generic one. I click the "end" button to ignore the call. *4 missed calls from this number*, it says. A possessive rumble takes over my chest. Who the fuck is blowing up Lyric's phone?

Before the light dims, I look at the number closely. 206 area code. That's Seattle, isn't it? There's only one person I know from Seattle that would call Lyric. Discomfort snakes through me as I think of the night in the club with Tony harassing Lyric, leaving me no choice other than to obliterate his face with my fist.

As much as I want to dig more to give me a reason to stake Tony out and end this now, I decide not to fuck up my relationship by snooping any more than I already have. I'll just ask Lyric when I see her. That's what a normal boyfriend would do. A normal boyfriend in an honest relationship. She'll tell me what's going on … I hope. Not that she's been very forthcoming with information so far.

Groaning against the growing weight of questions that seems to just keep falling, I make my way downstairs to the bottom level of the house where the gym, theater, activity room, and some guest bedrooms are. Bingo. The light is on in the gym, and the door is cracked slightly. Of course she's working out. It's second best to running, and running is no fun in this humidity.

I push the door open to see Lyric stretching on a yoga mat with her back arched, stomach exposed, and pelvis high in the air. Her feet press flat against the floor as she contracts, releases to press her core into the mat, and then she's arching her back again. The simple movement is sexy as fuck. And it doesn't help that she's wearing tiny pink shorts that cling to her body and a matching pink sports bra.

"Babe." I'm instantly hard.

She's got headphones in, but she must hear me over the music because she looks up in surprise and rips the buds out of her ears.

"Hey."

Her eyes move to her phone in my hand. She swallows uncomfortably, and my heart sinks. I can't take any more secrets.

Then Lyric adjusts herself, lowering herself to the floor and then sitting up, her eyes still on the phone.

"I tried calling you and found this," I say, setting the device on the table beside me. I hesitate before coming clean. "You had a bunch of missed calls from Seattle."

Her eyes narrow. "You looked through my phone?"

Heat burns my chest. What is she hiding? "No!" I pause, because it did feel like I was snooping a little bit. "Your phone rang after I found it in your purse, and it showed four missed calls. 206 area code is Seattle. So, who the fuck is blowing up my girlfriend?"

The shade of pink in Lyric's cheeks keep darkening, only adding to the growing number of secrets. As much as I want to practice my patience with Lyric, I think I'm hitting my limit.

I watch as she swallows, her eyes carrying a hint of worry among the many layers of emotions she manages to carry so well. "Did you listen to the voicemails too?" she asks, sarcasm dripping from her tone.

"Should I?" I demand. "Is that the only way to find out what you're hiding from me?"

Her eyes soften, and she shakes her head. "I have nothing to hide from you."

"Then who is calling you?"

She lets out a deep sigh and raises her eyes to the ceiling. "Tony. I don't recognize the number, but he left a voicemail. It's no big deal. He wants me to call him, but I won't. I already called Doug and asked him to talk to Tony, so hopefully soon he won't bother me anymore."

I clench my jaw. I believe her, but I'm no less pissed than before. One confession doesn't negate all the other secrets, all the reasons I felt compelled to snoop in the first place. That's not like me, but Lyric has me feeling paranoid and possessive.

She peers up at me through her lashes, sweat beading from her chest and stomach. "Come here," she pleads. And just like that, my anger starts to fall away. All I see is Lyric. She's all I want.

I remain standing to show her I won't give in. Meanwhile, my mind and my dick have already given up the fight. My eyes peruse her body, fantasizing about taking her over the workout bench ... or maybe right there on that pink yoga mat. My eyes meet hers.

"I know what you're doing. It's not going to work this time, Lyric."

She sighs with frustration and looks down, but I won't let her shy away from facing me. There's too much at stake.

"At least look at me when you're going to deny me a piece of you," I say, gritting my teeth to stop myself from raising my voice.

She flinches at my tone.

I take a few deep breaths before continuing, trying a new approach. "I get it, Lyric. You have secrets. You aren't ready to tell me. But fucking *look* at me. I'd rather have you here with me than have you run away to deal with your secrets alone. You know I'm here when you're ready to tell me. I can be patient. I promise. Doesn't mean I'm happy about it, but I'm not letting you go."

She lets out a relieved breath and nods, then stands up and walks to where I'm inclined against the wall. I let her lean in and kiss the side of my mouth. "I love you," she whispers. Then she sighs again.

I think she knows I won't say it back. It's not that I don't love her. I might love her more than she loves me. I'm just not ready to give her those words again. Not until she fully trusts me. Maybe I'm a jerk, but I'm holding those words hostage.

"So what are we going to do about all these secrets?" I keep my lips flat, but I can't help the grinding of my teeth that hardens my jaw.

She leans back and looks me directly in the eyes. "Do you know when everyone will be back?"

"Not a clue. Maybe another hour or so," I say. My heart beats faster with hope. "Want me to check?"

She nods. "If you don't mind. There's something I want to show you, but I'd rather it just be us."

Before I can ask any questions, she steps away and walks toward the door of the gym. Before leaving the room, she turns to face me. "Meet me in the family room. At the piano." As she says this, she bows her head slightly, but I catch the pain in her expression.

She's about to let me in.

The moment she's gone, I don't waste a second. I send a group text telling everyone to stay away from the house for the next hour. The house is massive, but Lyric made it clear that she wants complete privacy, so that's what I'll give her. I'll put Rex at the front door to make sure they don't come in if I have to.

I freshen up in the bathroom and meet Lyric in the family room. She's sitting behind the piano, looking down at her hands with a slight frown on her face. She's changed out of her workout clothes and is now wearing a long, black jersey knit dress, her hair hanging loosely over one exposed shoulder.

"You okay, babe?"

She smiles as I approach, but not at me. "I am. Honestly, I worry more that my secret might sound silly to others. I don't know why I refuse to tell anyone. I guess I'm just embarrassed that my childhood was less than stellar. I mean, growing up with Hollywood's elite, you'd think I'd have it all. There's nothing to complain about, right?"

"Babe, you're talking to the right person. I've been there. You have every right to feel like you missed out on things. It's the price we pay. There ain't no heaven in fame." I reach for her hand, which is still hovering over the piano keys, and squeeze. "You don't have to prove a thing to me."

This time her smile reaches her eyes. "I trust you."

147

Chapter Fifteen

Lyric

I play the first verse and then stop. Wolf is slowly making his way around the grand piano, waiting patiently and probably trying to not distract me, but his movements are making me anxious more than anything else.

"Come sit by me."

He sits close, but not so close as to restrict my movements. He must sense that I'm about to unleash something fierce on this piano. I am.

I start the song over again, the soundtrack filling the cracks of my broken heart, caused by the story I'm about to tell.

"When I was sixteen, I moved in with my mom. You know that part." I smile. "Playing piano was my getaway, always. I could have been in a packed mall on Christmas Eve or in the middle of an interstate, but if I was behind a piano, I was in my happy place. Untouchable. I was four when I started lessons, and by the time I was a teenager I could play anything by ear.

"When I moved in with my mom, I was bored to death. That's when I started putting my lyrics to music. Composing became my escape from my lonely, shitty situation. And it all just came naturally. I was obsessed." I smile as my fingers continue to dance along the keys. "I breathed, slept, ate, and drank my music. It was the only thing that kept my mind off the pain of my father sending me away. Of my mother not being there when I'd come home.

"On the few occasions she did come home, I barely saw her. She was always on her phone, going on dates with the wealthiest men she could find, and having spa days with women from the athletic club—you know, the ones that appear on that *Housewives* show? Yeah. Well, then one day she came home and heard me singing at the piano. I'll never forget it. She finally saw me as something other than an unwelcome houseguest.

"She sat next to me, just like you're doing now. She listened. It was the most attention she'd ever given me. Soon, we were smiling and laughing together. For the first time, thanks to music, I had a mother. I thought we finally had that bond that would keep us close, you know? The kind that mothers are supposed to feel for their kids before they're even born. She seemed so proud of me.

"From then on, every time she came home, we spent hours together while I composed, and she would sing from my songbook. It was magical. When I was seventeen, I remember she had just come home from the recording studio and she was frustrated about something, so I played her a new song, knowing it would make her feel better. It was one I had been working on for a while, and I was excited to finally share it with her."

At this point, my emotions are almost overwhelming. I let my fingers do the storytelling as I play the acoustic version of my mother's greatest hit, "Innocence."

Destruction finds me at every turn

I've gotten good at running
But there's nothing more to learn
Just let the fire burn
Just let the fire burn

Ashes carried with the wind
That's me, floating away
You tell me there'll be better days
I have nothing left to say
Just let me float away
Just let me float away

You made me, saved me, destroyed me
Wanted nothing but the best
But what about the rest?
What about me? What about my innocence?
What about my dreams? What about my fairytale life?
There's no pause, no stop, no rewind
My innocence was left behind

Tossed overboard, it's sink or swim
You love me, but it's me or them
Whether I'm standing tall, or forgetting it all
Now I face it all alone
I face it all alone

You made me, saved me, destroyed me
Wanted nothing but the best
But what about the rest?
What about me? What about my innocence?
What about my dreams? What about my fairytale life?

There's no pause, no stop, no rewind
My innocence was left behind

Tears are streaming down my face by the time the song is over, and Wolf is pulling me into his arms. He already knows why I'm crushed by the words of my mother's song. It was my way of dealing with my pain at the time. Lyrics are supposed to heal, but this song didn't heal me. Instead, it was stolen and used to propel Destiny's career.

I don't have to tell Wolf anything more, but I choose to anyway.

"After that night, she took off for a while. It wasn't anything unusual, but I remember feeling disappointed. I thought we'd bonded, and then she just … got busy. Two months later, I was driving home from school when my song came on the radio. A music video came out that same day.

"My first reaction was excitement. I was ecstatic that Destiny loved my song enough to record it. I waited for her to call to tell me the big news or come home so we could celebrate. Back then, I didn't want to believe my mother was capable of something so horrible." I let out a sarcastic laugh. "I was a pathetic kid. I convinced myself that she put the song out there to surprise me. Because she was proud of me.

"When she finally came home a month later, she brought her soon-to-be-released album with her. Wolf, I listened to the entire thing and almost died. Every single song came from my songbook. She was recording my compositions when I wasn't paying attention. And then she added in her Auto-Tune crap and ruined most of them."

"Babe, I'm sorry." He's rubbing my back, throat thick with emotion.

I wipe my eyes with the back of my hand and shake my head. "She's horrible. I can't tell you how many times I tried to give her the benefit of the doubt. Every time I approached her about my songs, she was either too busy to talk or she would wave me off like I was being ridiculous. When she realized I wasn't going to drop the subject, she just stopped coming home.

"I didn't see her again until I was packing for Seattle. She'd missed my birthday, didn't even realize I had graduated. And then she had the audacity to try and stop me from moving by telling me she missed 'collaborating' with me." I laugh dryly.

"She's my mother, but I hate her for what she did to me. I couldn't trust anyone after that. She sucked my dreams of becoming a professional songwriter right out of me and tossed them out the window. I've never been able to stop writing lyrics, but sharing my music … that wasn't something I was ever going to do again. And I didn't … until you."

I smile at him because I'm happy that things turned out the way they did, even if the reasons behind it are awful.

"You were furious when you heard me sing your song," he says, as if everything finally clicks for him. "You must have been dying inside. If I had known any of this—"

I shake my head. "What you did and what my mom did are two completely separate things. You know why I gave you my song? It wasn't because you told me you liked it or because I had the hots for you. It was because you gave me the choice. I still wasn't ready for the world to know I wrote it, but it thrilled me that it was out there."

The crushed look on his face shifts to hopeful. "Really? I don't know what I'd do with myself if I ever made you feel the way Destiny did. That's just ... evil."

I nod. "I know." It's like a dagger hits my heart every time I have to agree with that statement, but it's true. "Now you know why I hid my music from the world and why I will always try to hide it from my mother."

"You have every right to hate that woman for what she did to you," Wolf says. "It's a shitty thing to take something that isn't yours. Something so personal. No sane mother would ever do that to her child."

I lean into Wolf. He's so warm, and his hold is strong. It makes me feel strong, too. "She treats me like an accessory that she uses only when she needs me. She never cared about my well-being or how I was doing in school. If I got sick, she had someone else tend to me for fear of getting sick herself. What kind of mother would hate her child so much to never care to see them, or wonder about them, or want them around?"

His chin rests on the top of my head and it moves as he talks. "A horrible one, Lyric. You realize her actions don't reflect on you, right? She sounds like an unhappy and selfish woman who lives in an alternate reality. I don't know, maybe that's where she met Crawley."

This makes me laugh a little, and Wolf smiles in response.

"She'll forever miss out on true happiness because she already had it," he says. "It was within her grasp, and she destroyed it without a second thought. The way I look at it, I feel sorry for her. But Lyric, you were put on this earth to do better than her. Your father seems to make up for some of her awfulness."

I snort sarcastically. "Well, he may be a hell of a lot better than my mother, but he's still the one who dumped me on her."

"He's sorry for that. He really loves you."

Something about Wolf sticking up for my father warms my insides, but at the same time, I'm confused. Where is this coming from? I sit up and look at him. "How do you know he's sorry?"

Wolf shrugs. "I saw the way he was with you. There was love there—between you both. You may still be angry at him, but the fact that he came here for you and made an effort to see you with no expectations is huge. Don't you think?"

I sigh. "I was happy to see him today, which surprised me. I've been mad at him for so long, but you're right. There's a difference between what he did to me and what my mom did."

Wolf smiles. "See?" He touches my nose with his and holds me tightly, waiting until I relax in his arms before speaking again. "Will you play something else for me? Your voice just might be even sexier than your lyrics."

I laugh, realizing how much lighter I feel after telling Wolf my story—a story I don't tell anyone because I'm ashamed of my pathetic excuse for a mother. I've gone through all kinds of emotions over what she did—confusion, hurt, pain, regret, anger, grief. All over the loss of my mom. She may not be dead, but my dream of what a mother should be certainly is.

Wolf adjusts his body so he's kissing my shoulder, soft kisses that make my heart flutter and my knees weak.

"Okay," I agree, because I can't imagine saying no to him about anything right now. My secrets are out. All of them. And I want to thank Wolf for helping me get to this point, and for being patient. But also, I want him to know this side of me. A side I thought I lost long ago. A side that somehow felt so right when I was singing on that stage back at the studio today. I don't think I would have ever let myself experience that moment if it weren't for all the confidence Wolf has given me, whether or not he realizes it.

I take a deep breath and start a melody I know he's more than familiar with. "Darkness Wins" is one of his earliest songs. I've never actually played it before, but I've had every chord memorized since before I met him.

When I open my mouth to sing, the words bleed from my soul and seep out my pores. I feel every single ounce of the emotion in his lyrics as if they are my own. The song, contrary to the title, is about *not* letting the darkness win. Not giving in and succumbing to the pain and letting it control you. The moment I heard this song come on the radio, I became an instant Wolf fan. He has no idea that his music carried me through a lot of hard times.

The last note punches through the air and lingers a little before Wolf sinks his teeth into the skin between my shoulder and neck. "That was the sexiest thing I've ever heard. And seen." He groans and presses me back until I'm lying flat on the piano bench. "I think you were made for me." His eyes are on my lips and then back on my eyes. "Don't ever keep anything from me again. I get why you feel like you need to keep those parts of you hidden, and you can continue to do it if it helps you, just not around me. I want all of you."

He presses a hand onto my chest, motioning to my heart. "Everything."

Tears well in my eyes at his sincerity. My throat is clogged with emotion and I'm not sure I can speak, so I just nod. He leans down and presses his lips to mine. He's been so patient with me through all of this, forgiving me even when I hurt him, loving me when I'm broken. I grip a handful of his hair and hold him as tears stain my cheeks.

When I finally get my emotions under control, I pull my lips from his. "You have my everything for as long as you want it."

"Forever, then. I want all of you. And I want you forever."

The blood running through my veins is pumping so fast as his eyes bore into mine. Our connection has been intense from the moment we met, but this … this might be the moment I realize how strong it truly is. How strong it has been since we first met at the Aragon at just fifteen years old.

I lift my hand to his face and run one finger across his cheek. "I'm so in love with you. I know I messed up when I left. I know it hurt you. I'm so sorry. You're the last person I ever want to hurt. Forgive me, and I promise I'll never keep anything from you again. Never."

His smile tells me everything I need to know as he leans down and brushes his lips against mine. "You're forgiven."

I giggle when he plants his face on my neck and tickles it with his unshaven jaw. "You know what I miss?" I ask.

"Hmm?" he moans while alternating between sucking and licking my sensitive skin.

"Writing together. Can we write something?"

I can feel the shake of his head against my skin. "Aren't you hungry, babe?" he asks as he nibbles my neck. "I'm starved."

As he works his way down my body, lifting the bottom of my dress as he goes, I stifle a moan and hold onto his shoulders. "Wolf, I'm serious. We haven't written a song in a long time. I have the itch."

When he reaches my thighs, he parts them smoothly and brushes a finger up my center. "Let me scratch it."

"Wolf," I laugh, but it feels too good to tell him to stop again. He stands but remains hovering over me. His hot mouth works its way down until it finds my center through my panties. And then he's running his teeth lightly along my core and stealing the deep moan I'm trying so hard to suppress.

I'm ready to give myself over to Wolf completely, but a sound at the door makes us jump. I sit up, smoothing down my dress while Wolf adjusts himself in his shorts next to me. My lips curl at the frustration written all over his face.

"Let's go to our room," he growls. Wolf is sexy when he's impatient and horny. I laugh and he shoots me a glare.

I bite my bottom lip, loving this way too much. "How about you grab us some food—since you're so hungry—and I'll meet you in your bedroom? I'll grab my songbook so we can write."

"*Our* room."

"Our room."

His lips meet mine as he nods. "Deal." We manage to break apart just as a rowdy crowd surges through the doors.

"What the fuck have you two been up to?" Hedge calls out, his voice slurred. He's swaying as he walks toward us, a girl tucked under each arm. One is already slipping her hand between his skin and the waistband of his jeans. I watch, stupefied, as he laughs and steers both girls down the hall toward his bedroom. Wow.

Derrick and Terese stroll in next. Terese gives me a knowing smile and walks my way.

Derrick calls after her. "Our room. Ten minutes."

Her cheeks flush and she giggles. "Yes, sir."

Who would have known Terese and Derrick would click so well? I've been majorly preoccupied lately, but I'm not blind. None of these guys are ones to settle down with someone easily. They know how much commitment it takes to keep a relationship afloat in this business. With temptation at every turn, a nonstop schedule that makes the days blur together, and the potential for disastrous fallout if things end badly—relationships are not ideal in this world. But I can already see things are different with Derrick and Terese.

"You missed an awesome session today. Please tell me I'm going to see more of you this week." Terese frowns as she plops down next to me.

I laugh. "If you're not too busy face-sucking your new boy toy over there. And I have a lot of making up to do with Wolf."

She catches my smile and returns it. "I take it you two are good?"

I nod. "We are now."

"That's a relief. Derrick and I were talking tonight. We should go on a double date this week. You know, let the guys woo us a little."

My eyes light up. "I love that idea." A double date sounds so ... normal. And drama-free. That's a foreign concept to me.

"Okay, good." She turns her head, glancing over her shoulder anxiously.

I laugh and push her jokingly. "Go ahead; go back to Derrick."

She winks before walking off and calling over her shoulder, "He is kind of addicted to me."

Still laughing, I head down the opposite hall to the master bedroom and let myself in. I have no idea where to start looking for my songbook. I haven't seen it since I left the tour a week ago. It was in Wolf's nightstand since that's where we always wrote. Rory and Rex promised to pack up everything in the drawers, so it must be in one of the bins they dropped off this morning.

I start my search. The first container is full of Wolf's clothes, my songbook nowhere to be found. I sigh and open the second bin.

Interesting.

This one is full of goodies—Wolf's condoms and lotion and some very interesting gadgets I've never seen before. My eyes grow wide as I pick up one of the objects. Wolf must have an even kinkier side than he's shown me.

"What are you doing?" Wolf comes in with a plate of food in his hand and shuts the door behind him.

I hold up the furry pink handcuffs, an eyebrow raised. "And who have you used these on?"

His eyes narrow and darken a little. "A fan gave them to me last week. I was holding on to them in case you decided to beg for forgiveness."

"Excuse me?"

His lips quirk up at the corner. "Are you upset that I accepted a sex toy from a fan? Or that I wanted you to beg?"

I narrow my eyes back at him. "I'm supposed to believe that you've never used these before?"

A chuckle rumbles from his throat as he sets the plate on the nightstand. "Relax. I've never used them. You'll just have to trust me."

Wolf approaches me as I kneel in front of the container. In one swift move, he moves my hair over my shoulder. "I wouldn't mind using them tonight. I'm getting hard just thinking about you strapped to our bed, naked. I can do whatever I want to you."

I swallow, and suddenly there's a dampness between my thighs. "You find my songbook and I'll let you do whatever you want to me." *God, please find my songbook quickly.*

Wolf sees how serious I am and kneels by my side. "It's got to be in one of these bins."

"I've been looking," I say, unconvinced.

We spend the next hour searching. By the time we finally give up, our room is a disaster. I panic, pacing from one wall to another and trying to remember the last time I saw it. Wolf sits at the edge of his bed, hands in his hair, trying to keep me calm.

"When's the last time you wrote in it?"

"With you!" I say as I throw my hands up, exasperated. "We were in bed and got distracted, like usual. But I remember picking it up off the floor after and putting it back in your drawer. That was the night before the Tony fiasco. When did you last see it?"

Wolf thinks for a moment before answering. "The day you left, I was so pissed. I grabbed it and handed it to Crawley. Told him to ship it to you. And then I thought better of it and took it back. I put it right back in the drawer."

My heart stops at his words. "Crawley knew about it. And he knew where it was? Shit. Did you see it after that?"

Wolf shakes his head, the color draining from his face as we come to the same realization. "No. Every time I looked at that damn drawer, I got pissed. There were pictures of you, your songbook, condoms… Everything reminded me of you, and it pissed me off. So no, I didn't open it again."

"You know what this means, right?"

He looks at me, his expression filled with dread. "You think?"

I nod. "I guess we know why my mom was with Crawley in your bedroom the other night. They probably went back there to take it and ended up fucking."

Wolf's face turns red as he realizes I'm right. I've got to be. We've looked everywhere.

"Before we keep going down this path, let me talk to Rory and Rex. And Doug, too. They probably put it somewhere to keep it safe."

I nod, appreciating Wolf's calm tone, but I'm not convinced. Still, I'm hopeful as he reaches for his phone and starts dialing. Ten minutes later, my worst fears are confirmed. Doug's phone rings to voicemail, but no one else has seen my songbook, and Rex made a point of mentioning that damn purse hanging off my mom's arm when she was escorted off the premises. My heart sinks.

Wolf looks at me, defeated. "Looks like your mother stole your lyrics. Again. And Crawley is in on it. I wonder how long they've been planning this." He shakes his head. "Shit. Crawley was trying to fuck with your tour contract, too."

"What?" I ask, shocked. "No one mentioned anything to me."

Wolf growls. "He didn't get away with it. He was trying to sign the rights of that three-song deal that included 'Dangerous Heart' over to him, but someone at Wicked Records caught it. I just found out a few days ago, and with everything else going on I didn't think to mention it."

I watch him pace around the room, speaking his thoughts out loud. "Wow. Somehow Destiny and Crawley bonded over their intention to steal from you. Now we know why they were together."

I'm still looking at him as he speaks, but my ears have started to ring and his words are becoming muffled. Rage has possessed me. But with every second that passes, I will myself to regain control, using the strength of Wolf's eyes to hold my focus. The rage begins to dissolve. The pace of my pounding heart slows, and I'm able to take a deep breath.

Wolf's eyes search mine, his determination evident in his hardened expression. "Destiny already hurt you once. I'm not going to let it happen again," he promises. "Destiny and Crawley won't get away with this, Lyric. I'll die before that happens."

Chapter Sixteen

Wolf

Lyric doesn't sleep. She's restless and rises at least dozen times to go to the bathroom, for no other reason than to get up. I can tell her mind is working a million miles an hour, and it makes my heart ache, but there's nothing I can do. She's refusing my comfort. Doesn't want to talk about it. She's mad. She cries. But she's silent.

When she slides the silky white comforter from her body and leaves our bed for what feels like the hundredth time, I sit up and wait. Her feet barely make a noise as she sneaks across the marble floor, stopping just long enough to shut the door behind her and flip on the light. Even in her despair she's worried about waking me up.

After a few minutes of hideous silence in a California King bed that feels far too empty, I stand and follow her tracks across the room. As soon I approach the bathroom, the light through the crack at the bottom of the door fades to black and the door opens to reveal my beautiful, puffy-eyed girl.

She sees me but avoids eye contact as she tries to move around me, so I step to the side to catch her and wrap my arms around her instead.

"Not right now," she pleads.

This time I don't listen. I tighten my hold and bury my nose in the long, wavy strands of her sun-kissed brown hair near her ear. Lyric still smells the way she did after her shower, of green apple shampoo and apricot face wash. Sexy and vibrant and good. Just like her. Seeing her like this is like taking a blow to my gut.

"I promise you, Lyric, we're going to get your songbook back. If that woman even thinks about stealing another song from you, she's going to pay for it."

Lyric lets out a choked breath, and I pull her even closer. Her weight falls into me, letting me hold her as she plants her face in the crook of my arm and cries. "Why can't she just leave me alone?"

My jaw clenches. "She's sick, Lyric. There's no use making sense of her actions. I don't think it's possible. What I do know is that you've got more talent and heart inside you than she's ever had. It must drive her crazy to have a daughter with more talent in her pinky than she does in her entire body."

Lyric shakes her head. "Stop. That can't possibly be true," she says, and I hate that she gives her mother this power. "Destiny spent an entire decade in the limelight. She had everything she could possibly want. And then I came along and she acts like I ruined her life just by existing."

What do I need to do to convince Lyric of how amazing she is? That her mother is nothing but a washed-up mess who had promise, but zero heart to back it up. Looks and talent can only get you so far in this industry and Destiny's time ran out. I can't say any of that to Lyric, because as much as she despises her mom right now, she still loves her. She wouldn't be crying otherwise.

"Babe, listen to me." I lean back and bend at the knees to meet Lyric's eyes. "Destiny Lane doesn't deserve your tears. Or your pain. She doesn't have the first clue what it means to be a decent human being, let alone a mother." I swallow against the ache in my chest as I watch Lyric's expression crumble again. "It's time to focus on what's best for you. Your career. Your life. Baby, this is your time. Don't let her take this from you."

When she leans into me again and continues to fall apart in my arms, we stay there for a few minutes before I finally lift and carry her to bed. I pull the covers over her and sit beside her while her breathing steadies. Her eyes are still wide open.

"Do you want me to get you something? To sleep?" I hesitate, because the last thing I want to do is give Lyric a way to shut reality out. But so help me if I let my girl suffer for another second tonight.

She nods, almost eagerly, so I lift myself from the bed and walk to the bathroom. I search my bags for my Tylenol PM. I rarely have time to sleep on the road, so when there is and my mind is on overload, I take one of these suckers. It kills my energy for a couple days, but a lack of sleep might kill me faster. I grab Lyric a tiny blue pill and a bottle of water from the counter and rejoin her in bed.

She swallows it down and then pulls me into her arms. "I don't know what I would do without you."

I kiss the top of her head and let out a breath. "Lucky for you, you'll never have to find out."

It's two in the afternoon when we break from the studio. It's supposed to be a two-hour lunch, but I'm not sure if I'm coming back. I tell the guys to record without me if I can't make it. Mitch has been diligently providing advice and feedback, and since I told him about what happened with Lyric and why she had to skip their lunch, he told me to go check on her and call him later.

She's still asleep when I get home, which explains why my dozens of calls and texts went unanswered. I've been a wreck all day worrying about her. I lie next to her and stroke her back as I watch her inhale and exhale gently. I think it was four in the morning when she finally drifted off in my arms, and after that pill, she could easily be knocked out for twelve hours.

When she starts to shift an hour later, I breathe a silent sigh of relief. She moans and rolls over. "How long did I sleep?"

"About eleven hours." I smile and stroke her cheek. "Those pills are potent."

She groans again. "I was supposed to have lunch with my dad. He probably thinks I blew him off."

I kiss her nose. "He knows what happened."

"You told him?" she asks, sounding panicked.

"Lyric," I say, my shoulders falling in defeat. She can't be mad about this. "I'm sorry. Mitch was asking where you were, I figured he should know. He's your father, and he cares about you."

She still doesn't respond, so I continue.

"He wants to do something about it. He said he'll call her label and threaten to sue if she does anything with the songs. But he wanted to talk to you about it first."

"I can't think straight right now. Can you just hold me for a minute?"

"Yeah, babe." I tighten my hold and watch as she drifts off again.

A half hour later, I'm standing over the stove, when Lyric walks into the kitchen wearing only a sports bra and panties like it's the most natural thing in the world. I see my future flash before my eyes as I imagine Lyric barefoot and pregnant in our kitchen, cooking while I try to grope her from behind.

I want all of that with her. Three months ago, I couldn't even see myself having a girlfriend. Everything changed when Lyric came into my life. Music had always been my purpose, but Lyric waltzed in and gave substance to it all. My world became brighter, like anything was possible, and the darkness I'd carried with me since my mother's death four years ago began to fade away.

Chapter Seventeen

Lyric

The moment I peek my head around the thick, Italian column to peer into the kitchen, my chest swells with emotion. Wolf has never looked sexier than he does in this moment, managing a stainless steel spatula with the same finesse he has holding a guitar. With a flip of his wrist, he pops a thick piece of toast in the air, picks the pan up from the stove, and catches it.

Not even in my wildest dreams—and I've had a few—did I picture Wolf the way I see him now. So ... domestic, and wearing nothing but boxer briefs that reveal every cut and swell of his body. I glance around, quickly, confirming what I suspected. No one around. So I untie my robe and let it fall open before continuing my approach to Wolf.

He must hear me enter because he turns and takes in my attire in one slow sweep. His lips turn up, and when our eyes connect, the heat I feel between us is just as strong as it's ever been. Maybe even stronger after last night.

I step forward as he turns back to the steam and sizzle of oil against the pan, such a satisfying sound to my ravenous belly. It's been starved for way too long.

"What's cookin', good lookin?" I ask teasingly, wrapping my arms around all his sexiness and placing my cheek on his back.

A deep rumble of laughter vibrates through him as he turns off the burner and tosses a pair of perfectly golden and extra cheesy grilled sandwiches on two plates. My mouth is practically salivating when he turns his body toward me.

I can see the slight lift of his cheeks as he slides a hand under my chin and searches my expression carefully. It's in this moment I remember all the ways Wolf made the worst night of my life a little less awful. The respect he showed as he allowed me space to wrestle with my emotions. The loyalty that kept him up every second I stayed awake, as if every ache of my heart was his. The softness in his touch. The gentleness of his words. And the relief he offered when he slipped me that pill.

I may not be able to move past the horror that recently became our reality, but this time I'm not alone. I have Wolf. And it was Wolf who reminded me last night what I need to focus on right now. *Me.*

No words are necessary as he leans in and kisses me hard on the lips. Looks like I'm not the only one who's starving here. Wolf breathes in through his nose and crushes me against him, holding me at the waist and dipping me back slightly. When his tongue sweeps inside my mouth and he bites down on my bottom lip, I'm ready to let him take me right here.

To my disappointment, he's the first to pull away, but he makes up for it when a sweet smile lights up his face and turns my insides soft.

My nose brushes his playfully before I kiss the tip of it. He growls in response.

"You need food," he speaks sternly. "I'm feeding you, and then we're going to handle your mother and Crawley."

I frown at the reminder and bury my head in his chest. "You mean that wasn't just a bad dream?"

I look up in time to catch his expression darken. "I'm afraid not. You okay? Last night was rough."

Of course I'm not okay. How can I possibly be okay when the person who killed my dreams is playing an unwelcome encore in my life? Reality can be a bitch, and so is Destiny Lane.

As much as I want to stand here and be strong and tell Wolf the anguish has passed, that would be a total lie.

"I'll be fine," I say.

But the doubt is clear in Wolf's expression.

"Honestly. It's just … six years ago, I needed her to do the right thing. Because she's my mom, and I thought I needed that dream version of what I always thought a mom should be. But I just don't care anymore. All I want is to move on and have my own life."

He nods slowly as if he's thinking about something. "You're living this life for you."

I smile, remembering our first conversation on the rooftop of the Aragon like it was yesterday. "Wise words from a wise little boy."

He shakes his head and pulls me close, a wicked gleam in his eyes. "Never been anything little about me, doll."

I try to stifle my giggle as the cocky man I love with every ounce of my heart glows like he's just won the lottery. Still, I roll my eyes and watch as his expression grows serious again. "You're the strongest person I know. Everything is going to work out, babe."

I'm about to respond by telling Wolf how much I love and adore for believing in me when my stomach grumbles angrily. On second thought...

"How about that grilled cheese now?" I ask, moving to the side and checking out the warm sandwiches. "Oh my God." I moan as I lift both plates from the counter and take them into the dining room. "I don't think food has ever looked this good. Where's Alice, anyway? I can't believe she's letting you work in her kitchen alone."

He chuckles. "She ran to the store."

I barely hear him. My mouth is already full.

By the time Wolf joins me at the table I've already downed an entire sandwich. I'm moaning with my last bite as I reach for the other one, but Wolf manages to snatch up half of it before I can get to it.

"You're in a weird-happy mood all of a sudden." He eyes me suspiciously.

I narrow my eyes back at him. "Weird-happy? Isn't that some kind of oxymoron?"

I really do feel okay, and I think he can tell because he smiles and takes a bite of grilled cheese in response.

"You're feeding me," I say thankfully. "And I slept better last night than I've slept in a long time." Just talking about it stirs up unwelcome emotions, but I know better than to hold them back. "I'm pissed, yeah, but there's nothing I can do about it right now. And I trust you. You said she's not going to get away with it this time. I have to believe that's true." I peer deeply into Wolf's eyes, determined, but it's also a plea for help. "I'm not going to let her get away with it again. I'll do whatever I have to do."

There's admiration in Wolf's eyes. We both know a week ago I would have shut down and refused to do anything about it, because facing this means potentially facing the spotlight. I'm not sure exactly why I'm okay with finally ending this battle between the child in me who's always wanted a mother and the me today who knows I'm better off without her, but it feels good. It feels right.

"Then let's call your dad." He watches me as he speaks, as if waiting for me to argue. "If anyone can help guide us through this mess, it's him," he adds.

"Okay," I say. "I agree."

It really is that easy. As much as I've pushed back against my father's previous offers to help, I know he's the best chance we have of fighting this. With his connections and his reputation in this industry, we could actually get my songbook back.

We finish our food and shuffle off to the den, which I've been using as an office. Wolf sits on the desk chair and pulls me to his lap to call my dad.

"Hey, Wolf. You called just in time. We're finishing up at the studio. I think you'll like what the guys did today, but we'll need you here all day tomorrow."

Huh? I look at Wolf, wondering what I missed during my sleeping spell. Why is my father in the studio with the band? Wolf glances at me, and I raise my brows an inch in a silent question. *What the hell is going on?*

"Yes, sir," Wolf responds.

"Why is my father telling you what to do?" I hiss quietly, letting my amusement show through my smile.

Wolf moves his mouth slightly away from the phone. "Mitch is filling in for Crawley. We asked for some help in the studio. That's cool, right?"

My shoulders shake as I laugh quietly. "Yeah, I guess so." There's no time to ask more questions, but the thought of my father and Wolf working together on a song I wrote is kind of ... amazing.

"How's Lyric?" My dad asks next.

Wolf catches my half-smile and returns it. "I'm here, Dad," I say, loud enough for him to hear me.

I can sense my dad's smile. "Hey, pumpkin."

"We wanted to talk to you about Destiny," Wolf explains.

There's shuffling on the other end of the line and a faint cheer that sounds like it's coming from Wolf's band. Mitch chuckles. "Sorry about that. The guys are heading out. Can you two meet me downtown? At the Italian place I used to go to with Lyric. I can get us a private room, and we can talk there. How's eight-thirty sound?"

Wolf catches my eye, and I nod in agreement.

"We'll see you there," he agrees.

I'm off Wolf's lap and heading down the hall to our bedroom before he even hangs up the phone. Not only am I ready to fight for what's mine and Wolf's, but I'm ready to fight this battle with my two favorite men.

On the way to the restaurant, Wolf holds my hand in the backseat, our heads turned in opposite directions. Slow, heavy breaths, air conditioning, and the steady roll of the tires fill the air as we travel down Miami's side streets. Other than that, all I can hear are my thoughts.

I guess I've been in somewhat of a daze since we left the house, wondering what comes next. It's all so surreal. How yesterday, I could be confessing my story to Wolf as the ultimate announcement of my trust in him, and us. And then to be blindsided by the ultimate betrayal. Again.

We pull up to the restaurant right at eight-thirty on the dot, and my dad is already there, waiting for us in the private dining area. Just like so many of the places I've been since coming to Miami, this room is present in more than a few memories of my father. We used to come here for band dinners, birthdays, and private events. He always called me his date, and I felt so proud to be on his arms, or shoulders, or wherever he'd put me. He kept me close, and that's what mattered.

That's why my heart shattered so completely when he told me it was time for me to move in with Destiny. I'd never felt that kind of love from her. Not even remotely.

My dad spots us first and is already closing the distance. He wraps me in his embrace, and my lids squeeze together as my heart swells in my chest. He holds me for as long as I let him as he rubs circles at the center of my back. "It's going to be okay, pumpkin," he whispers, and that's all it takes for the first tear to spill as my heart rattles in my chest.

"You ready to talk about this, baby girl? It's okay if you're not."

I take a deep breath, which feels healing to my insides that have otherwise been riddled with pain. "I'm ready," I say with a nod.

A calm washes over me. As angry as I've been at my parents for so many years, my father and I have an unbreakable bond, one I regretfully forgot about until seeing him again. That realization is enough to center me as I step into Wolf's arms.

After my two favorite men shake hands, a silent exchange of thanks between them, Wolf pulls out my chair directly across from my father and then takes the seat next to me.

A member of the waitstaff comes by to pour our mineral water, carefully filling each glass an inch from the top. "Bianca will be your waitress tonight," he says. "She'll be by shortly."

We thank him and each take a sip of our water, almost awkwardly, as if we aren't quite sure if we should make small talk.

"Is it okay if we jump right into it?" my dad asks, breaking the ice.

"Yes, please," Wolf says with a brief laugh. "So, what's the plan, Mitch?"

"I have an idea, but only if Lyric's okay with it."

My heart rate spikes at the sound of my name. I sit taller in my chair and pull my shoulders back, ready to hear my father out. "Whatever we do, it needs to be legal," I say quickly. "Other than that, I'm ready to fight for what's mine. I may have been a weak little girl when she stole my songs before, but she can't get away with it again. It's not right, Dad."

"No, it's not right," he agrees. "And we all know that talking to her and Crawley won't do us any good. I think we need to take it to her label. I already made some phone calls. I didn't tell Soaring what it was about, but I have a meeting with them tomorrow. You two need to stay here and work. Let me handle things in California. At least, I'll try. I'll see what they say. I have a great relationship with Alex, the CEO. We've worked together for years. He's not an unreasonable man, and he's aware of Destiny's ... mood swings. He's not a huge fan of Crawley, either. And I know the last thing he wants is a scandal on his hands."

I panic slightly at the thought of my father facing Destiny's label alone. I should be there. Maybe if they heard the truth from me, they'll realize she needs to be stopped.

"What will you say?" I ask.

Wolf's grip tightens against my sweaty palm.

"I'll tell him the truth: that Destiny is a thief and Crawley is bad for business." My dad looks determined. "Do you still have the recordings of the original songs?"

Wolf gives me a curious look, his eyes drawn together inquisitively.

Just then, our waitress, Bianca, steps in the room, silencing our conversation as she approaches. Her hair is twisted into a bun and her lips are a rose pink to match the decorative rose barrette in her golden brown hair. A wide smile blooms on her face as she sees us, and I'm not sure if it's because she recognizes the two men at the table with me or if she's just a natural smiler. Maybe it's both.

She greets us and goes over the specials of the day before taking our drink order and exiting quietly. Eyes are on me, so I know they're expecting me to answer Wolf's silent question.

I turn to Wolf. "I completely forgot about the recordings until he mentioned it, but I have my original music." I pause, needing to get something off my chest. "I should mention that I'm not worried about those old songs anymore. I just want to stop her from taking any more from me. Besides, most of what's in that songbook is Wolf's, too. We wrote those together, so she's not just stealing from me this time."

Mitch nods. "I know, but if we have proof that she did this when you were a minor—stealing from her child and claiming the music as her own under the label's name—then we win. It's an easy battle. We won't even need the recordings in hand. We just threaten to out her for that entire album and sue everyone involved. There's no way they'll allow Destiny to move forward with the new songs unless she can prove they're hers."

God, I hope that's true.

Bianca's back to take our order, and I immediately request a round of whiskey shots for the table. After the last couple of days, we deserve it. And I need it.

Wolf looks at me with wide, amused eyes. I know he likes this side of me, and I don't want tonight just to be about the Destiny and Crawley drama. We should be celebrating Wolf's upcoming tour, too.

For the next two hours, we talk strictly music. The latest trends, bands, and videos that are making a splash. Mitch tells us about his decision to take a break and how it's been a long time coming. We drink and laugh, which is the easiest thing in the world to do with these two men.

I squeeze my dad hard when we say goodbye, and I tell him I love him, which I think makes him tear up a bit. And then Wolf and I leave the restaurant brimming with hope and confidence. I feel it the moment we hit the pavement and walk toward our ride. Everything is going to be fine.

Chapter Eighteen

Wolf

The moment we arrive back at the house, Lyric is on a mission. I follow her to the bedroom and watch as she tears through her bags until she pulls out a tiny black bikini. I shut the door behind me and groan. She doesn't even have the thing on yet and I'm already planning how I'll get it off her.

"What'd you have in mind there, babe?"

Her eyes carry a wicked gleam. "Skinny dipping is out of the question since everyone is home." She tosses my swim trunks at me and starts peeling off her clothes. "Let's go swimming."

Her tits are bare and beautiful in front of me. It's instinct for me to touch them. I approach and wrap my arms around her from behind. She giggles as I slide my hands up her smooth skin and grab hold of her breasts, squeezing while pushing into her ass with my hips.

"Wolf," she warns, before turning around and slipping her arms around my neck. She kisses my neck right below my chin. "Swimming first," she whispers, huskily before I hear her swallow. "And then I want you to handcuff me to the bed and fuck me like there's no tomorrow."

She pulls away to secure her bikini top, a flirtatious smile lighting up her face. My hand dips down to my waistband, and I remove my shorts before grabbing my cock and stroking it slowly. "I can do that now, babe. The pool will still be there after the world ends."

She eyes my length and bites her lip, stifling a laugh. "You better hurry your ass up." She walks toward the French doors and pushes them open, then takes off running toward the pool. I watch in amusement as she tucks her knees up and wraps her arms around them before landing in the pool with a splash.

Cheers erupt from outside, and that's when I realize there's a party happening by the pool. I scramble to pull on my shorts and join Lyric in the water. She's already doing a lap toward Terese, Derrick, Stryder, Melanie, and Lorraine when I get in. Misty is sitting at the edge with her legs swinging beneath the water as she sips from a beer can, her golden hair streaked with pink highlights. Probably Melanie's doing.

Everyone else is scattered around the giant yard, drinking, dancing and having fun. It's the first night everyone seems to be letting loose. Or maybe it's the first time Lyric and I are going to join them. That is why I booked this place, after all. Every now and then we get time off, but we rarely get time off together.

"Wolf, catch!" Hedge says from the deck. A beer can zooms toward my head and I catch it easily, cracking it open as I walk-swim toward my friends scattering in and around the pool.

Lyric's all smiles as she slides up to me and wraps her arms around my neck. Her legs lock around my waist and her head tilts flirtatiously. "Hi, sexy."

My heart beats like crazy, and I'm unable to suppress the smile that breaks out across my face. This side of Lyric is pretty fucking incredible. Confident, sexy … ignoring the weight of the world that could be weighing her down.

"Hi yourself," I respond. I study her expression for any signs of stress.

She catches my examination and laughs. "I'm happy," she confirms, reading my mind. "For the first time in a long time, I feel like I'm right where I should be."

"Because of your father?"

She nods and leans in an inch. "And because of you." Her eyes move from my eyes to my lips and back up again, almost bashfully. The shit this woman does to me is insane. "You make this big, cold world feel safe when I'm wrapped up in your arms. I'll never give that up, Wolf."

My chest swells, heavy with love, adoration, and trust. Trust … the final piece of this crazy relationship we've found ourselves wrapped in. I finally feel it. I put my beer down at the edge of the pool and grab Lyric's face, pulling her mouth toward mine. It's an innocent kiss. I just want to show her how much I love her after being unable to say those words since the first night they passed my lips. I needed to be sure that she wouldn't slip away from me again at the next sign of disaster.

Lyric's hands begin to roam my body—first my chest, then my arms. I love when she feels the need to run her hands all over me, but when she sticks her hand down the back of my shorts and squeezes my ass, I'm pretty sure it's time to drag her out of this pool.

I deepen the kiss instead, exploring her mouth with my tongue. Sucking, pulling, and nipping at her lower lip as I push against her and groan into her mouth, letting her know what she's doing to me.

"Hey lovers, get a room." Terese floats up to us, and I want to growl in protest, but Lyric's already pulling away from my mouth and turning to her friend.

If it weren't dark out, my hard-on would be a problem. Thank God for the cover of night. I take a second to breathe and calm the erection that is more than ready to take full advantage of my girl.

A deep chuckle comes from a few feet away. I look up to find an amused Derrick nodding at me with his beer raised in a silent toast. My eyes narrow in his direction, and he laughs knowingly.

"Dude, our session today was the shit. You're going to love it!" Stryder says, swimming up next to Derrick. He takes a pull of his beer and sets it on the edge.

That's right. The session today. The one I walked out on. Once again, my mind is in the fucking clouds because of Lyric.

"I can't wait to hear it tomorrow," I say. "Mitch said it was great. Sorry I had to leave."

Derrick waves it off. "Nah, you had shit to take care of. You can lay down the rest of your vocals tomorrow, and that leaves Thursday for final tweaks after Vana mixes a rough cut. You know what that means?" He looks between me and Stryder, eyes bright even in the darkness. "We get a three-day break before we head to Europe. Can you imagine? We can have the biggest fucking party."

Hedge must overhear us because he lets out a high-pitched whooping noise from the swimup bar several yards away, grabs a fifth of alcohol from over the counter, and begins pouring a round of shots. Maurice, our bartender just shakes his head in amusement.

Lyric turns to the edge of the pool, grabs my beer, and finishes it off before taking a couple of shot glasses from Hedge's tray and winking at him. Hedge winks back, and I remember the crush he had on my girl. Aside from the other night at the hotel, it never worried me. If anything, it just made me up my game whenever the two of them were in the same room together.

I laugh at the memory and take the shot Lyric hands me. Throwing a look at Hedge, I grin. "Dude, you are way too good at this bartending job. Don't get any ideas."

He shrugs. "Someone's gotta be the life of the party. I'm surrounded by couples that wanna fuck nonstop."

Throwing my head back, I laugh and point my finger at him. "The love bug is going to bite your ass one of these days. Just you wait. I bet you find yourself a hot European on tour and worship her for the rest of your bushy-haired life."

Hedge rolls his eyes and shakes his head. "Not going to happen, fuckface. Just cause you have monogamous dick doesn't mean you need to spread that shit around like herpes."

"Ironically, it's the monogamous ones that don't spread herpes, you shit. C'mon. Let's take these shots. And then I need to take care of my girl." I wink to rub it in a little further, not that it actually bothers him. Hedge probably has a girl—or two—on the way to the house right now.

Back in the pool, we toast and toss back our shots. My arms are wrapped around an already tipsy Lyric, her back to my front. I'm slyly walking us toward the edge of the pool. My erection, which is still going strong, is telling us it's time to take this party inside.

My face moves to her neck so I can nuzzle her wet skin, and then I bite down on her shoulder. "You should know

I've been hard since you made that comment about the handcuffs. I'm hurting here, babe."

She laughs and wiggles against me playfully. "Shouldn't we try to socialize a little? You know, with other people."

Hell no. I look around. "Looks like everyone is busy. I need you in my bed. Now." I nip at her shoulder again and snake my hand down her stomach until I'm in her bikini bottoms. I only graze her clit before pulling away.

She tenses, and a tiny breath escapes her mouth. I don't need to look at Lyric to know she's frustrated too. That's when I know I'm winning.

"Suit yourself," I say, making my way around her to lift myself onto the edge of the pool. "Take your time. Socialize. I have a problem to take care of."

Chuckling to myself, I climb out of the pool and let myself in the French doors of our bedroom, heading toward the master bath. I'm not really going to take care of myself. I'll wait for Lyric, but I hope she hurries her sexy ass up or I'll be blue balling it for a while.

After washing my hands, I leave the bathroom to find my Lyric standing there. The doors and curtains leading to the patio are shut behind her but the bedside lamp is on, illuminating her wet, naked body as she stands next to the bed holding the fuzzy pink handcuffs.

"Fuck me," I mutter under my breath. The look in her eye tells me she wants this just as much as I do. "You're trying to kill me." I walk toward her and grab the handcuffs from her as I take in her perfect curves. Lyric's body deserves to be cherished. And that's exactly what I'm about to do.

"Take control." Her voice is raspy. "Do your worst, Wolf." She leans into me and places a kiss on my chest as her hands finger the waistband of my shorts. She undoes the string and tugs the material down my waist, freeing my needy cock.

"I want this," she says, batting her eyelashes, and I almost let go right there.

My beautiful girl is giving up control. Something has changed in her, and I love it. I love that she's trusting me with everything, especially with pleasing her. But I also know it's the distraction she's after. I saw it in the pool, when my reserved girl became a chatterbox, floating from one person to the next. She's suppressing the hurt, and if she needs me to help keep her thoughts from drifting to the surface, even for a night, that's exactly what I'll do.

"I can do that." I kiss her cheek, careful not to touch any other part of her. Not yet. "Sit against the headboard."

Her breaths are heavy as she turns to face the bed, but I wrap my arms around her before she can move. "Go slow. I want to see your ass in the air."

When she starts to climb onto the bed, I see her body tremble a little. There's no bigger turn on than watching the way Lyric reacts to my demands.

I give her ass a smack. Water droplets spray in all directions, and I groan at the pink mark my hand leaves on her soft skin. She sways slowly, deliciously, as she crawls up the bed before turning and propping herself up against the headboard. I swallow when she spreads her legs, her perfect pussy glistening and begging for my attention.

I move quickly onto the bed, taking one of her wrists and placing it above her head, locking her to the bar of the headboard with the first cuff. My breaths are heavy and quick. I'm too fucking turned on to play around right now. I capture her second wrist and place it near the first, locking this one in place too.

My mouth skims her lips and lands above her ear, but I'm careful not to touch her.

"Just tell me if it gets too intense, okay?"

Her eyes widen in surprise, but she nods. I smile and reach for the bedside table where I stashed the oil. Lyric prefers to be on top, something I'll never complain about. I've never let anyone else take control, but Lyric handles me like she was made for me, tending to my needs while she moves wildly above me. And man, can she move. I especially love when she pulls her hands through her hair and tugs when she's lost in the feel of me.

But this right here is out of her comfort zone. I know what it means for her to give up control like this, and that only makes it that much better.

"First rule," I say, squirting some oil on her chest.

"There are rules?" she asks, her eyes wide.

I grin. "Yeah, babe. My game, my rules." I eye her, silently telling her I mean business. "First rule. Your eyes stay open. I want you to watch everything I'm about to do to you." I lean down to make sure I get the point across so that I'm at her ear. "No matter what. Other than blinking, your eyes stay open. Got it?"

She nods, and I hear her swallow.

I chuckle and move back to a sitting position, rubbing in the oil around her rib cage and then up to her chest. Her breasts are full and firm and ready as I flatten my hand over one, tweaking her nipple when I get there. I can feel her legs spread further apart below me. I lean forward, letting my length push into her belly as I kiss her deeply, giving and taking all at once. Her groans become moans and then whines as she jiggles on the cuffs.

She's already going crazy and we've just begun our little game. My lips move from her mouth to her neck and then down to her breasts. As I suck on her nipple, she moves beneath me. I look up and see that her eyes are drooping to a close, so I bite gently down, making her gasp out a scream.

"Eyes open," I command. "Don't make me tell you again."

Her eyes open wide and her breathing quickens. Exactly how I want her. Panting and restless. It's going to feel so good when I unleash on her. But the torture leading up to that moment is what makes it so satisfying.

I lather her in even more oil, massaging it into each breast, then her stomach, and then her legs, one by one. My hands are slick when I slip a finger down her center and into her entrance, finding her depths and flicking fast as she gyrates below me.

"So wet, babe. What are we going to do about this?" I add a second finger and listen as she moans.

My other hand palms her stomach, moving down it until my thumb covers her clit. It's intensity I'm going for, and I know I'm succeeding when her mouth parts and her breaths become pants. When her eyes find mine again, they're dark and needy. Her stomach muscles and skin ripple as she clenches and unclenches, going crazy under my touch.

I bite my lip and scoot down the bed so my mouth is directly above her slick opening. "Eyes open, babe. I'm about to eat your pretty pussy, and you're going to watch me."

Then I taste her, licking from the bottom of her slit to the top before licking my lips. She shudders beneath me. I blow on her gently, causing another scream to leave her mouth.

"It's too much, Wolf."

I chuckle again and shake my head. "I'm just getting started, babe. Don't make me give you rule number two."

She pouts and looks at me with need in her eyes. "There's more?"

I nod and kiss her pussy before sucking her clit into my mouth. I let go and grin. "You can moan, talk dirty, tell me harder, softer, more. You can scream. I don't think you'll be able to help that. Other than that, no talking."

She takes a deep breath and bites down on her lip. I want to laugh again at the desperation on her face. Instead, I concentrate on tasting every inch of Lyric's clit as I pump her with my fingers. Flicking my tongue and sucking her into my mouth again, I can feel her tense and relax beneath me.

She lets out a gurgled scream as I drive her over the edge with my mouth. I don't go easy on her. Not tonight. I torture the first orgasm out of her, slowly at first, and then when I feel her about to unravel, I unleash hell, pumping furiously.

Her convulsions seem to last forever as she shakes and screams like no one can hear her. She throws out my name like a curse word, only making me want to punish her with another orgasm.

"You're trying to kill me," she pants.

I laugh at her urgency. "No, babe. No one's dying today."

She throws her head back in frustration, moving her pelvis up so it grinds into my face. With my hands, I push her hips down on the bed and then run them up her torso, my mouth latching onto her breast again. "I'd flip you over, but I'm not taking those cuffs off. This is too much fun." I grin and move so that I'm in between her legs.

"I need you," she says.

This time, my confidence goes out the window. Her pleading reaches into my heart and squeezes. She's so damn beautiful.

The water from the pool has dried on her skin, but the moisture of her body's sweat has replaced it. She's glistening, and I can practically see every inch of her tingling.

I can't stay away anymore. I hover above her and lean into her mouth to kiss her as I slide in between her legs. She moans happily into my mouth.

My thrusts are slow and deep, and I pull back for a second to look her in the eyes. She's looking back at me with a love so deep, so pure, that I'm caught in the moment. This woman is it for me. She's my everything.

Before Lyric, music was my everything, but as much as I loved it, it became a way to fill a dark void of depression within me. I suffocated in my music because it was better to drown in that than in darkness.

Then Lyric came along, and she not only filled my void with light, but also gave music a new meaning. My music may have been good before, but now, it breathes life.

My eyes are still locked on Lyric, my body still rocking deeply into hers. Before I think about it again, I remove the handcuffs and bring myself back down to her lips, kissing her hard as she moans and wraps her arms around me, running her fingernails up the length of my back. I need Lyric's touch as much as she needs me inside her right now. We suffocate each other with tightly woven limbs, our oiled bodies moving as one. Not a crack of air between us.

She removes her mouth from mine. "Is the game over?"

I look at her again and smile. "No games, babe. I just needed you to touch me." My nose skims hers, my heart pounding like a fucking gorilla on its cage. "I love you." I push into her again and growl into her neck, "So fucking much."

She bites down on my skin and reaches around, feeling for my ass and squeezing. "I love you too." Her legs spread even wider and she pushes me deeper inside her. *Holy fuck.* When her muscles contract, I'm ready to come.

We move together, fucking like there's no tomorrow as she greets each of my movements. I'm warning her of my release and she nods, telling me she's ready too.

It doesn't take long before we're swallowing each other's moans and she's begging for the world to end, just one more time.

Chapter Nineteen

Lyric

I've never felt so loved in my life. Wolf reaches a deeper part of me that has nothing to do with his skills in the bedroom. He touches my soul. He shows me love, even in his need for a release. Every single time. I don't question it.

I've never questioned Wolf's feelings for me. It might have taken me longer to get here, to this point where trust solidifies our connection, but the journey was necessary. Now—I'm never letting him go.

As I watch him sleeping soundly next to me, gently snoring and drooling ever so slightly, all I can think about is how crazy I am for this man. He'll take care of me. Put my needs first. Never hurt me. Never make me question his love. He'll stand by me during the lowest points in my life. I want to do all those same things for him.

I grab my silky, silver robe from the bathroom and walk down to the kitchen, where I find Terese standing by the toaster, yawning, coffee brewing beside her. Alice here, too, prepping ingredients for breakfast at the island. The rest of the house is silent, everyone still sleeping off the late night of partying.

"Hey, Alice," I say before turning to Terese. "Hey, sexy," I greet her. "Late night?"

Terese groans, grabbing her stomach in pain. I laugh, sympathetic but amused.

"Never drinking again," she moans.

Grinning, I grab some ingredients from the refrigerator. "Is that right?"

She shakes her head. "Probably not, but saying that is supposed to make me feel better, right?"

I nod, wide-eyed with sarcasm. "I'm making eggs. Want some?"

"How many, dear?" Alice asks, giving me a warning look that tells me I better not argue.

"Two for me. Scrambled with cheese, please." Alice nods and turns to Terese.

Terese holds a hand up and shakes her head. "No, thank you. Toast and coffee for me. But Derrick might want some if you have leftovers."

"I'll make extra," Alice says. She cracks a half dozen eggs and lets them sizzle on the stove while chopping up some vegetables and throwing them on a separate skillet. As she slides a pan of bacon in the oven, I lean back against the counter where Terese is sipping her coffee lazily.

"So, what are we doing tonight?" I ask her. "Double date, right?"

Her posture straightens and I can see her eyes lift excitedly. "You up for it?"

My smile grows, realizing that I am. The chance to spend the evening with my boyfriend, my best friend, and my best friend's boyfriend—who also happens to be Wolf's best friend— sounds perfect. "I am."

Terese grins. "Derrick said he'll figure it out with Wolf and they'll surprise us."

My gaze floats to Derrick and Wolf, who are wandering into the living room right on cue, in animated conversation. I almost can't believe I'm here. For the first time in a very long time, I'm happy.

Wolf catches my gaze from across the room and winks at me before returning to his conversation.

"You coming to the studio today?" Terese asks as she grabs her coffee off the counter.

I take the plate Alice has just made for me and nod. "I'll be there later this afternoon. I'm going to work in the office this morning. Crawley had all the Europe information, so I'm scrambling to put the pieces together."

"Okay. Maybe I'll hang here today and go in with you later. I'm in Miami, for heaven's sake. My skin should be bronze and glowing by now." She winks at me and takes her coffee out onto the deck.

I take my plate outside to join Terese in the outdoor lounge. It resembles a living room, with white and tan striped chairs and couches arranged in front of a wood fireplace. From here, there's a view of the clear blue infinity pool and the white sand beach beyond that.

The mansion is set in a cove in Coral Gables with the shore of the beach about a hundred yards away. There's a line of palm trees separating the edge of the pool from the shore, except for a slight gap where the sidewalk leads to our private beach. The sky is almost free from clouds, and we can hear the waves rushing the shore as the morning breeze flutters through the palm trees.

Terese and I chat about our days in Vegas and promise we'll take the boys to visit soon. Now that everything is out in the open between Wolf and me, I'm looking forward to so many things. Vacations together. Traveling. Writing. A future—whatever that may consist of.

I fill Terese in on what's going on with my dad and Destiny, and although she knows about the strained relationship I have with my mother, she's still appalled.

"The only reason she still has a following is because of the album that saved her career six years ago. You're telling me you wrote the entire thing?" Terese asks, incredulous.

I nod, amazed that I don't have that sinking feeling I'm used to whenever I talk about Destiny. My mother's betrayal hasn't left my mind; it's more like the weight of it all just bobs like a buoy unanchored in the middle of the ocean, simply drifting with the currents as I wait for my father to return with news that will free me from this hell.

"She hasn't been able to come up with anything decent since, and before that, she was a joke in the business." Terese is still going off, unable to comprehend how a mother could take advantage of her daughter like that.

She's criticizing my mother, and here I am agreeing with every word. I should feel compelled to stick up for Destiny, but I'm done. She'll never change.

"Maybe she's having some sort of midlife crisis," Terese says, her face twisted up like she doesn't believe her own words.

I pick at my food with a fork and sigh. "I don't care to know the reason why anymore. I just want my songs back. I think it's time I start falling back in love with what I'm passionate about. Letting her take that all away from me was the worst thing I ever did."

"So. 'Dangerous Heart,' huh?"

I smile. "Yeah."

"How did that happen if you weren't sharing your music with anyone?"

I fill Terese in on the rest. About how Wolf found the lyrics by the pool and put them to music. The way it felt to hear him sing my words to thousands of people that night in San Diego. She's wide-eyed throughout my entire story.

"No fucking way." She laughs. "I can't believe you just gave him the lyrics. I would have at least gotten my share of royalties."

I laugh. "I know. He and Crawley were both shocked. The guys still don't know it was me, but I'm going to tell them."

"What?" Terese screams this time, and I laugh so hard, tears spill down my eyes. She stands up and waves to the guys through the open sliding door.

"What are you doing?" I whisper in horror.

She looks down at me in a challenge, daring me to fight me on this. "Look, if you want to do this right, the guys need to know. Right now, so I can witness their reactions."

Clearly confused, the guys start filling out the patio. Wolf takes a seat beside me, giving me a strange look. My face must be beet red. Terese looks at me, asking for my approval. I know she wouldn't say a word if I asked her not to, but I'm ready. I give her a nod.

"I have an announcement," Terese tells everyone as they spill out onto the deck. "Lyric Cassidy has been keeping something from you all. So has Wolf." She glares at him. "Lyric gave me permission to spill the beans, so brace yourselves for this one."

I bury my head in my hands while Wolf tries to get my attention. I can't even look at him.

"I know who the writer is behind 'Dangerous Heart.' And the last three songs you all started playing on tour." I look up finally to see Terese pointing down at me.

Everyone grows silent at first, and then the silence turns into hushed whispers as the guys make the connection, and then … it's all-out pandemonium.

"What?"

"Why the hell didn't you tell us?"

"We should have known. Her name is fucking *Lyric* for Christ's sake."

"Babe, you okay with this?" Wolf is asking me, his strong arms pulling me close to him. I hear the concern in his voice, and I nod.

He smiles at me, and I can't help but smile back. "That's my girl." He looks up at the guys and raises his hands as if in surrender. "Now you know why I fell in love with the girl. And I was legally bound to silence, so you can't be mad at me for keeping it a secret."

"Shit, Lyric. Why didn't you want us to know?" Derrick asks, taking a seat next to Terese.

I sigh. "It's really a long story. Let's just say, people in the business have a habit of disappointing me, and it was just something I wanted to keep to myself." I nudge Wolf and laugh. "But this one here was nice enough to give me an out. Instead, I signed the song over in exchange for his silence. I've kept my songwriting a secret for so long, but I'm done hiding it."

Chapter Twenty

Wolf

Lyric has not only come out of her shell, she's ripped it apart and stomped on the pieces that once sheltered her. I love everything about this side of her. Happy, free, and exposed to the world. At least, she will be when Mitch Cassidy is done destroying Destiny Lane.

It's late in the afternoon and we're about to head back into the recording booth when Lyric bursts into Studio Gold, a trail of girls behind her. Misty, Terese, Melanie.

They all look eager about something, but it's Lyric who I'm focused on. She's holding her phone and I notice her hand trembling slightly. But it's the expression on her face that quiets us immediately. Just the sight of her flushed cheeks and wide eyes, and the sound of her fast, heavy breathing make my heart flip and then flop in my chest.

"This just came in from my dad," she says. She takes a deep breath and reads off the message on her phone. "Record label is in agreement. Destiny Lane is toast when she gets to their office. She arrives tonight, and they are ready for her."

I can't describe the relief and happiness that rushes through me the moment I realize the battle is over. Lyric's songs are safe, and Destiny can't touch her. My smile stretches so wide, the corners of my mouth ache. The room explodes in celebration.

I lift Lyric into the air and swing her around before pulling her close and crushing her mouth to mine. This is how things should be. The music. The love. The friendships. This is our family. As dysfunctional as it might be, it's perfect.

The afternoon recording session is flawless and full of energy. We put the final touches on "Dangerous Heart," and I'm so happy Lyric is there to witness it. She's humble, but I know her well enough to recognize the pride in the moisture glistening around the rims of her eyes.

We wrap with a half dozen bottles of Ace of Spades champagne, a gift Mitch left behind, knowing he was going to miss this. Vana passes champagne flutes around the room as Lorraine pops the cork like a badass, howling as the stopper shoots across the room, almost hitting Hedge in the head. He ducks just in time and howls along with her. Liquid spills down her hands, so she does what any respectable musician would do and laps it up with her tongue, not wanting to waste a single drop.

Lyric is laughing, wrapped in my arms right where she belongs while we toast. The only person missing in this perfect moment is Mitch.

"We're done a day early! Fuck yeah!" Hedge offers in his usual overly confident tone. He's got an arm around Melanie, rattling her a little as she chugs back her flute. When a drop of liquid falls down her chin, she glares at Hedge and smacks his stomach with the back of her hand.

I roll my eyes and feel the need to remind everyone that there's still more work to be done before we can officially call this week in the studio wrapped. "We're a wrap *until* we get the rough cut back. We might have to come back in for some cleanup."

Hedge makes a face. "Sounds like we're wrapped to me." He raises his arms. "Party all day tomorrow, you got that, assholes? Invite everyone."

This time I chuckle and cheer with the rest of them, tossing back my glass. Derrick is there to refill it with a wink. I wink back and take the bottle from him, filling Lyric's flute too.

"I love you, babe," she says softly.

I swallow, leaning into her ear. "I love you, too. So fucking much."

She laughs lightly at our favorite phrase and then tugs my shirt to pull me down for a kiss. Pressing my hand into the dip in her back, I deepen our lip-lock. I can almost forget that the room is filled with chaotic celebration—almost. I groan. Sliding my lips to her ear, I brush a strand of hair away and whisper. "Why don't you and Terese go home and start getting dressed for tonight?"

She leans back with amusement and question in her eyes. She knows Derrick and I are taking her and Terese out, but she has no clue where. Suddenly, celebration shifts to anticipation and I couldn't be more fucking excited.

"Why?" she questions.

I slap her ass and wrap my fingers around her wrists before pulling her arms away. "No questions. Just go get dressed. Something I can slip off easily later."

She grins and presses her body into me so I can feel her firm breasts just under my chest. I lean in a little so she can speak into my ear, feeling the rush of goosebumps spread across my skin. "Panties on or off?"

Fuck.

"Off. Definitely off."

When Terese and Lyric strut out into the foyer where Derrick and I are waiting, I swear I forget to breathe. I only glance at the silver fabric of Terese's short dress for a second because the moment Lyric comes into view, my eyes are glued on her.

Her off-white tube dress is snug on top and flowy at the skirt, revealing every perfect curve of her sexy body. No doubt Lyric will make more than a few heads turn tonight. Her legs are long, shiny, and smooth, especially with the sexy leopard print heels strapped to her feet.

She does a little turn to show off the back of the dress, which gives me an instant hard-on. The fabric lands softly against the curve of her ass, and those sexy-as-fuck heels raise her up a couple inches, just enough to reveal the definition of her calves.

But my God. When Lyric faces me, I can't get enough of her. How the fuck did someone like me wind up with her? Every natural inch of her is beyond gorgeous. And her hair is just the way I like it. Loose, long, and wavy, just brushing the rise of her breasts.

Even with all that beauty in front of me, all I can think of is her question earlier.

"Panties on or off?"

Looking between her legs, I almost have a panic attack. One wrong step and her pussy will be all over the internet. I narrow my eyes, and she laughs. She knows exactly what I'm thinking.

My heart almost jumps out of my throat when she struts to me, her dress swaying slightly with her movements. "What's wrong, Wolf?" she teases.

My eyes move to her face, my teeth clenching as I take her in. "That dress safe tonight?" I run my finger in a line from her thigh, up past her waist, all the way to the fabric hugging her chest. When she takes in a stuttered breath, my lips curl upwards. I love how my touch affects her.

"It's secure." She blushes.

Her face is extra sexy when pink stains her cheeks. I brush a finger across her lips, considering what I want to do to them later. "You look beautiful, Lyric. Almost too beautiful, if I'm being honest."

She smiles, pleased. "Honesty is good."

"Just—" I cringe before I speak again. "Don't bend over or anything. No sudden movements."

She gives me a playful smile. "You said to wear something sexy."

I lean in because I can't help myself and kiss her on the cheek. I let my hand slide up her arm until I'm holding the back of her neck, my mouth poised at her ear. "You don't even have to try. You are sexy. And beautiful. And mine."

I kiss her hard, waiting for her lips to part so I can slip her some tongue, and leave her dizzy when I finally break away. She recovers with a slow flutter of her lashes. I grin.

Tonight will be fun.

"No fair," she pouts. "I was supposed to do that to you."

I chuckle. "I think you know what you do to me, babe." I pull her into me so she can feel what I mean. We haven't even left the house and I already can't wait to have my girl alone.

My mouth grazes her ear. I need to know. "Are you—" I rub my hand against her lower back, slyly feeling around for material under her dress.

She just smirks and pulls away. "You'll find out later tonight."

"What?" I can't help the gruff tone of my voice. I could throw her over my shoulder and drag her to the bedroom right now, demand to see what's under that little dress. "When?"

"When I say so."

The look she gives me. She owns me, and she knows it. With a sly smile, she meets Terese in the middle of the living room while Derrick and I assess them from the front door. They have no idea what we have planned for them. After the end of tonight, we'll see who owns who.

Derrick meets my eye, probably thinking something similar, and then he winks to confirm my suspicion. "Ladies, the car is waiting," he announces.

Lyric's smile grows bright. "We're ready to be schmoozed."

I weave my fingers through hers when she approaches me. "Oh, I'll schmooze you." I squeeze our hands together and lean into her ear. "If you don't drive me crazy tonight first."

She winks. "That's the plan."

Fusion sits on top of the Grand American Hotel in downtown Miami. The restaurant has a modern elegance we thought the girls would appreciate. Their specialty: American tapas. Lyric's favorite. And from what I hear, the wait to get a table at this place is months long.

This is one of those times I'm not ashamed to admit that it's nice to be a household name. Not only did Derrick and I have no problem getting a reservation tonight, but we were able to make special accommodations that we hope will impress the girls.

We're escorted to a private event room that takes up a quarter of the entire top floor. The large windows are wide open, overlooking the city. It's still light out, but the Miami city lights are already beginning to make their vibrant appearance.

We've hired an acoustic guitarist to set the mood, and he's already mid-song when we arrive. The bartender approaches immediately, so we order our first round.

While the girls take their drinks and snack on sample appetizers from various trays situated around the room, they scope out the modern canvas art and the unusual décor made out of recycled materials. Derrick and I keep our eyes on the girls as we toss around stories about early years with the band.

"A few months ago, we'd be at the bar every single night. What happened to us?" Derrick jokes.

I smile at the girls, who are giggling as they sip from their champagne glasses and stand in front of a bicycle made from recycled trash. "The most beautiful women ever."

Derrick nods. I know my friend well. He's never been a douchebag, scoring chicks every night like the rest of us, but he's also never found someone he wanted to attach himself to like Terese. Often times I felt like Derrick was afraid of relationships because of our time on the road. He's one to want to give his all with things, and I don't see that being any different with a relationship.

Maybe Terese makes him want to take a risk. I may be consumed with Lyric lately, but I can see that my best friend has got it bad. It's good for him.

"Is Terese coming with us to Europe? Have you talked to her about that yet?"

Derrick's smile immediately turns down and I cringe, realizing this could be a sensitive subject. I'm just lucky that my girlfriend tours with the band. Terese has a job in San Diego and was barely able to get time off to vacation with us in Florida. Now I'm full of regret, wishing I never asked the question.

"No. I'm not done working on her, though."

"What's the problem? Her job?"

Derrick nods. "The company is already on edge because of what happened with you and Lyric, but that's not all. She's worried if she leaves her job, she won't have one to return to when things don't work out between us."

"Ouch," I say. My face twists as if I've been hit. "She said that shit?"

Derrick rolls his eyes and shifts his stance. "Yeah, dude, but I get it. We just started up and we're into each other, but it's a lot to ask her to pick up and quit her life to have a fun few months in Europe. Anything could happen, I guess, and she loves her job."

"We could give her a job," I suggest, the idea just now coming to me. "If that's something you want. She'd love working with the crew, and she could still be employed by Perform Live."

Derrick puts on his thinking face and tilts his head. "Shit. Not bad, dude. Maybe she'd go for that. You think Perform Live would let her tour?"

"Ask her if she's into it. I can handle the rest. Shouldn't be a problem since she's been hanging out with the band so much. We'll say she helped out a lot this week and we could use her on the tour." I shrug. "They won't say no. Trust me."

A smile lights up Derrick's face, and for the first time, my chest feels lighter for someone other than Lyric. All seems to be heading in the right direction.

"You and Lyric seem to be good now. Glad to see it, bro."

I nod, knowing there's more to his comment than he'll ever say. Derrick and I have always been the closest out of all my bandmates. He's seen me through my worst. My rock bottom after my mom died. He never judged. Never let me stew in my misery for long. He was always there, reminding me why we needed to keep going. To move forward. And I'm forever grateful for it. For him.

Just then, tiny arms wrap around my waist and a head snakes under my arm. I look down to see Lyric gazing up at me with a smile on her face.

"Am I on this date with Terese or my hot rock star boyfriend?"

I wink at her. "Me, babe. What do you think?" I gesture around the room with my head.

"It's beautiful up here."

"You're beautiful up here."

Her cheeks turn pink. "Okay, charmer."

"I mean it. You make this place look good."

Lyric slaps my chest and laughs. "You're on a roll." With a smirk, she grabs my hand and pulls me toward the small square floor in front of the stage. "Dance with me."

Derrick and Terese follow, finding space to dance several feet away. Lyric's in my arms and I'm leaning down, touching her nose to mine before she flattens a cheek on my chest and sighs deeply. I place a hand at the dip in her lower back and bask in the feel of my girl in my arms.

It's amazing how someone can feel like they're made for you. Like nothing could ever feel better than holding them.

Lyric shifts to peer up at me, a smile pushing up her cheeks. "You want to do some writing tomorrow? Before the big party?"

I chuckle. "If Hedge has anything to do with it, the party will start before we even wake up. But we can hide out for a while if you want to write." I tuck a strand of loose hair behind her ear, brushing my thumb across her cheek. "Or we could write at the piano."

My expression must reveal the hope radiating from my chest because Lyric looks hesitant at first. I don't want to lose this moment with her, so I change the subject. "We need to get you a new songbook," I say.

She wrinkles her nose. "My dad should get my book back from Destiny, right?"

I shrug. "I don't know what his plan is. I assumed he would just have the label mail it or something so he doesn't run into Destiny. He's supposed to meet with them tonight. We can call him in the morning."

She smiles and nods "Okay."

"I like you like this." My thumb moves to her lips, and I trace them softly. "Happy. Carefree. Relaxed." I smooth my free hand along her ass and squeeze. I practically groan when I realize there's no panty line. My thorough search confirms it.

The glimmer in her eyes gives her away. "What are you looking for, rock star?"

I lean in, my thickening cock making me bite my lip to keep from yanking her to the floor and ripping off her clothes.

"Are you wet?"

I can just imagine the slickness between her thighs. Her pink lips begging for my finger to push its way inside as I delicately torture her nipples with my—

Damn. I *was* on my best behavior. But now...

She lets out a whispering laugh straight into my ear, then bites the outer rim. I have to take a deep breath to keep my shit together. Fuck.

"You are, aren't you? You imagining my mouth down there?" I pull her close so she can feel me.

She shifts, her expression matching my desire. I can't wait to get this girl home, but I need to be careful. Tonight is about wooing her. Showing her I'm a gentleman and that I love her for more than what comes after dinner. I pull away to put some space between us, and then I lean in to kiss her cheek. "Need another drink?"

She nods and I take her hand, spinning her around before leading her to our table. Derrick and Terese join us, and soon we're chatting about Europe. Derrick has let Terese in on our discussion, but she's not as optimistic that Perform Live will agree to transfer her. Not after what happened with Lyric and me a few days ago.

"Does your boss know you're dating Derrick?"

She shrugs. "Possibly. I haven't said anything to her directly, but the girls I work with know." A flush spreads across her cheeks and she darts a look at Derrick, who sits back with a smug look.

"Talking about me at work, darlin'?" he teases.

She smacks his chest with the back of her hand, and we all laugh.

"I'm sure it will all work out." I wink at Derrick. "I'll make a few phone calls tomorrow."

I can tell Lyric's hopeful. It must be nice for her to have a close friend again. One that won't try to sleep with her boyfriend. Not that I'd ever pull that shit on Lyric. Tony is a grade-A ass, but whatever happened that led Lyric to me, I'm selfishly grateful for it.

We work our way through our five-course meal. By the time we get to the tiramisu, the girls are struggling. I, for one, love watching Lyric eat. The way she savors every bite as if the food is melting in her mouth. But we're all groaning from overeating when it's time to finally leave the private dining room. I wrap an arm around Lyric's waist to guide her to the elevator.

The girls think we're going home, but Derrick and I have other plans. Instead of taking the elevator down to the lobby, Derrick pushes the button that will bring us to the roof. The girls are oblivious as they lean on each other and complain about all the incredible food they managed to stuff into their tiny bodies.

The door to the elevator opens, revealing the rooftop. It's loud and windy from the helicopter that sits on its pad in the middle of the roof. The girls' eyes go wide at the sight.

"You're shitting me," Terese says. She's the first one to step out onto the roof. I turn slightly to find Lyric's eyes lingering on mine, something I've never seen before settling in them. Before I can ask or try to figure it out myself, she smiles and steps out behind Terese.

We lead the girls to a man in a black suit who stands at the edge of the pad. His cheeks lift as he greets Lyric and Terese. And then he turns to Derrick and me.

"Mr. Chapman. Mr. Kennedy." He shakes our hand. "I'm Benjamin Stahl, your pilot for the evening. Are you ready for your tour of the city?"

I'm still focused on Lyric, who is nodding with excitement. Her hair whips around her viciously, and she laughs through it. The skirt of her cream dress tightens around her as wind from the propeller promises everyone a show, but she reaches for it just in time. Now I'm laughing. Thank God Derrick takes care of the talking.

Derrick helps Terese in first, and then it's Lyric's turn. She gives me that look again, the new, different one that makes my heart beat like a stampede of wild horses in my chest.

"Well played, Mr. Chapman."

"This is only the beginning, babe." I help her into the helicopter, careful to keep her dress down as she slides into the seat, and then I hop in behind her.

After Benjamin straps us in, I nudge Lyric's side to get her attention. She smiles.

"Surprised?"

Her eyelashes flutter slightly, and she nods. "You've never stopped surprising me, Wolf."

"I'm surprising myself, to tell you the truth."

This makes her laugh, and I catch some of the sound in my mouth when my lips touch hers. "I love you."

"I love you," she says against my lips.

The pilot announces that we're taking off, so we put on our headsets and I grab hold of Lyric's hand. She squeezes.

"Ready to see Miami, girls?" Derrick calls out into the headsets.

"Hell yeah!" they cheer.

And we're off.

Chapter Twenty-One

Lyric

"You got a freaking helicopter ride? I swear, I need to reevaluate my relationship goals." Melanie flips onto her front and lifts her chin onto her hands.

The party is in full swing before noon. Wolf promised it wasn't a big deal if we skipped it and did some writing like we'd planned, but I told him no. He deserves this time with the guys, and I'm looking forward to lounging by the pool with the girls.

Lorraine, Melanie, Misty, Terese, and I claimed our lounge chairs around breakfast time, and we have the perfect setup. A stack of magazines sit at our feet, our Kindles are charged up and ready to be devoured, and a cooler rests beside us, bursting with drinks and snacks. Still, we somehow haven't touched the copious amounts of reading material because we've been chatting it up for hours.

Listening to Terese gush about last night causes my lips to curl into a smirk. "Except Terese and Derrick were too busy sucking face to see much of anything."

Terese waves me off and reaches for her beer. "Shut it, sister. You and Wolf are no better. He always looks like he wants to hump you."

"He does always want to hump me," I fire back. Everyone laughs, except Melanie. She seems to be pondering something.

"Maybe Hedge and I could be a thing. We flirt." Melanie's suggestion comes with a thoughtful expression, followed by a smirk. We all know she's full of shit. Melanie flirts with all the guys. The only thing that makes Hedge stand out is the fact that he's the only single guy left in the group.

"Scratch that," Melanie responds to her own comment. "Rock stars don't turn me on. Even if some do prove that it's more than partying and fucking"—I think she says this for Terese and my benefit—"I've been in this industry for as long as the boys, and I've never succumbed to the rock cock."

We all burst into laughter.

"A little rock cock might be just what you need." Terese smacks Melanie's ass.

"If I'm getting some, it better not be little," Melanie adds with all seriousness.

Again, we laugh. All of us but Lorraine. She seems amused, but not as into this conversation as the rest of us— probably because her sexual preference has no cock size.

"You can't tell me you've never thought about sleeping with a rock star," Lorraine says to Melanie.

Suddenly, Melanie's cheeks turn pink. "I didn't say I've never thought about it." She squirms in her seat, then waves off her own confession with a movement of her hand.

"Who?" Misty pries, pulling in closer to Melanie. "One of the boys?"

"God, no!" Melanie cries and we all laugh.

It's crossed my mind that Wolf could have messed around with someone from the tour, but I decided early on that I didn't want to find out. It would make things awkward with whomever it was, and Wolf has never made me feel remotely jealous when it comes to other women. Well, except for little Suzie, but even that is already old news.

Lorraine's still stuck on the subject. "You've been in the business for what—six years, Mel? Don't lie. Even I've done a rocker boy."

In unison, we all turn to Lorraine to see if she's full of it. She's completely serious.

"What?"

She's sitting next to me, so I tap her tummy with my toe. "You mean before you knew you liked girls?" I'm so confused.

Lorraine rolls her eyes. "Why does everyone assume I only like girls?"

I laugh, and I'm not alone. Looking around, we're all a little confused.

"So you swing both ways?" Melanie shrugs. "That's cool. We've only ever seen you with the ladies. And you've been with the guys forever. I'm surprised you haven't done one of them then."

Lorraine makes a face. "No way. They're like my brothers."

I sigh with relief, happy no one can see me. If I had known Lorraine liked guys, too, I might have been worried about her friendship with Wolf.

Terese stands up and adjusts her bathing suit. "Bathroom break. Be back, bitches."

I scramble to my feet and follow her, hoping to find Wolf to see if he's heard from my dad.

As soon as we enter the house, we hear cheering and hollering. The guys are watching a recording of some fight they missed last week. It's not something I'm into, so the girls and I were happy to let them be. There are about a dozen or so guys in the living room and a few more in the kitchen. The chicks who were invited—mostly by Hedge and some of the crew—are scattered around, drinking and making themselves readily available for whoever takes notice.

Laughing, I continue down the hallway to the bedroom I share with Wolf to use the master bathroom. Using the tip of my finger, I move the strap of my red bikini top to check my tan line and notice that I've already gotten some color. After peeing, I reapply my sunscreen and then head back out to find the girls.

I'm approaching the kitchen when I find Wolf leaning against the island, shoveling a handful of peanuts into his mouth like he's in a race. That's when I notice the group of guys that had been crowding the television just minutes before are gone.

"Where'd everyone run off to?" I ask Wolf as I snake my arms around his waist.

He rolls his eyes. "Mel's putting on a show out there. Saw it. Left. Just eating my peanuts and waiting for you."

I laugh at his expression and stilted words. "What are you talking about?"

He tips back his beer and swallows. "Mel's topless."

My expression twists into annoyance. "And that bothers you why?"

He gives me a look as if I'm crazy. "It doesn't bother you?"

I shrug. "Not really. I'd do the same if I didn't think it would bother you."

His eyes flash with anger. "No fucking way are you taking your top off. Nobody sees those tits but me."

I stifle a laugh "See? But I guess I'm a little happy this is the first time you've seen Mel's tits." I'm teasing, I think. Melanie's one of those hard to look at types, with her piercing blue eyes, light brown hair that manages to take on new streaks of color every week—and tall, modelesque frame.

"You're not going to be pissed at me, are you?" Wolf asks.

Shit. I step away, glaring at him. "Why? What did you do?"

He shakes his head, pulling me back. "No! Geez. Nothing. She likes to do that. I've seen 'em before. Never bothered me before today."

"Why does it bother you today?"

He chuckles. "Because I wasn't in love with someone else's tits before." He bends down and kisses the top of my breast. "I don't need them feeling all jealous and shit."

I chuckle, feeling the tension release from my body, and then lean in to kiss his cheek. Loud voices interrupt us as Terese walks inside yelling while Derrick follows, frustrated and embarrassed. When Terese pushes him away and walks toward the hall leading to their bedroom, he pauses a minute before following her.

"Shit," Wolf and I say in unison.

"See, *that's* what I was trying to avoid," Wolf says pointedly, pulling me against his chest. "Mel should know better with you girls in the house."

A door slams, and Derrick storms into the kitchen and grabs a beer from the fridge, slamming that door, too. When he pounds a fist into the wall, Wolf pulls away from me and approaches him. "Whoa. Let's go outside."

Derrick shakes Wolf off and points to the patio. "I'm not going back out there."

Wolf looks at me, and I nod. "I'll go tell her to cover up."

When I reach Melanie, she's already pulling her swim top back on. "Shit, Mel." I drop into my lounge chair with a smile. "We know you have nice tits and all, but you're really stirring it up in there."

She rolls her eyes. "I heard. I'll go talk to Terese. I feel like a rock skank now."

I frown. "You didn't do anything wrong. Don't feel bad. This thing with her and Derrick is just new, that's all. It's natural for her to have some insecurities at the start, especially since he's asked her to come to Europe."

Lorraine rolls her eyes and cuts in. "Honestly, Lyric, if Terese is going to get upset about Derrick checking out a set of lady lumps, it's going to get ugly if she comes on tour with us. We don't need that kind of drama. You and Wolf are enough."

My stomach rolls. I understand what Lorraine is saying, but it's also unfair to expect Terese to accept things as they are without really seeing firsthand what this life is all about. Girlfriends in the business need thick skin to survive. Not that their men should get away with anything, but if there isn't trust, jealousy can quickly make a relationship ugly.

Unfortunately for me, I had too much trust in my relationship with Tony when he threw up all the red flags that should have warned me away. Derrick isn't like Tony, though. I know Terese will be fine.

Wolf, on the other hand, had enough sense to walk away. If he hadn't, it wouldn't have bothered me to the extent it did Terese, but the warmth settling around my heart makes me a little grateful for my own situation. I like that my man thinks of me even when I'm not around. Derrick could learn a few things from Wolf.

I somehow convince Melanie that talking to Terese won't help anything—not right now, anyway—and we all toss ourselves in the pool to cool down.

A half hour later, Terese hops in with us and glares at Melanie. For a second I'm afraid I'll have to break up a hair-tugging contest, but Terese surprises me. "Thanks a lot, bitch. Your tits are perfect. Happy?"

Melanie looks shocked until Terese cracks a smile, and then she lets out an awkward laugh. "I'm sorry, babe. I didn't think it was going to be an issue."

They hug it out and I'm left on the side of the pool stupefied from the bizarre drama that just unfolded in front of me. How did Terese get over it so quickly?

Derrick takes a seat beside me … grinning.

I turn to him, impressed. "How did you do that?"

He shrugs, a cocky expression playing on his face. "I'll never tell."

Wolf sits on my opposite side and hands me a cold beer. "How the hell did you do that, you dick?" Wolf asks Derrick over my head.

Derrick is still grinning. "Precisely. She can't stay mad at me. What can I say?"

Wolf chuckles. "Good job, dude. I was sure that fight was going to last the rest of vacation." Wolf's arm snakes around my waist.

I smile and look up at him, his sunglasses hiding his eyes. "I'm relieved, too. That could have been messy."

Wolf leans in, touching his lips gently to mine. When he pulls away, he raises his brows. "Hey, your dad called a bit ago. Wants to meet up with you tomorrow. He says he won't steal you away from me for too long."

I smile. "I'll call him back later. Do you want to come with us?"

He shakes his head. "Nah, you two spend some time together. I'll be here when you get back." A buzzing sounds from his pocket, and he reaches for it, sighing at the distraction.

"Wow, your ears must be burning," Wolf says to the caller with a chuckle.

I open my eyes wide in Wolf's direction, trying to get his attention. He looks at me. *"My dad?"* I mouth.

He nods, his expression quickly shifting from humorous to stony. Panic begins to grow in my chest. To my utter horror, Wolf pulls me to my feet and leads me through the doors of our bedroom.

We sit at the edge of the bed, my heart beating a hundred miles an hour in my chest. He pushes a button on his phone, and my dad's charismatic voice comes through the speaker. I watch Wolf's face, trying to understand what his expression means.

"Lyric's listening now. Go ahead."

Wolf is watching me. I turn my eyes down to the phone, dread growing with every second as I wait for whatever bad news is coming. I knew this life was too good to be true.

"Pumpkin, you there?"

"I'm here, Dad. What's going on?"

There's a long sigh on the other end before he speaks. That pause is enough to confirm every fear that's now seeping into my system. "I talked to the label yesterday," he says cautiously. "They were in complete agreement with me regarding your songs. But Destiny never showed up to meet them last night. They met with her this morning ... and she wasn't alone, sweetie. I guess Crawley was there. Turns out he's managing her image transformation. They had your songbook with them."

"Okay," I say, growing angrier by the second. I couldn't care less about Crawley and whatever position he fills for Destiny. "I just want what's mine."

My dad sighs again. "I know, pumpkin. I tried."

"What do you mean, 'tried'? I thought it was a done deal?"

"It was ... until Crawley showed them the contract that you signed regarding the rights to Wolf's songs."

"You mean for 'Dangerous Heart and the other two?'"

Wolf's expression shows his confusion. He looks like he's about to burst into flames. "Those songs were signed over to me, Mitch. It was a three-song deal that included 'Dangerous Heart.' Besides, all that was handled by our label's legal team. There's no way they messed that up. The only thing that was missing on that contract was Lyric's request for privacy."

"Crawley has a clever way of handling legal contracts. He likes to doctor the final copies after they've been reviewed by legal and before everyone signs, hoping his revisions will be overlooked in the final review. But I'm not talking about the contract you and Lyric signed for 'Dangerous Heart' and the others. Those are clean."

"What?" Wolf's rage grows as he tries to comprehend what's going on. I'm trying to understand too. If Crawley didn't do something shady with our song deal, then what could he possibly have on us now?

I jump in. "I don't understand, Dad. The label should be ripping my songbook from Crawley's disgusting hands by now and overnighting it. He has no claim."

"Pumpkin, it's not that simple." He pauses, and the sinking feeling grows. "All they can do is drop Destiny from the new label, and they're doing that. They're done with her, based on my word alone. But they can't take the songbook. Not after hearing Crawley's claims."

"What claims?" Wolf growls, just as confused as I am.

My dad sounds helpless when he speaks. "Wolf, I'm sorry. Crawley doctored your initial agreement with him six years ago. Apparently, you boys were new and had an agreement prior to going to the label."

"Right," says Wolf, "and that deal ended the moment we signed with our label. Crawley hasn't worked directly for me in four years. There's no way that contract is still valid."

By the sighing on the other end of the line, I can tell my dad's already been through all of this with Destiny's label. My balloon of hope is quickly deflating.

"You'll need to speak with your label and their lawyers," Mitch says. "There should have been a new contract drawn up between the band and Crawley the moment you were signed. Your label will need to take some ownership in this if they failed to rewrite those terms. That would be a major fuck up on their end, but still, you can win this. There's nothing gainful for the band in that contract. The contract states that everything benefits Crawley the moment he gets let go. That alone would have a judge rolling his eyes in court."

Wolf's jaw is working overtime, clenching and unclenching. "What were the terms?" He asks through tight lips.

"If you fire Crawley, he gets royalties for all previously published songs and the rights to anything unpublished up until the time he's released. He's claiming he owns every single lyric written in that songbook since it was in your possession. He's also sending notice for you to turn over the rights of 'Dangerous Heart' to his client."

"Destiny." Wolf's teeth are clenched, his grip on the phone tight.

"That's right. I'm sorry."

"This isn't over, Mitch. Why are you talking like it's over?" Wolf stands, taking the phone with him.

I move toward him, trying to wrap my arms around his waist. I'm less concerned about my songbook now. This is years of Wolf's hard work being stolen from him in the blink of an eye. Because of me.

He shrugs out of my hold as he moves to the window and places a palm against it. I freeze, unsure what to do or say to make this better. I know I can't.

"Hell no, Wolf!" my dad says emphatically. "Look, we need to proceed with caution; that's all. My sources tell me Crawley looks like he's in bad shape. He's hanging on by a thread, but you still need to play your cards right."

The confidence in my dad's tone fills me again, but I'm not so sure that Wolf hears him. His eyes are blazing, his knuckles white around his phone.

"I'll meet you in the studio tomorrow," Mitch says. "In the meantime, call your label and your PR team. Get them on a flight to Miami as soon as possible. We're settling this before we leave for Europe."

"We?" Wolf snaps out of his spell at my dad's words.

"I'm coming with you to Europe. If that's okay with you both ... and the band. You guys need a manager, and I'm looking for a change right now. Especially if that change includes spending more time with my little girl. And when we win this war, I want to be there."

My throat tightens with emotion, and tears immediately spring to my eyes. I look at Wolf, hopeful, but he doesn't hesitate for a moment.

"I don't know what to say, Mitch. We'd be fucking honored."

"Lyric?" my dad asks.

"Yes." I laugh, realizing how croaky my response sounds. I never would have considered this a possibility, but it's like a dream come true. "Yes!" I say again, with more enthusiasm this time.

My dad chuckles. "Okay, good. Phew, I was worried for a second."

Wolf looks back toward the window.

"Lyric," my dad starts again. "I'll call Davis and get him to Miami, too. He'll be representing you. This is about to get messy, and we'll need a ferocious team on our side."

Davis has been my dad's legal counsel for years, and 'ferocious' is a polite term for his methods. My dad's never walked away from a case unhappy—even in cases when he's technically lost.

Unfortunately, lawsuits weren't that uncommon when I toured with my dad. He tried to keep my ears free from the shenanigans that went on, but I picked up on a lot. Once he was sued by an audience member when they fainted at a show. It was an outdoor show in Texas, in midday, on the hottest day of the year. The woman was pregnant but went to the show anyway, neglected to stay hydrated, and fainted from heat exhaustion.

Davis worked with the woman and her family to settle outside of the courtroom. Mitch paid for the hospital fees and nothing else, which he would have done anyway. But Davis somehow convinced the woman not to move forward with a court case. Something about her neglecting to care for her unborn child in natural climate conditions, or something equally terrifying.

My father has always been a fair man, but he's not someone you'd ever want to push into a corner.

"See you tomorrow, Dad."

"Thanks, Mitch." Wolf ends the call, but his cell phone is still in his hand. It's clear that whatever momentary happiness he felt about my dad coming on tour has dissolved. He could possibly lose everything because of Destiny Lane— the woman I'm supposed to call mother. A woman *I* brought into his life. Sure, Crawley is involved too, but without Destiny, Crawley would have no leverage.

Wolf's face is redder than I've ever seen, and it looks like he's about to crush his phone into pieces. I gently remove it from his grip and reach for him again. "Babe?"

Wolf turns but makes no move to wrap his arms around me. Instead, he shakes his head. "I can't..." He chokes on his words, then tries again. "Not right now."

"Wolf," I plead, unsure what's happening.

I know he's pissed. He has every right to be pissed. But he can't be pissed at me. We've been through too much to let Crawley and Destiny win. Is he starting to regret everything?

Deep down, I know we'll be okay. I also know that Wolf has a lot to lose if we don't win, so his emotions are completely justified. But still, his actions suffocate me with unease, and I'm helpless to remedy his pain.

He moves away, grabs his wallet from the nightstand, and walks out of the room without a word. Seconds later, I hear the front door slam.

She's wrapped up in a sheet, her small fist clutching the pillow under her head. She stirs as I stumble into the room. I've had quite a bit to drink, but not enough to forget how much I love this woman in my bed.

I remove my shoes first, kicking them to the side. Then I slide off my shirt, saving my shorts for last before climbing into bed and pulling Lyric to my naked body.

"Wolf," she moans. She's facing me, and even in the dark, I can see the pain in her eyes. I walked out to calm down, but in doing so, I left her with nothing. Left her alone.

"I'm here, babe. I'm sorry. Fuck, Lyric. I'm so pissed. Not at you. I shouldn't have left like that. I just—"

"Shh," she tells me, pulling herself closer. "It's okay." Her hand moves up my arm until it lands on my cheek. With gentle strokes, she forgives me, and I fall in love with her all over again.

I move down her body, placing my head on her chest. She holds me, and I wrap my arms tightly around her waist. "This is so fucked up," I say into her shirt. "Crawley knew he had me by the balls, but he would never tell me what he had on me. He *wanted* to get fired." I can hear myself slurring a little, but my mind is clear. "I thought it was weird he didn't start trouble as soon as I kicked him off the tour. I'm so fucking stupid."

"No!" Lyric says, her voice trembling with anger. "You are *not* stupid. Crawley is the stupid one. He's not going to get away with this, Wolf. You said it yourself; he wanted to get fired.

"I did some research while you were gone," she continues. "His termination wasn't a layoff or an amicable parting of ways. It was him, trying to steal from you *while* he violated your property. And it wasn't his first offense. You had no choice but to let him go. Not only that, but you need to look into his ties with your legal team. Someone should have caught on to what he was doing."

My beautiful, smart Lyric. I should have known she would do everything in her power to make this better, even when she's hurting, too.

"You just have to hang on for a bit," she continues. "Let's talk to my dad, your label, and the lawyers, and we'll figure out our options. My songbook is the least of my worries while I help you fight this. Before, this was about principle and showing Destiny that she can't control me anymore. Now, it's so much bigger than that. I love you, Wolf. Destiny and Crawley shouldn't fuck with the people I love."

I look up. Lyric has tears in her eyes to match the thickness in her voice. Shit. My love for this girl runs deep.

It's funny how fighting for someone you love gives you more strength than fighting for yourself. Lyric sounds like me when I was determined to get her songbook back. I still am. And she's right. There's got to be a way to win this. But right now, I just want to forget about it all. I want to bury myself inside Lyric where my world is right. Where we're both safe.

I slide her shirt up slowly so it gently skims her skin before I pull it up it over her head. Her dark hair cascades around her face, and I'm overwhelmed by her beauty and strength. It's everything I fell in love with, and just one of the many things that holds my heart hostage.

"You know what I realized when I was out feeling sorry for myself?"

"What?"

I move a strand of hair from her face and tuck it behind her ear. "At the end of the day, I'm not worried about a royalty share or songs getting taken away. You and me—we'll just create more where that came from. But there's one thing no one will *ever* have the power to take from us." I lean in and kiss her neck, breathing her in and letting out a deep sigh. "If we walk away from this and all I have left are the clothes on my back and you in my arms, I'll be a happy man."

"I feel the same," Lyric agrees. "We're in this together, babe."

I use my knee to spread her legs wide and press my lips to hers. "Forever."

Lyric nods, then moans when I thrust myself into her. "Forever."

We make sweet, slow, torturous love, neither of us speaking about Destiny or Crawley for the rest of the night.

Tonight is ours.

Tomorrow, we fight back.

Chapter Twenty-Two

Lyric

Friday is a freak show of epic proportions as representatives and lawyers of all kinds descend on the house, turning it from a vacation home to a battle station. It's early evening and no one has had a drop to drink—which maybe we should reconsider. There have been no celebrations. No work. Just repurposing the mansion's game room to host a cutthroat team of entertainment professionals.

My dad and the entire band are here as we greet Wolf's label rep, his publicist, a legal rep from the label, and Wolf's lawyer and his associate, who drew up the original contract in question. Five professionals coming together to put a stop to Crawley and Destiny before they can revel in what they set out to destroy—at least, I hope.

Wolf and I spent the earlier part of the day talking with my dad at the studio. The band had some cleanup work to do on the song, but the rest of the time was spent filling everyone in on the drama and preparing for the long night ahead.

My dad is convinced Crawley's ship is sunk in more ways than one. He's done for. Our mission now is to come up with the best approach to end him and get back what's ours. He's an idiot for thinking he could destroy Wolf's career and steal from us. Using my mother, no less. And in the fallout, Destiny will be left in the dust.

But there are still so many questions. Things we need to understand before we make our next move.

First, who allowed Crawley to rewrite the terms of the original contract? Obviously Wolf wouldn't agree to something like that, and any judge would see right through it. But why didn't Wolf's legal team catch it?

Even then, doesn't the contract Wolf signed through the label override the old contract? If not, why wasn't a new contract drawn between Crawley and the band once the band signed with the label?

And finally, the most perplexing question of all: how did Crawley and Destiny become allies in this dangerous game they're both playing?

Questions and answers are flying around the room as the legal team reads all versions of the contracts line-by-line to see what was changed and when. And by whom. That might be the most important piece of information here.

My dad sits with me at the opposite end of the room as Wolf. We're speaking to Davis, my dad's attorney, as he reviews the latest three-song deal I made with Wolf.

And once again, I have to explain why I wanted no compensation. This, apparently hurts our case, because it leaves me with no monetary tie to the situation at all and a record of my agreeing to relinquishing my rights, giving me zero leverage and zero claim to what's mine. And Wolf's. Even Davis admits he understands Crawley's argument that the songbook is now his—because some of the songs were co-written with Wolf.

My head hurts, and I place it into my palms as my elbows rest on the table. My dad wraps a strong arm around me and squeezes. "Stop thinking you did something wrong here, Lyric. You may not have claim to what you signed over to Wolf, but that songbook is yours. Same with the original songs she took from you and made millions off of."

"What original songs?" Davis asks, leaning in, forehead crinkling as he waits for my response.

I vaguely remember meeting Davis before when I was younger, but he's changed so much he almost looks like a different man. With white hair, light gray eyes, and tan, leathery skin, he's intimidating at first glance. I guess that's a good thing.

My dad turns toward me. "Is it okay if we talk to Davis about this? Destiny's label already knows."

I nod. I have nothing to hide anymore. Nothing is more important than getting Wolf his songs back, even if that means outing Destiny for the record she plagiarized—and outing myself for letting her get away with it.

My dad goes on to explain my mom's betrayal just as he remembers it, letting me fill in the gaps. The only reason he knew about it to begin with is because I confessed to Doug at work right after the album came out and I'd realized what I fool I had been to believe she meant well.

Doug was livid, understandably, and he wanted to get my father involved. I was okay with it at first—until Destiny threatened to end his career. That's when I called everything off and told my dad to stay out of it. I could live without my songs. What I couldn't live with was being the cause of my parents putting each other through hell.

"Who else knows about these recordings?" Davis asks. "You said Destiny's label knows."

I look at my dad, and he sighs. "Yeah, I told Destiny's label when I went to LA yesterday. They're letting Destiny go—at least, that's what they say."

Davis nods. "Got it. I need to make a few phone calls." He looks around at the madness. "In private."

I nod and stand, leading him down the hall to my makeshift office and switch on the light. "Take your time."

"Thank you, Lyric."

For a shark on the job, Davis' presence is calming and very much welcome right now. The tension in this house could slice a brick.

I head for the stairs, wanting food and distractions. And possibly a stiff drink. I'm almost to the staircase when a dark, shadowy figure moving through the hallway makes me freeze. Whoever it is appears to be searching for something. When the figure's head angles toward me slightly, I realize it belongs to the associate on Wolf's legal team. He looks to be around my age—and permanently nervous.

I smile to ease the tension. "Can I help you find something? This house is massive; I know."

He jumps and swivels to face me, his eyes widening. His mouth opens, then closes, his gaze fixed on me as he swallows.

"Bathroom is taken," he says finally. "Is there another?"

I smile, pushing away my unease. He may be awkward, but he's harmless. "I'm heading upstairs. There are a few up there. You can follow me."

We get to the main floor, and I point him toward the nearest bathroom. Then I busy myself making snacks and pouring drinks for our guests. It's a nice break from the chaos downstairs.

I'm just about done loading up a tray when my dad runs upstairs with Davis and Wolf on his tail.

"Lyric," my dad says, his voice almost frantic, "where are the recordings you have of your original songs? Do you have them on you?"

My heart speeds up. "No. They're in Seattle at my storage locker." I look around at the faces, wondering where this is going. "Why?"

"We need those tapes in our possession before we move forward," Davis says. I wait, still trying to understand. "I just got off the phone with my connection at Wicked, Wolf's label. They mentioned the recordings to Soaring, trying to get them to give up their pursuit of Wolf's songs. Destiny and Crawley were in the room during the call. They heard everything. If Destiny gets her hands on those tapes, we lose the only evidence we have."

My face falls. I look to my dad, who looks as if the weight of the world is on his shoulders. "What happens now?"

Davis looks between us all. "We need those tapes in our possession to win this thing."

My dad grabs my hand and squeezes. "Do you have someone you can trust in Seattle who can overnight the package, pumpkin? Better yet, do you know someone who can get the recordings and fly here with them? Tonight?"

My immediate answer is no. But I rack my brain just in case. Trust has never been an easy thing for me. Not after my dad sent me away, my mom stole from me, and then Tony cheated on me with my best friend. Do I trust anyone in

Seattle enough to give them access to something so important? I don't think I do.

I'm about to shake my head when Wolf comes up behind me and wraps his arms around my waist. "Babe, what about Deloris? Doesn't she live in Seattle now?"

Deloris. My heart skips around in my chest, and I widen my eyes. Oh, my God. Deloris.

"Yeah! I mean, I could ask her. She has a job. I don't know if she could get away, but I could ask."

"And you trust this Deloris?" Davis asks. "We can't afford to take any risks right now."

I nod heavily. "Yes. I trust her with my life."

Davis nods. "Okay, then give her a call. If she agrees, I'll arrange the flight. You'll just have to tell her how to access the tapes and pick her up when she arrives."

I reach for my phone and search for her number, still not exactly sure what's happening. "What do my original recordings have to do with Wolf's songs, though? They'll prove Destiny stole from me when I was seventeen, but that still leaves Crawley."

Davis shakes his head. "It's all the proof we need. Not for court, but this is how we encourage Destiny to work against Crawley. Think about it. If Destiny gets outed, she'll lose all credibility. No one will want to work with her. But we can cut a deal with her if she gives up Crawley. He won't even be able to start an indie label in his mom's basement with the reputation he'll earn once everyone knows what he's been up to. And *that's* how Crawley loses his leverage, and then he will return your songbook." He looks at Wolf. "As for the rest, we're working on it."

My head goes fuzzy with his words. I hope he's right.

With a deep sigh, I pick up my phone to call Deloris. The moment her voice comes over the line, I start crying.

"Oh honey, what's wrong?" Her sweet, velvety voice pours over me just like I remember. It hurts how much I miss this woman. A woman who was more mother to me than my own flesh and blood.

I wipe my eyes and take a breath. "I'll explain everything. I promise. But I need to ask you a favor. Something has happened—*is* happening. You're the only one I could think to call. You're the only one there I can trust."

"Sweetie, take a breath and just ask. I'll do whatever I can to help."

I laugh between sobs. "You don't even know what I'm going to ask you."

She laughs right back, her voice just as melodic as I remember. "It doesn't matter. I'll still do whatever I can to help you."

With that reassurance, I take a deep breath to steady my voice and let it out. "Do you think you could fly to Miami? Tonight? If you can, there's something I need you to do. I'm so sorry to be asking you this."

"Don't be silly, Lyric. You have nothing to be sorry for. I have the kids tonight, but I could leave here in the morning as long as I'm back first thing Monday."

My eyes widen, and a relieved breath leaves me in a whoosh. Deloris was never the type to questions my motives. She's always trusted me to do the right thing. And she knows I never ask for help unless I really need it.

I cover the mouthpiece and relay what she said to Davis. Everyone scrambles into action to plan for Deloris' mission. The storage unit is locked by a passcode, so I tell her to call me in the morning so I can give it to her when she's at the facility. At this point, I don't feel comfortable transferring that information over phone or email.

She's booked on the first flight from Sea-Tac, which will get her to Miami International by eight twenty-five in the evening. That's a lot later than we wanted, but it will have to do.

We decide not to tell the others our plan. This is safer staying between us for now. In the meantime, we'll let the rest of the team work out how to prove that Wolf's original contracts were illegally modified by Crawley.

It's nearly ten o'clock when I start to head back downstairs with a tray of fresh fruit and veggie slices. Exhaustion slows me down a little, making me jump when I see a figure rounding the corner from the hallway. We collide, food tumbling from the tray as it crashes to the ground and I look up, wide-eyed and heart pounding.

"I'm sorry," he says quickly, stooping down to fill the tray with the fallen goods. It's the associate from Wolf's legal team. Has he been up here the entire time?

I stumble back, my side pressed against the hallway wall as I examine the odd man with his long, light brown hair, thick-rimmed glasses, and rosy cheeks. "It's okay," I say, my voice catching a little in my throat when I notice the sweat beading on the man's forehead.

He's still stacking fruit and veggies on the tray while I examine him. He's shaking, like he's afraid I'm going to punish him for spilling veggies all over the floor. What's his problem?

"Thanks, Lyric." As sorry as I feel for the guy, the way he says my name as if we're old friends drags a rake down my spine.

I dump the tray off in the kitchen and join Wolf and the rest of the band on the sofa downstairs in the game room. Wolf pulls me onto his lap and I curl up into a ball, letting him hold me.

But my eyes never leave the strange, jittery man, who only seems stranger as he takes a seat beside his boss. He's not helping him. At least, it doesn't appear that way. Instead, his leg jiggles anxiously and his eyes wander around the room.

"You okay, babe?" Wolf asks in my ear.

I nod, but he finds my focal point and now is watching too. "Guy's kind of creepy, yeah? What did you say his name was again?" My heart is pounding like it's leading a freaking marching band.

"Cole Matthews," Wolf responds easily. "He's been with the team as long as I've known them. He was just an intern back then."

My eyes widen, and I look up to face Wolf. Does he hear himself? "What? As in the same legal aid that tried to pass off Crawley's updated legal terms to your label to own the rights to the songs I gifted to you?"

Wolf gives me curious eyes. "Yeah. Doug says he's a bumbling idiot. Why? What's wrong?"

"I don't know. He seems awfully nervous, don't you think?"

Wolf lets out an airy laugh. "Oh, that. He's a fan, babe. Don't judge. Almost shit his pants when I shook his hand earlier. I think he has a crush on you, too. He keeps staring at you."

I look at Cole, who stares down at the contract beneath his pen with a wrinkled brow. He seems to be concentrating on something important. And for a second, I decide that maybe Wolf is right. Maybe he is just a superfan who happens to be the same one who missed the fact that Crawley tried to steal my songs from Wolf.

What am I thinking, anyway? That Cole had something to do with the legal revisions from years ago? He was just an intern. There's no way any lawyer would put that much trust into a kid.

Just then, Bradley from the Wicked's legal team stands and clears his throat to get everyone's attention. "Crawley is mentioned in the label's agreement," he announces. "A small section on page 44."

"We already know this, Bradley," says Fredrick, Wolf's lawyer. He looks annoyed, like this is all a waste of his time. "The problem is," Fredrick explains, "that it just notes his base salary from when the contract was signed with the label and says the contracts will be renewed in five years. That doesn't override the fact that the band made a separate deal with him prior to this contract being signed."

"That's where you're wrong." Bradley pulls up the original agreement, grinning, then throws it on the table for Frederick to view. "Read who the agreement was established between."

Frederick rolls his eyes. "Beowulf Chapman and Lionel Crawley. So what?"

"So," Bradley explains, "the original agreement states that if Lionel Crawley is *fired* by Wolf, then he is owed. No one fired Crawley during the time these contract terms were valid."

My dad jumps in, grabbing the document from Fredrick's hands. "You're right. Crawley was never fired by Wolf during the terms of this contract. Simple as that. Crawley was written into the label's agreement when the label became his employer." My dad looks up. "Meaning the old contract is void. Wolf's music is protected under the label's new contract, and there isn't a thing Crawley can do to fight that."

Bradley beams and takes the document from my dad's hands. "That's correct. There is nothing binding Wolf, the person, to Crawley any longer. In simple terms, Wolf may have kicked Crawley off the tour, but it was the label who terminated his employment for a list of acceptable reasons. Manipulating legal documents, unprofessionalism, and insubordination to name a few. Wolf and the label are in the clear."

The room lights up with excitement. Wolf's arm tightens around me, and I turn in to hug him hard. My heart pounds in my chest. Can it seriously be this easy? Is it over? I can't be so quick to assume we've won this thing yet, but it sure sounds like everything is going our way.

As celebration consumes the room, I'm rooted to my seat. Instead of joining in, I find myself examining Cole, who has stepped away from the excitement to take a call on the other side of the room, I can't shake the feeling that this battle isn't over. Maybe I'll feel differently once my songbook is safely in my hands. I'd also love to see a new contract drawn up with bulletproof protection against assholes like Crawley.

My phone buzzes on the table beside me. I grab it when I see Doug's name and excuse myself to an empty room down the hall, shutting the door behind me.

"Hey, Doug," I answer. I want nothing more than to fill him in on everything that's just gone down. But maybe I shouldn't. There's still so much to be done, and I wouldn't want to compromise any of our plans. Not that Doug would tell a soul. He's one of the good ones.

There's a crackle on the other end of the line, some quick breaths, and then a familiar voice breaking through the static. Air freezes in my throat as I listen.

"Lyric, it's me." Tony's voice is low and rushed, immediately filling me with a boil of anger.

"Goddammit, Tony." I hiss into the phone, livid that he still won't give up. And now that I've blocked his new number, he's calling me with Doug's phone. "Don't you ever listen? Leave. Me. Alone."

"Fuck. Lyric, stop. I need to talk to you."

I pinch my noise to control my anger, fill my lungs with air and then shake my head even though he can't see me. "No, Tony. Just—no. Whatever you want to talk about, there's no point. It's over."

He starts to talk again, but I'm faster. "I'm hanging up. I can't block this number because it's Doug's, but if you try to contact me again, I will get a restraining order, and I won't hesitate to spill your every misdemeanor to the press. Goodbye."

I power down my phone and am shoving it my pocket when the door opens and Wolf enters quietly,

"Babe."

I feel my body shaking from my brief call with Tony, but I try to contain it for Wolf's sake. The last thing we need is more drama getting in the middle of all this chaos. But I can't shake the unsettled feeling that has stayed with me since I first laid eyes on that legal aid. I'm worried that there's something we're all missing. Something Crawley will blindside us with. And I'm terrified this won't be as easy as we all think.

"Let's get you to bed," Wolf says gently.

I nod, no energy to argue. I'm tired. Everyone thinks the battle is over, but I'm not so sure it is.

Wolf leads me to our bathroom and leaves me in front of the shower while he starts it, testing the water and then turning to me.

He must sense my exhaustion because he takes my long dress and lifts it above my head, careful to avoid snagging my hair. When he's tossed it aside, he reaches around to unclasp my bra, gently sliding it over my shoulders, his fingers gliding along my skin until the cloth drops to the floor.

His kisses are soft, his lips gently kneading mine and shaking me from the inside out. Fabric lifts from my hips and slides down my thighs as Wolf removes my panties. He lowers himself to a kneeling position, and his eyes lock on mine as he places a kiss on my pelvis. My skin warms where his mouth touches, and as he stands again, my entire body buzzes.

Wolf moves me into the shower, continuing to be gentle. Loving. He's always been able to read me, and he knows this is what I need right now. He places me under the hot water, getting my hair wet before lathering it with shampoo. He massages my scalp with his strong hands, his strength comforting, making me feel every bit as cherished as I always do with him.

He takes a washcloth and rubs gentle circles on my skin, starting between my shoulder blades and working his way down to the small of my back. A kiss lands on my shoulder, almost distracting me from the hand moving around my waist to my stomach, lightly brushing the skin below my left breast. Nothing about it is sexual, but it's all so intimate still, and I never want him to stop.

I'm reminded once again how perfect we are together. How I never realized how much I was missing until Wolf showed up in my life. How my life was just a series of rock tours, glass windows, and empty, convenient love. And how the one man I should have never fallen in love with managed to claim a piece of my soul.

I turn to face him, swallowing when I see the way he's watching me, his caramel eyes heavy with love and yearning. But for once, the yearning isn't for sex. We're far more than that. We've become two people in a war that has the power to rip us apart, but we'll only ever be fighting together.

My hand moves to his heart and I lean in, angling my chin to grip his eyes with mine. "No matter what happens, we're going to be okay," I say with conviction. We've already come to this conclusion, but I'm just now starting to grasp the sentiment with my whole heart.

Wolf nods. "We will always be okay." He tips my chin up with his fingers, making my heart soar in my chest. When his lips find mine, he's weaving his fingers through my hair and deepening the connection.

He knows what I know. Nothing else matters, as long as we're together.

Chapter Twenty-Three

Lyric

She'll be here any minute. I'm wringing my hands in the back seat of the band's hired SUV, unsure if I'm more nervous about seeing Deloris again or about the tapes she'll be bringing with her. Those recordings. The only proof I have of what was stolen from me years ago. Memories I've tried to bury along with my anger at the woman who ended up being the evil in the world that she was supposed to protect me from.

If it weren't for Deloris, I may never have made it through my teenage years. She was everything I needed, even though I may not have realized it at the time. She never let me miss a meal. She was a tutor when I needed one. And she was my companion when all I wanted to do was lock myself in the house and binge on bad food and television.

When everything changed, after I realized what Destiny had done, I started to thank my lucky stars when she didn't come home. I wouldn't have been able to stomach the sight of her. Working out a transfer to Seattle with Perform Live was the easiest decision I ever made. With my diploma barely in my hand, I kissed Deloris goodbye and headed straight for the airport.

No regrets.

What I didn't expect was for Deloris to follow me to Seattle, and take a full-time nanny position for a family in Fremont, just north of downtown. With her own kids fully grown and living in different parts of the country, there was nothing tying her to California, and Destiny had no reason to keep her around. Not that Deloris would have stayed.

My phone buzzes, and the moment I see Doug's name on the screen I answer it, praying it's not Tony again. I could kill him for continuing to pop up in my life like he owns me, like he has any right to speak to me after his betrayal—and worse, after meddling in my relationship with Wolf.

"It's me," says the panicked voice on the other line. "Please don't hang up. This is important."

I swallow my anger, knowing in my gut I need to hear him out this time. "Fine. You have two minutes."

"Thank you," he sighs. "Look, Doug…" There's a pause on the other end of the line, and I'm gripped with fear. "He's missing."

"What do you mean? He's missing?"

"Well—have *you* heard from him?"

Confusion fills me. Why would I—? "No. I haven't heard from him since the end of Wolf's tour. Before he left to babysit you. But you're calling me from Doug's phone. What is going on?"

A frustrated huff of air leaves Tony. I remember that noise. He made it a lot during our final weeks together. There was always something frustrating in his life, and I always felt like it was me.

"That's what I'm trying to figure out. Something fucking weird is going on, Lyric. Doug has been getting a lot of strange phone calls lately. He'll step away to take them, but

I've heard him get into these intense arguments. And then he never came back to the bus after our last show two nights ago. No one's seen him. We've been stuck in Tampa, waiting for his ass to appear. He left his phone, his wallet. Everything is here ... except him."

"Jesus, you're serious? Did you call the cops? Maybe something happened to him." I grip the leather seat hard, my knuckles whitening at the pressure.

"Yes, I called the cops today but there's not much they'll do for me since he's a grown ass man and I have no proof that anything bad happened."

"Did you check to see who the calls were from? It could just be the label."

Tony sighs. "His call log was deleted. But I heard him address whoever it was by the name Crawley. Isn't that Wolf's band manager?"

My chest grows heavy with worry. Fuck. What the hell does Crawley want with Doug? And where is Doug now?

"I've called everyone I can think of," he says. "I just— hoped maybe you knew something." Tony pauses. "You believe me, right?"

I narrow my eyes even though he can't see me. I wasn't questioning his honesty until he asked me to trust him.

"Prove it," I say.

There's a gasp on the other end of the line. "What?"

"Prove that you aren't lying."

"How?" he explodes.

I search for an idea—anything for Tony to say or do to make me believe he's truly panicked and that Doug is really gone. Why would he just disappear? It makes no sense at all.

"Tell the media what really happened between you and me, and you and Wolf."

There's a longer pause now, and I can almost see Tony's face flame with rage. "Lyric, I'm not fucking around. I think whoever Doug has been talking to hurt him. And you want to play fucking games with me?"

"I'm not playing games. It will take you two seconds to post a message on social media saying that you're to blame for getting beat by Wolf."

"That's stupid!" Tony explodes again. "That shit's already died down. And anyway, I didn't get beat."

I shake my head, not allowing him to give him. "Just do it, Tony, or I'll know you're full of shit about Doug."

I end the call with Tony just as we're pulling up to the airport and immediately dial Wolf's number. After ringing a few times, it goes to voicemail. I want to scream. What nightmare am I living in now?

Wolf's voicemail picks up telling me to leave a message.

"Babe, it's me. Look, Tony just called from Doug's phone, so I answered. He says that Doug is missing. I don't know if he's telling the truth, but I can't imagine why he would lie about something like this." I take a deep breath. "What if Doug's really missing? Tony says that Crawley's been calling him. A lot. Anyway, I'm at the airport. Just call me back soon. I love you."

It takes me a few minutes to get my bearings back, to try to push all thoughts of Doug to the back of my mind so I can look for Deloris. When I see her round figure emerge through the sliding glass door of the airport, I'm flooded with memories of getting my hands sticky in the kitchen as I'd roll dough in sugar to make churros. Of learning to drive at the cemetery, since there was no way I could kill anyone. Of playing Scrabble by the fire "just one more time" so I could finally beat her. I never could. I smile, unable to stop myself.

The driver, whose name I forgot to ask in the flurry of activity, opens the car door, and I jump out to greet Deloris. She hasn't changed much since I last saw her. She's still just as vertically challenged as me, with fuller curves than I remember, curly, dark brown hair, and small, brown eyes that always seem to disappear when she smiles.

My arms wrap around her shoulders, and I squeeze. I might even squeal. And then I burst into tears, unable to hold back the thick build-up of emotion in my chest.

"Sweetie, shh. I'm here, baby girl." I always loved when she called me baby girl. It made me feel protected, which is something I hadn't felt again until recently. Until Wolf.

After our long embrace and my cry session, we shuffle into the SUV.

"So," she prompts, turning toward me with narrowed eyes. "Care to fill me in on why I just took an eight-hour flight to Miami of all places? In the summer?" She fans herself dramatically. "My old bones won't stand for this humidity, you know."

I laugh and roll my eyes. "Your old bones will be just fine. And yes, I'll explain everything back at the house. Do you have the tapes on you, or did you pack them in your luggage?"

"They're right here." She reaches into her carry-on purse and pulls out a large zip lock bag with a dozen or so tapes tucked safely inside.

I smile and take the bag from her. "Wow. I just had a flashback to the day I packed these up and shoved them in a drawer in the locker." Shaking my head, I meet Deloris' eyes.

While Deloris knows that there was tension between Destiny and me, and she may very well know more than she ever let on, we've never discussed her stealing my music.

"Does this have anything to do with that 'Dangerous Heart' song?" The smile that blooms on her face shocks me right to hell. My jaw drops.

"You know about that?" I let out a huff of breath. "Everyone knows. How does everyone freaking know?"

Deloris rolls her eyes. "You're still as clueless and stubborn as ever. You must have thought I was deaf when we were living together."

"No, of course not. But to recognize my lyrics when someone else is singing them is…" I shake my head. "It's been years."

She smiles sadly. "I know. But there's something about your lyrics I'll always recognize. Strength through sadness is how I thought about it. Always a fighter, you were. I've always been proud of you for that." She reaches over to cup my chin in her hands. "Looks like that hasn't changed a bit."

When she drops her hand, I let out another laugh. "It's really good to see you, Deloris. I'm sorry I haven't made it back to Seattle. Between Tony's show and touring schedule and then accepting the job with Wolf, there wasn't an opportunity. I was planning to go there this week, but…"

She's shaking her head. "Nonsense. You're doing great things for yourself, which is what I've always wanted for you. I know it's never been easy for you, Lyric."

Swallowing, I try to get a handle on my emotions. "My dad is staying at the house where we're headed." I catch the questioning look she gives me and smile. "I'll explain it all later, but it's been nice having him around again. I'm just … trying to let the past go and move on." I hold up the bag of tapes. "Hoping this helps."

Deloris nods knowingly and faces front. "Well, you don't need to tell me anything more than you already have. I'm just here to deliver, let you spoil me for a couple of days, and then head back to Seattle to see my new babies." She winks at me and I smile.

"Lucky kids."

She reaches for my hand and squeezes. "Just don't tell them I've already got a favorite."

Laughing, I nod. "Our secret."

I feel so at peace in this moment, knowing that everything will finally be okay. In less than an hour, the most important people in my life will all be together. And soon, Destiny and Crawley will be out of the picture.

But everything changes in an instant.

With a squeal of tires as our car comes to a screeching halt, I'm thrown into my seatbelt, my head falling forward, and then I'm flung backwards against my seat. I look over to find a terrified and wide-eyed Deloris, staring at something in front of me. My eyes track her stare to the driver's seat.

What the hell?

I peer around the headrest to find the company driver facing forward, tightly gripping the wheel and shoulders tense. There's a gun pointed at his head through the window, a beady-eyed Cole standing behind it with his finger on the trigger. I gasp.

As if on cue, Cole's eyes find mine. *Shit.* I sink into my seat. He's staring at me with the same dark brown, beady eyes that stared at me last night in the hallway. Nervous, a bit off the mark.

The corner of his mouth twitches, but not into a smile. It's more like an anxious tick. Like he's on a timed mission. For what?

Where are we? I try to look around me, but I'm too afraid to remove my gaze from Cole's. Not with that weapon in his hands.

It's late, so the streets are dark, but we must have taken a turn off the highway at some point because we've stopped somewhere in the outskirts of the city. Streetlights glow dimly in the distance, but directly around us, there's nothing but trees and a small playground nestled in the center of some park I don't know the name of.

I swallow and slowly reach for my phone, which is tucked under my leg. If I can just get to it and unlock it, then I can speed dial Wolf.

A light tapping sounds at the driver's window stops and chills me to the bone. Cole's eyes are still on me, and he's shaking his head. *Shit. He knows what I'm doing.* But he makes no effort to stop me because he's too busy opening the driver door and gesturing for the driver to get out of the car.

"Stand over there," Cole tells the man with nervous confidence.

"What about the money?" the driver asks, desperation heavy in his breath.

Cole rolls his eyes dramatically, grabbing an envelope from his back pocket and handing it to him. "Now move!" Cole yells. He waves the gun in the direction of the sidewalk.

The driver nods cautiously, raises his hands up slowly, and moves around Cole until his back is to him and he's walking away.

Everything is happening so fast. Cole turns his body to face the driver and lifts the gun to aim at his head—and then a shot rings through the night.

Deloris clutches my hand as we scream and watch our driver jolt forward from the hit, fall to his knees on the sidewalk, and then land on his face. By his lack of reaction to the impact, I'm guessing he's dead or close to it.

Cole tucks his gun into his back pocket and runs toward the sidewalk.

While Cole is busy frisking the body, a panicked Deloris cries softly beside me. I squeeze the hand I'm already holding in an effort to calm her. But I'm not sure how convincing I am. "It's going to be okay, Deloris. Just breathe."

When I let go of her, I remember the phone near my leg and fumble to unlock the screen. Once it's open, I look up to gauge how much time I have. There's nothing. No dead body and no Cole.

What the fuck? I search the front windshield desperately for any sign of either of them, but all is black except for the beams of light coming from the front of the car.

My eyes are still scanning the street and sidewalk when Cole's body pops up from the ground, the car's headlights illuminating his light blue eyes and heavy breathing. "Shit," I whisper-cry as I fumble for my phone again.

I don't have time to think, so I open my last text to Wolf and quickly send the only thing I have time to send.

Cole. It goes through almost instantly, thank God, and I'm deleting the message just as Cole steps into the driver's seat.

"If you think you're about to call your boyfriend, you're wrong." Cole practically has his entire body facing me in the seat, a shiny black revolver now aimed straight for my head. I freeze, and my heart beats rapidly in my chest. "Hand it over," he demands.

I'm still frozen in place, my thoughts a jumble of incomprehensible alerts. When I don't react quickly enough, he leans over the seat and shoves the gun to my temple. Pain radiates through my head, and for a moment, everything goes dark.

"Lyric, honey, just give the man your phone. No one needs to get hurt today." Deloris says this as calmly as she can manage, but her voice is shaking and close to tears. There is obvious fear in her tone, and I'm the reason for it. Why did I think it was a good idea to drag her into this mess?

Because you didn't think a crazy legal aid with a gun would intercept you on an abandoned road in the middle of nowhere and then steal your phone.

Cole sneers at Deloris and then turns to me. "Hello, Lyric. I'd like to apologize to you and your guest in advance for what comes next. But first, I'm going to need you to hand over your phone and then that pretty zip lock bag with the recordings. Your friends are waiting."

"My *friends*?"

"If you need me to be specific, fine," he huffs in annoyance. "Crawley and your mother have plans for you."

"My *mother*? Does she know you're holding a gun to my head?"

His lip curls. "Of course, your mother. She hates you just as much as my father."

What? I look at the man again. And that's when I see it. It's all in the eyes. "Crawley is your father?" I swallow.

His eyes narrow in confirmation. "You and that boyfriend of yours should really be careful when letting people into your home. You never know what kind of psychos are gonna just walk right in."

The pressure of the gun only gets stronger, and I cringe with discomfort. "What do you want, Cole?" The man is sweating profusely, worse than last night when I found him wandering around the house supposedly looking for a bathroom.

"I told you what I wanted!" he yells, mouth glistening with saliva. "Give me the damn tapes before I'm forced to shoot you in the head."

"Do it, Lyric," Deloris says, a tremor filling her voice.

I narrow my eyes. "He won't shoot me, Deloris. He wants something from me, and he won't get it if I'm dead. Besides, my mom may be a bitch, but she would never ask for this." I shift away from the gun, wedging myself into the corner of my seat. "*Why* are you doing this for him?"

His face twitches again, this time in multiple places, and for a moment I think he's considering putting down the gun. Instead, he points it right at Deloris' head, never once looking away from me. Her scream shreds any resolve I had to challenge the psycho in the driver's seat.

"I'm going to say this one more time, you stupid cunt," Cole spits. "Hand over your phone and the tapes before I blow this lady's brains out. You seem fond enough of her to want to keep her safe, don't you?"

"Fine!" I shriek as I toss my phone into the front seat, followed by the bag of tapes. "Get the gun away from her."

Cole laughs and pulls the gun back. He aims it at the roof while he powers off my phone and stores my things in the glove compartment. "Okay. Now, Deloris. Hand over your phone, honey."

Deloris doesn't give him a reason to press the gun to her head again. She digs into her bag and hands him her phone.

"What do you say we go on a little drive? I have a delivery to make."

My fists clench and I shake my head. "No. You have what you came for. What's the point of keeping us now?"

His sneer practically glows in the rearview mirror. "Oh, Lyric. You don't actually think you're going to live past tonight, do you? You've seen my face. You know my name. For fuck's sake, you saw me kill a man." He chuckles nervously. "Once I hand over your possessions, all that's left is deciding how to end your life. And my father is quite looking forward to that last bit."

"She should've been back an hour ago. Did you check the status of Deloris' flight?" My words feel forced. Heavy. I'm not even sure who I'm speaking to.

The band is milling around the kitchen. Mitch is on the other side of the island trying to get ahold of Deloris. I've tried Lyric's cell phone a million times, but it keeps going straight to voicemail. Everyone else is downstairs, worrying about building our case against Crawley and devising a plan to use the original recordings as leverage to get Destiny and Crawley to hand over Lyric's songbook.

But we don't have the tapes. Because Lyric isn't here with Deloris, and no one is answering their damn phone. Not to mention, Doug is missing. Ever since I got Lyric's voicemail, I've been in panic mode, awaiting her return like a friggin' psycho.

Lyric left almost three hours ago. The airport is only thirty minutes away, and even with traffic, they should have been back over an hour ago. I shouldn't have let Lyric pick up Deloris alone, but I wanted to respect her, and I knew this reunion was important for her.

Mitch slams his phone down on the kitchen island and rubs a hand through his hair. "Deloris' phone is ringing, but no one is picking up. Which means she landed. She must have her phone on silent. Are you sure there weren't any accidents tonight?"

I look over at Hedge, who's got his laptop out, searching traffic reports. "No. Nothing like that at all."

"Have you tried tracking her phone?" Lorraine asks, wide-eyed with worry.

I let out a frustrated breath. "You think I track my girl's whereabouts like some sort of stalker?" Meanwhile I'm cursing myself for not being some kind of stalker. At least then I'd know where Lyric was.

Lorraine rolls her eyes. "No, jackass. I mean through the Cloud. You can detect the last place her phone was turned on. But you need her login information."

I don't know Lyric's Cloud account login. My mind reels, trying to remember the last time Lyric tried to find her phone using the Cloud. She loses the damn thing all the time. My eyes widen and my heart rate quickens. "Be right back."

I leap from the room, run through the foyer, and then down the stairs to her office. Her computer is but locked, but she keeps her password taped to the bottom of the damn thing. For once, I'm glad she didn't listen to me.

After logging in, I pull up the Cloud website, and there it is. The password auto-populates, and I'm in. After waiting for what feels like an eternity, the location pops up: about twenty miles away, northeast of here, nowhere near the route they should be on to bring them back to Coral Gables. Something is really fucking wrong.

My stomach clenches tight, twisting and turning, like it's wringing a sponge. Grabbing her laptop, I shoot from the chair and race down the hall and up the stairs until I'm back in the kitchen, showing everyone else. "Her phone is somewhere in Sewell Park." I look to Mitch. "Did you try the driver again?"

Mitch nods. "I called the driver directly, no answer. And then I called the company. No one knows where the guy is."

Who the fuck hired this company? I freeze the moment the thought enters my mind. *No fucking way.*

"Crawley arranged everything before he got fired. He rented this house, he hired the car service, the housekeeping, the cook, the bartender, everything. Shit."

Mitch peers at me from where he sits, eyes intense as ever. "What are you saying, Wolf?"

I clench my jaw, praying to God Lyric turns up before I set out to murder someone. If Crawley is behind Lyric's disappearance, he's a dead man walking. "I'm saying that dickhead knows where we're staying, and he's the one who hired the vehicle Lyric was supposed to come home in. She's not fucking here." I grip the counter and push off it. "I know this is a reach, but he could have intercepted her to get the tapes. He's clearly desperate. And Doug is missing too. Let's not forget that."

"The Doug thing is strange, I'll give you that. But it doesn't make any sense for Crawley to be involved," Mitch says. "Doug doesn't know what we're up to. And neither does Crawley." He shakes his head, and then his eyes wander the room.

A slow chill creeps up my spine as it hits me. *Beady brown eyes and sweat for days.* I remember how much Cole Matthews creeped Lyric out. I thought he was just a superfan, but maybe she was onto something.

"Hey, Derrick," I say. "Can you go downstairs and bring that Cole guy up here?"

Derrick shakes his head. "I would, but I don't think he's here. I saw that creep leave hours ago, right after … Lyric."

Mitch stands up, his chair flying out from under him and clanging angrily to the floor. My head falls into my hands as my elbows slam into the counter. I'm a fucking idiot. Lyric was trying to tell me how creepy the guy was, and I didn't listen. My ego loved the fact that I could make the kid sweat just by shaking his hand. I should have listened to her.

"That psycho has her. And he probably has Deloris too." I'm fuming. "If he touches a single hair on their heads, I will murder him myself."

Mitch stands near me, placing a hand on my shoulder. "I'll do worse. We need to get the police on this. We can give them her coordinates from the cloud, but who knows where they could be or how long ago her phone shut off."

"There's a timestamp on it," Derrick says, coming up behind me and pressing something on the laptop. "Seven fifteen. That was over an hour ago."

"Fuck." I slam my hand onto the counter and back away. I reach for my phone again to check it one more time for hints that Lyric may have sent me. "There's an unread text for her," I say to no one in particular, clicking into it.

Mitch walks quickly to stand behind me as I view it. "Cole" is all it says. That's the only confirmation I need.

My eyes move around the room until I find Rex. "Let's go," I demand. "Someone call the police and give them everything we know. And someone call the car service and find out who was driving Lyric. I want names. Maybe there's a GPS in the damn thing. And you might as well call Tony while you're at it to see if Doug has been found. It could all be connected." There's a sinking feeling in my chest that I can't succumb to, not while I need my focus solely on making sure Lyric is found safely.

"Let's go." Rex, Mitch, Hedge, and Derrick trail me to the front door.

The driver of another car must sense we're on a mission, because he starts to open the back door. I pull him back and eye the keys in the front seat, shaking my head. "No fucking way are you driving us. I'm borrowing the car."

"But, sir. The company won't—" I jump in the driver's seat and slam the door before he can say a word. I roll down the window. His eyes are wide as he reaches for his phone.

"We've already called the police, so don't bother. If I were you, I'd get inside that house and start talking."

Hedge is there to grab the driver's phone, and he gestures for him to follow him into the house.

I don't think about the fact that I'm stealing a car or the fact that Hedge is practically holding the guy prisoner in our rental home. All I care about right now is getting my girl back.

Derrick acts as my human GPS, directing me where to turn as he gets us to the last spot where Lyric's phone was, while I have Rex run a background check on Cole Matthews.

"What if she's not there?" Mitch asks calmly from the backseat. "Chances are she's not."

My jaw clenches. "Then let's pray the background check on Cole turns something up. He's connected to Crawley somehow. He's got to be. Why else would he want those tapes? And Lyric?" I shudder, remembering the way his creepy eyes roamed my girl's body every time he looked at her.

"What about Destiny? Let's not rule her out." Mitch adds sourly.

A heavy silence falls upon us as we realize that Lyric's mother could be behind some deranged form of kidnapping, but it's broken a few seconds later when a shrill ring slices through the air.

I scramble for my phone, push a button to put the call on speaker, take a breath, and pray to hear Lyric's voice.

"Hello," I say cautiously.

A deep voice chuckles airily. "Well, hello there, Wolf. Hope you haven't been having too much fun in Miami without me. That wouldn't be very nice, considering you're only where you are *because* of me."

My skin crawls at the sound of his voice. "What do you want, Crawley?"

Another laugh, this one louder. "Silly question. I think you know by now. Don't you? Lyric has been keeping me company. Don't worry, pretty boy, she's safe and sound. For now."

"And Deloris?" I ask, my jaw tightening at his last words.

"I haven't offed her yet, if that's what you're getting at."

My stomach drops, but before I can say anything, Mitch clamps a hand on my shoulder. I make eye contact with him in the rearview mirror and he shakes his head, warning me to stay cool. We need to figure out where Lyric is, and me flipping my lid now won't help us.

"What do you want, Crawley? Just tell me what you want, and then you can tell me where Lyric is."

I hear a whimper in the background. It doesn't sound like it belongs to Lyric, so I assume it's Deloris. My stomach twists as I bite my tongue.

"A little birdie informed me that our contract won't hold up in court, and Destiny got fired from the label yesterday, which means I have no one to manage, no money to start my own label, and my reputation is in the shitter. But none of that matters, does it? Because I have your precious Lyric and Deloris, the mother she always wanted. Do I have your attention now?"

A tortured scream tears through the short pause and my heart shatters into a million pieces at the sound. *That* was Lyric. I pull the car over to the side of the road and put it in park, gripping the steering wheel and imagining it's Crawley's neck.

What is he doing to her?

"If you touch her, you're dead. Do you hear me? Imagine the most excruciating pain you've ever suffered and multiply it by a hundred. You are fucking dead."

Crawley laughs, and I barely register Mitch leaving the backseat, opening my door, and pulling me out of the car. "You, take the back. We need to keep moving, and you need to keep him talking," he whispers. "For as long as possible. We're almost to the last spot Lyric's phone was detected. Try to get Crawley to turn it back on without raising suspicion." He turns to Derrick. "And you have Hedge keep alerting Lyric's phone until we know where she is."

I suck in a breath and nod. Why didn't I fucking think of that? Adrenaline surges through me like a wildfire. I like having a mission. A mission gives me something to focus on other than that scream.

Mitch nods to the backseat, where Rex is tapping something on his phone. I scramble in and return my focus to Crawley.

"I don't think you understand who's about to kill whom, Wolf," Crawley is saying. "I'm afraid you're about to get a hard lesson about who's the boss around here. It will always be me. Now listen up," he says. "I need money, and I need a plane out of here. When I get to where I'm going, I'll make arrangements for you to see your precious Lyric again."

I grit my teeth. "Alive," I huff out. "When I see her again, she better be alive. You don't have to ask twice about the money or the transportation. But we're doing this shit tonight. You're not touching a hair on either of their heads."

He chuckles again, and I swear, the first thing I do when I come face-to-face with Crawley—because I *will* come face-to-face with Crawley—will be to grab him by the throat so he can never laugh again.

"Easy now, tiger. Travel arrangements take time. And so do wire transfers. I have a contact waiting for you at the Miami airport. Be there in no more than two hours with your bank account information. You'll recognize him." He's talking about Cole. I grind my teeth to keep from saying something I'll regret. "He'll be assisting you in your wire transfer of ten million dollars. Once the amount is secure, I'll get on a plane—to where, you'll never know. When I touch down, and not a second sooner, I will make arrangements for Lyric to be delivered to you."

"What about Deloris and Doug?" Mitch asks from the front seat.

There's a second of silence as Crawley registers the new voice. "Mitch, you bloody wanker!" he says, his voice like venom seeping through my veins. "I'd recognize my old pal anywhere."

Mitch shakes his head, holding back his own retort.

"Congrats on the new gig managing Wolf," Crawley says, his tone dripping with sarcasm. "I think it's a fine choice, what with your music going to shit anyway. You have some pretty big shoes to fill, though. Your ex-wife got to take an extra close look recently, and I'm happy to report, she'd agree."

Mitch shakes his head as he continues. "Enough, Crawley. You have a deal. Ten million. We'll head to the airport now. What about Doug and Deloris?"

"I suppose I can deliver Deloris, but I don't know about Doug. Haven't seen the lad." I can almost see the creepy grin on his face, and I can't wait to wipe it off with my fist.

"Put Lyric on the phone," I demand.

Crawley groans loudly. "Shouldn't you be rushing off to the airport?"

"I need to know she's safe," I say, raising my voice.

"She's fine. Have I ever lied to you?" He laughs again, making my blood boil.

I look up to catch Mitch eyeing me, silently telling me to calm the fuck down and keep Crawley talking. I turn to Derrick, who is quietly giving Mitch directions. They know what they're doing. And they're calm because we've almost made it to the pinned location. Lyric is going to be fine. I squeeze my eyes shut, and for the first time in my life, I pray.

Rex nudges my side and hands me his phone. "We have a lead, boss."

I swallow, almost nervous to take it from him to see what he's found, but I do, because it's all we've got. Cole Matthews' background profile is on the screen, and when I see what Rex is referring to, I freeze.

Cole Matthews, descendant of Rebecca Matthews. Also related to a Lionel Crawley. Mother died in a home robbery seven years ago when he was eighteen. I dig deeper into his profile, the blood pumping fast through my veins as the connections become clear.

"Holy fucking shit."

Chapter Twenty-Four

Lyric

Crawley taunts Wolf on the other end of the line, a wicked smile playing on his face the entire time. I want to tell Wolf that I'll be fine. Coming here will only put him in danger too, and I couldn't live with myself if he got hurt. We're already in this mess because of me. Well, because of Destiny and what she wants to steal from me. It might as well end here.

The moment we arrived, Crawley and Cole hauled us in through a garage, into a family home, through an open door, and down a wooden staircase to the basement. They tied us up with ropes at the opposite end of the room against a wall, then grabbed socks from the laundry basket, balled them up, and shoved them in our mouths. I couldn't talk to Wolf if I tried. All I can make out are muffled moans and muddied sentences. I was happy to get one good scream in before Crawley stuffed my mouth. Unfortunately, I had to get kicked in the stomach to get it.

I've looked for any sign of my mother, but it doesn't seem like anyone else is here. Does she know that it's come to this? That her daughter has been tied up by a psychopath on a get-rich-quick mission? Is she going with him wherever he's going? I hope so. I'm not sure I could ever stomach the sight of her again.

"What in bloody hell are you talking about, Wolf? What message?" Crawley screams. Then he paces the cluttered room as he listens.

We're in a basement of a small, residential home. It must belong to someone Crawley knows because he seems awfully familiar with it. He knew just how to get in and where to go, and he didn't have to search long to find the supplies he used to tie us up here.

I work against the ropes, tugging and turning my hands to loosen them as much as I can, ignoring the chaffing of my skin as my wrists grow raw with the friction. I let out a silent cry when one of my wrists twists a little too far.

Deloris makes a sound next to me, so I look at her. She silently pleads with me to stop. I have to fight the tears when I make eye contact. Why did I bring her into this mess? She had a good life back home. No drama. She's done more for me than my own mother ever has, and this is how I repay her.

Crawley is still in a heated exchange with Wolf when he runs up the basement stairs and slams the door behind him. When he returns a few minutes later, he's holding my cell phone tight in his hands and his own phone to his ear. Then he places the call on speaker and kneels down in front of me.

His eyes are the muddied brown like his son's. No wonder Cole creeped me out from the moment I laid eyes on him. He's Crawley's spawn. Like father, like son—pure evil.

He yanks the gag from my mouth as he powers on my phone and then glares deeply into my eyes. "What is your passcode, Lyric? And don't even think about lying to me. If you do, you'll suffer greatly."

"Don't you touch her!" Wolf screams.

Crawley ignores Wolf and glares at me. "Your passcode, Lyric. Now."

"Seven, six, four, four." I look at the phone, wanting to say something to Wolf, to tell him not to bring himself any deeper into this. And to not give Crawley a penny of his money. If it were just me tied up in here, I would. But I need to get Deloris out of this psychopath's house as fast as possible.

Crawley scans my phone for whatever Wolf has him looking for. "Where is the goddamn message?" he growls.

Message? And then it dawns on me. Wolf must have told him about the text message I wrote with Cole's name and nothing else. But why? Before I can question it anymore, my phone starts pinging loudly. My heart takes off in my chest. I recognize that sound. A sound I've played more than enough times to know exactly what Wolf is doing. He's tracking my phone. I laugh, knowing I'll never forget the look on Crawley's face when he makes the same realization.

"What the fuck did you do?" Crawley roars. He tosses the phone across the room and it smashes into the wall, shattering into tiny pieces on the floor. Then he takes the back of his hand and slams it across my cheek. A searing pain radiates throughout my cheek and bones, my teeth ache, and I think I have whiplash from the impact.

I scream, but not because of the pain. I'm disgusted that he touched me. I can only hope that Wolf is close by. He's got to have made the connection between Crawley and Cole by now. And Crawley is over here losing his shit—not that he ever managed his temper well, anyway.

"That was the wrong move," Crawley spits before hanging up on Wolf. He presses a few buttons, glaring at me in the process, before placing the phone to his ear and walking away.

"Hey. Change of plans. Where are you?" He pauses and murmurs a curse word or two. "Turn around. Now. We're getting the fuck out of here." His eyes move over us like we're invisible. "After we finish the girls off."

The resolve behind his words make me shudder, but I'm not ready to give up. He must be talking to Cole, who's on his way to the airport to wait for Wolf. Apparently, though, Wolf is on a mission to find us instead. I take a deep breath, in and out, trying to calm my nerves. I need to focus.

When Crawley hangs up the phone again, I wait a few beats before speaking. "How do you know Destiny?"

Crawley laughs and shakes his head. "Is that what we're doing now? Is this the part where I tell you all my secrets? Give you all my motives? So you can understand why we're all in this predicament before I slice your goddamn throat?" He walks forward slowly, grabbing the back of a chair and dragging it forward. He spins it and sits down, crossing his arms on the chair back. He sets his knife on his lap, and I have no doubt that he has every intention of following through with what he said.

"Destiny Lane and I go way back. Back to the start of her career. Before princess Lyric arrived in this world. Did you know she was the first artist I ever managed? Her first demo became a hit so fast, she didn't know what to do with herself. We were on top of the moon. That was it for both of us. Our big break."

Crawley has a faraway look in his eye, but it quickly turns dark. "But then she met Mitch Cassidy, who promised her the world." His lip curls in disgust. "Mitch convinced her she needed someone 'established.' Someone that could make her into the pop diva she was born to be." He chuckles with a hint of sarcasm. "And then he went and got her pregnant. Refused to marry her." Crawley sneers in my direction and looks away. "Imagine my surprise when she showed up after the show last week to find you." He shrugs. "She was wasted. No surprise. Little cunt still can't control her drug problem. Never could.

"It worked to my advantage, though. When I met her at the show she was belligerent, crying about all the woes of her life. Her sinking career, the label's idea to give her one more shot, and the help she needed from her only daughter. You wouldn't help her on your own, so I offered. It was an opportunity to finally fuck over that cocky boyfriend of yours, and I took it."

Jesus. It wasn't just about getting royalties to Wolf's old songs. He wanted to rip his heart out, and mine, the way my mother did to him.

"But why?" I cut in, still not understanding. "Wolf treated you well. Respected you even, though I'm not sure why."

Crawley's lips curl in frustration. "Until you came along. The moment you joined the tour, I knew it was over. My time was running out. I wasn't about to let Destiny's offspring fuck up my career, but I guess it runs in the family. I tried to get you kicked off the tour after that hotel debacle, but it wasn't enough for Wright to can you. And then again after you and Wolf came out as a couple. Wright couldn't find fault since it wasn't in your contract." He shakes his head as if disgusted.

"You're not so different from your mother, you know? I knew you were the type to fuck your way to the top, and since I couldn't get rid of you, I leaked those photos from the club. But then you came crawling back to your meal ticket, didn't you?"

"You leaked those photos?" I say, my stomach twisting with anger. Wolf guessed it, but I couldn't comprehend why anyone would do something so cruel.

He sneers. "I already had plans to cash in one day if Wolf ever betrayed me. Turns out my plan was botched from the beginning. So here we are."

Crawley's phone rings, and he turns away to answer it. I twist my wrist one last time, finally working my fingers through the small opening of the ropes. Pain shoots up my arm, but I don't care. I continue to pry my hands through, grinding against the threads until I feel the sharp pain of my skin rubbing raw against the fibers.

My mouth opens in a silent cry from the sting, and I squeeze my lids together just as my fingers slip through.

I let out a breath, shake my hands a few times, and then work on my feet while Crawley's back is still turned.

He's talking to someone about a car. But what's going to happen to us? I look at Deloris, who has tears running down her face. I give her the most pleading apologetic look, and I keep working. I don't stop until I've loosened the ropes around my feet and the ones around Deloris' hands. I don't take them off completely just in case Crawley were to turn. If he sees what I'm doing, it'll be the end.

"Everything will be fine, I promise," I whisper. And then I reach up to the seat of the folding chair where Crawley left his knife and grab it, placing it behind my back before he can turn around to see me.

He growls something into the phone and walks toward the stairs as my heartbeat thunders in my chest. "I'll meet you in the garage. Leave the car running. You'll help me with the older one." Without another word, he hangs up and then takes off up the stairs in a half-run.

I work fast, kicking my feet free, then removing the rope from Deloris' wrists and legs and the gag from her mouth. She cries out a little, but I shake my head, holding a finger to my lips, in a motion for her to stay quiet.

I help her off the floor and over to the other side of the room, beneath the stairs where I can hide her in the shadows. I swallow as I think of my old hideout underneath the roof stairs at the Aragon. How I met Wolf for the first time at fifteen years old on what I thought was the worst night of my life. I think I'll need to reevaluate that. Tonight might just take the cake.

Searching around the dimly lit basement, I find the gun Crawley aimed at me when Cole dropped us off at the house. It's sitting on desk on the other side of the staircase, right where I saw him place it earlier. Why he wouldn't take it with him to go upstairs is beyond me. Something has him panicked. Distracted. Probably the fact that Wolf outsmarted him once again by getting him to turn on my phone.

I grab the gun and then dart back to the stairs where I wait. I stare down at the shiny, black revolver in my hands. It's probably the only time in my life I'll be happy to see a gun. When Tony first took me shooting, I thought he was crazy. But I understood. Originally from the South, he was raised on hunting and fishing. I drew the line when he bought me a pink revolver, though. As cute as the deadly weapon was, there was no way I would ever be comfortable having one so close to me on a regular basis.

A minute later, I hear the creak of the door at the top of the staircase, followed by the sound of it hitting the wall. A shallow light streams from above, illuminating the space where Crawley had left us tied up.

"What the fuck?" he yells when he sees we're gone.

I step into the light, gun already raised in the direction of his voice at the top of the stairs. With the safety already unlatched, I angle it at his chest. His eyes find mine just as I begin to pull the trigger.

I'm steady, focused on my target, and I don't wait another moment. A moment could mean I miss. A moment could give Crawley enough time to lunge for me. A moment could be the difference between life and death, and death isn't coming for me today.

I pull the trigger. The kickback shoots through my right arm, and a zing from the aftershock tingles through me like an electric current.

Crawley reels back from the hit, his hand moving to the spot where the bullet hit him. Blood seeps through his chest pocket. That's when I see a second figure appear in the doorway.

It's Cole. His mouth is agape as he watches Crawley fall to his knees and stumble down the first few steps, loosely gripping the railing to keep from falling down the stairs. He doesn't move, just watches me as if I've already won.

"What did you do?" Cole screams before dropping to his knees in front of his father. His hands reach for the wound, but Crawley pushes him away and points to me. "Get her," he growls.

Cole's eyes connect with mine. My gun is ready, poised in his direction, but this time I aim lower, for his stomach.

I watch as Cole reaches for the same gun he had pointed at me in the car earlier. And that's all I need to see to give myself the okay to pull the trigger again—but this time, nothing happens.

"Shit," I whisper.

I pull the trigger a few more times, but the damn thing is out of bullets. Seriously? What kind of kidnapper with the intent to kill only puts one bullet in his gun?

Disgusted, I drop the gun and reach for the knife I stashed in my back pocket. I back around the corner to where Deloris stands, shaking and wide-eyed. I gesture for her to remain silent, and she nods.

Turning back around, I wait and listen. The footsteps are slow to move down the staircase, but they're coming. I hold my breath until I can't hold it any longer. And then I hear hurried footsteps above us. When I hear the familiar voice at the top of the stairs, hope soars through me.

"Put the gun down, Cole."

It's Wolf. Tears spring to my eyes as I take my first real, deep breath of the night.

There's a clattering of feet as they move quickly down the stairs.

"Don't move another inch or I'll shoot you dead. You wouldn't be the first tonight," Cole says, but his voice sounds terrified. Between killing someone, seeing his father slowly bleeding out at his feet, and the fact that Wolf's probably double his size and angry as hell, he's got every reason to be scared.

By the charge of feet and the *oomph* of one body running into another, my guess is Wolf didn't listen to Cole's threat. There's a loud scuffle against the cement floor, and the room is filled with what sounds like fist blows and animal-like grunts.

I can't make out what's going on, so I push away from under the stairwell to catch a glimpse and see how I can help. Deloris tries to hold me back, but I plead with her with my eyes. She lets me go and places a hand over her mouth.

I need to get to Wolf.

I make out two bodies rolling around on the ground. Fists are flying, and I don't know which limbs belong to whom. I creep forward, readying my knife.

And that's when I see Cole raise the gun to Wolf's chest.

A deafening shot rings through the air, and a bloodcurdling scream flies from my throat as I fall to my knees. "No!" I cry. "No, no, no, no."

Then everything goes black.

Chapter Twenty-Five

Wolf

She's screaming, and I'm not sure if it's from pain or because she thought I was the one shot.

Cole lies on the floor below me, the gun he's holding pressed into his chest by my hands. He's dead. I don't have to check a pulse to know the body under mine is lifeless because of his own gun. Sure, I redirected his aim, but he's the one that pulled the trigger.

The first thing I want to do is go to Lyric, but I can't. Cole may be dead, but Crawley is still alive, and that gives me no comfort, even if he has been shot. I lunge for the stairs, taking them two at a time, to find Rex with Crawley in a chokehold with one hand. The other hand is emptying Crawley's pockets of whatever he's carrying. There's barely a fight as Rex tightens his hold, getting him to drop something that clatters onto the floor. His phone gleams in the light at the top of the stairs before it hits the floor.

Rushing the last few steps, I grab his phone, just as something silver slides across the floor toward me. I look up to see the most beautiful sage eyes looking at me from across the room, filled with tears but mostly relief. My Lyric is still alive. Alive and fighting.

A surge of energy rushes through me as I yank the knife from the floor and hold it to Crawley's throat.

Everyone stills. Rex, Crawley ... me. Derrick is keeping watch at the front door, waiting for the cops to arrive, and making sure Crawley and Cole stay put.

The tip of the blade has already broken skin. Blood begins to drip, but that's not what made me freeze.

A circle of blood soaks Crawley's chest pocket, and even in the dim light I can see his face turning white. He's losing too much blood, too fast. But I don't care about that.

I focus on why we're all here in the first place. Lyric's songbook.

As if on cue, sirens fade in from the distance. Time is running out ... for all of us.

I dig the blade into Crawley's neck and lean in. "Tell me where the songbook is. And then you just might get to live, you piece of shit."

Crawley growls, but it's cut short by a scream of pain. He's not going to last much longer. "Destiny ... has it," he sputters.

I pull the knife away and look at Rex. "I saw some rope down there." I point to the bottom of the stairs where I know Lyric must have been with Deloris. My chest squeezes and bile rises in my throat. I want to kill him. He doesn't deserve to live after this. But I don't want to be the one going to prison tonight. "Tie him up and call the cops."

Rex nods and I fly back down the stairs to where Lyric is standing. Tears stain her face, but she's still the most beautiful thing I've ever seen. She practically collapses in my arms.

"Baby, are you okay? Are you hurt?" I ask, holding her tight.

She shakes her head. "Just from the ropes, but that was my fault," she smiles up at me through her tears, only confirming what a badass my Lyric is. I wipe them away with my fingers and press my lips to hers, which are soft and comforting, but too soon she's pulling away. "Is Cole dead?"

I nod. "He's dead."

She clings to me, her body racked with sobs. "I thought it was you. I thought you were gone."

"Never," I say, swallowing the buildup of emotions in my throat. "I will always be where you are, do you hear me?"

She nods, and I can feel her shaking.

"Pumpkin?" a voice calls from the stairs. "Wolf, do you have her?"

Lyric pulls away turns toward her father's voice.

"She's here, Mitch. Both of them are." I look behind Lyric to a terrified Deloris and give her a sympathetic nod. What a horrific reunion that must have been. "You okay, Deloris?"

She nods and walks forward slowly. Lyric tears away from me and pulls her into a hug. They cry together, and Mitch quickly joins them, wrapping his arms around them both.

I jog toward Rex, who has Crawley secured with the ropes, and I lean in, ignoring the fact that he's practically dead. "This is what you get, asshole. You don't get a dime from me. Instead, you'll live the rest of your life behind bars for attempted murder, kidnapping, theft, and whatever the fuck else we can manage to throw at you. You're done."

"I got him, boss," Rex says gently. But even Rex's gentle voice isn't one that would lull me to sleep at night. "Go on. Wait upstairs. The police will be here any second."

I hesitate for only a second, not wanting to leave Rex alone with the bastard, but one look at a semiconscious Crawley tells me there's nothing to worry about.

"Mitch," I call. "Let's get the girls out of here."

Everyone seems okay enough to climb the stairs and exit onto the front porch, just as the police and ambulance pull into the driveway.

Lyric hangs onto me while Mitch wraps an arm around Deloris, and we all take a seat on the porch stairs to wait for the police. The rest of the hour is a blur. Derrick appears by our side as police move into the house to check out the scene. When they're done, EMTs, firefighters, and more cops rush through the front door of Cole's home, escorting Rex out to wait with us and carrying Crawley out on a stretcher. After they've cleared the house, a duo of officers joins us on the porch to ask us questions.

An EMT tends to Lyric's hand wounds as she answers every question thoroughly, and I'm so proud of her. What a horrifying chain of events, but she handled it like a fucking ninja. Note to self: never fuck with Lyric Cassidy.

"I think that's all for tonight. We'll need you all to come to the station tomorrow to give your official statements," Officer St. Claire says.

"Yes, officer. We'll be there after the girls get some rest." I look to Lyric for confirmation, but her eyes are in the distance, focused on the body bag being carried out of the house.

"What about Lionel Crawley?" I ask the officer, then swallow as I watch the body being lifted into the ambulance.

The officer looks over his shoulder to glance at my object of focus and then swings his head back around with an apologetic expression registering on his face. "He's in critical condition, but he'll be on full security watch at the hospital."

Lyric lets out a loud breath beside me, and I can tell she's relieved. I'm not sure from what exactly. Maybe it's relief knowing she hasn't killed a man—at least, he isn't dead yet. Or maybe it's the fact that she's safe from more violence. Whatever it is, it just makes me want to get her home faster.

Jesus, it's been a long night. It's almost three in the morning when we finally arrive back at the house. Lyric settles Deloris in the guest room down the hall and then goes to our bathroom to shower. Derrick and Terese happily moved for the night so Deloris could be downstairs closest to us. Mitch stays in one of the guest rooms too, which I know makes Lyric happy. After the hellish night we all had, keeping everyone together is so important.

"Hey, Wolf," Mitch calls before I leave his room. I walked him up since Lyric was preoccupied with her shower.

I stop at the door and lean in. "Sir?"

He smiles. "Stop that shit. It's Mitch."

Cracking a smile of my own, I nod. "Mitch."

"Thank you for being a man Lyric can trust."

As much as I've always admired Mitch Cassidy for his talent and charisma on stage, I never, in a million years, dreamed of hearing these words come out of his mouth. Turns out, they're the only ones I care about.

"For as long as she'll let me, si—Mitch."

Mitch winks and turns away, reaching for his pillow and fluffing it. "Good to hear."

As soon as I enter my bedroom, the shower shuts off. I walk into the bathroom to find Lyric wrapping herself in a fluffy white towel. All the while, she's staring into a foggy mirror with a faraway look in her eyes.

"Hey," I say gently, slipping off my bloodied shirt and wrapping my arms around her from behind. "Are you okay?"

She clutches my hand with hers. "I wanted to kill him."

"Me too." I don't say the words she doesn't need to hear right now. That Crawley is hanging on by a thread, and he very well could be dead when we wake up in the morning.

"How did you make the connection between Cole and Crawley?" she asks.

I let out a laugh, though there's nothing about this that's funny. "We already suspected Cole was involved since he disappeared when you left for the airport, but your text confirmed it. I had Rex dig into his background, and we found that Crawley was connected to him, but the background check didn't say how. It did say that Cole's mom, a Rebecca Matthews, died years ago. So after we tracked your phone and Crawley hung up on us, we found the number for Cole's aunt and she told us everything. Crawley abandoned Rebecca when he found out she was pregnant. Cole looked him up after his mother's death and has been trying to impress him ever since.

"The dick never told us he had a kid. My guess is he wanted to keep it under wraps since he had Cole helping him sabotage contracts."

Lyric is shaking her head. "I knew something was off about that guy."

I squeeze her hands. "You were right, babe. I should have listened to you. Crawley tried to set us up years ago, and Cole was part of the plan. Crawley bribed Fredrick. Wolf's legal representation in exchange for hiring his son."

I'm still pissed as fuck to find out how badly my original lawyers screwed me.

"But that's a conflict of interest." There she goes again, reading my mind. "Why would your lawyer agree to that?"

"Fredrick admitted he was desperate for the business and didn't see the harm. When Hedge told him what was going on with Cole and Crawley, Fredrick spilled everything. I don't think he had anything to do with what happened to you tonight. I don't know. I still fired him, and the cops took him to the station to question him further."

"Well, they all deserve to fry."

I chuckle at Lyric's animosity. "Anyway, having Cole working at the firm gave Crawley the perfect opportunity to get close to the contract and amend it as he pleased without us being the wiser. Rookie mistake on my part."

She leans against me and places her check on my chest. "Crawley represented Destiny, you know? Before she met my father. He managed her debut single and then got cut loose because my dad talked her into different management. He's been holding a grudge on our entire family ever since.

He saw an opportunity when Destiny came to the show last week, and the rest is history."

I grind my teeth as I chew on that information. "Well, thank God it's over." I press my lips to Lyric's temple. "Are you okay? I know I keep asking you, but that was fucked up back there. You must have been scared."

She turns and wraps her arms around my waist, placing her cheek on my chest. "I was scared. But I'm okay. If anything, I feel bad that I dragged Deloris into all this. She's never going to want to talk to me again."

I feel a tear fall on my bare chest. "Baby, that's not true. This isn't your fault. You keep saying it's on you, and it's not. Crawley is dirt, and he's going to rot in prison."

"If he lives," she reminds me.

I nod. "If he lives."

She sighs. "Whose house was that, anyway? Crawley knew his way around pretty well."

"You were in Wynwood, and it was Cole's house."

The questions just keep coming. As soon as one gets answered, there's another on the tip of her tongue. "What about Destiny? Where is she?"

I sigh and shake my head. "I don't know. That's the final mystery to all of this. She and Doug are nowhere to be found."

When Lyric's breathing regulates, I lift her onto the counter and place her face in my palms, searching her eyes. "Stay here. I'm going to shower, and then I'm taking you to bed. You need rest."

"I need *you*," she says.

I smile and press my lips to hers. "Baby, you need rest. You have me for the rest of your life. Tonight, you sleep."

She shakes her head. "No. Wolf, I almost lost you tonight. I saw him point that gun at your chest and then I heard the shot. I thought—"

"Shh," I say when she begins to get worked up again. "I said I'm never leaving you, and I meant it."

"Make love to me. Please. I need you to make love to me. I need to wake up from this nightmare. At least help me try."

Jesus. I can't say no.

I take one of her wrists and kiss the inside where it's been bandaged. And then I slowly work my way up her arm, to her shoulder, and then to her neck. My eyes meet hers with caution.

"Are you sure?"

Her nod is slight, but firm.

With a finger, I pull on her towel and let it fall to the ground. Her legs open for me and I wedge myself between her thighs before taking her mouth in mine and giving her what she wants and more.

Her hands are on my jeans, unbuttoning them and working my pants down over my ass, taking my boxer briefs with them until I spring free. I growl tenderly into her mouth, and she moans softly into mine. I'm pulling her closer so my cock nudges up against her entrance, but I don't try to enter her yet.

I run a hand up her sides until I brush the underside of her breast. "I love you," I murmur against her lips.

Her words are incoherent as she murmurs something back and then wraps a hand around my length and tugs. My next breath catches in my throat. Feeling Lyric touch me now after everything we've been through the last few days—hell, the last couple weeks—is a gift.

She strokes me, and I push myself into her hand before tilting her back so I can grab hold of her breast with my mouth. I give it a little lick before swirling the peak with my tongue, and then I take it in my mouth, sucking and nibbling until she moans my name.

Her hold on my cock tightens and blood rushes to my head as my heart rate speeds up. Fuck. I can't come like this. I push her hand aside and slip a finger into her sweet folds, preparing her for me, but she's already there.

With one slow thrust of my hips, I ride into her, wanting to go deeper. I take her ass and pull her forward so she's right at the edge of the counter, pull out halfway, and then slide in again, groaning when the lips of her pussy meet my base.

She's fucking beautiful as she leans back, her head tilted and her hands gripping the counter's edge. Her abs tighten every time I pull back, and her breasts move with each thrust. I watch her carefully to ensure it's pleasure registering on her face and not pain. When her breathing quickens, I know she's close.

I pull her forward, pressing her mouth to mine again, just in time to swallow her ecstasy as it rips through her. Her muscles clench around my cock, and I fill her in two final thrusts.

My lips are still on hers as I lift her from the counter to take her to bed. I'll shower later. Our mouths tangle together until we're under the sheets, and then my cock is thickening for her again.

We make love again, this time slower, more intensely, just like those times on the bus that I'll always cherish. Because being inside Lyric is almost as good as writing the sweetest melody. Soft, slow, intense, addicting ... perfect.

I've found my perfect song. And there will never be a sweeter melody than Lyric.

Chapter Twenty-Six

Lyric

It's almost noon when I finally wake up. The French doors leading to the pool are open, letting fresh waves of heat and wind pour into the room. From where I lie, there isn't a cloud in the sky, but a row of palm trees sways with wild grace, and waves are rushing the shore.

Today is new beginning for everyone. A new day where we don't have to live in fear or question the motives of those around us. A day when my family is all here under one roof.

Family. My chest warms at the word. The definition of family isn't what I once thought it was. It's better.

I slip out of bed, feeling the aches and pains of the night before, heavier on my mind than on my body. With each twist of my head, I remember the car jolting to a stop and the powerful slap across my face. With each roll of my wrists, I remember the ropes. My throat is dry and my jaw aches, which is when I remember the sock gag in my mouth.

It's safe to say I'm a little banged up, but it was the fear of what could happen to the people I love that hurt me the most.

I slip on a pair of shorts and a tank top, brush my teeth, and step out onto the patio. There's light chatter coming from the other side of the pool. Everyone appears to be out here.

The band and crew, my dad, even Deloris. I'm walking toward them slowly to avoid damaging myself further.

Wolf stands when he sees me approach and pulls out a seat for me between Deloris and Mitch. I smile in thanks, kissing his cheek before sinking in between them.

Deloris has a smile on her face, which brings me the most relief. I hug her, my throat clogged with emotion as I remember all that she went through just to bring me some stupid bag of tapes. "I'm so sorry," I whisper.

She squeezes me, just as I knew she would. "Nonsense. You have nothing to be sorry about, dear. Those men were monsters, and you saved my life." She runs a hand over my head and pulls away, wiping the tears now falling from my eyes. "But who taught you how to use a gun?"

Laughter fills the air, and I look around and smile, my eyes catching on Wolf's. "Tony, actually."

His eyes widen in surprise and then he smiles. "I guess the guy was good for something."

Mitch clears his throat, and I turn to hug him. "Hey, pumpkin. Speaking of Tony."

I frown. Do we really need to talk about Tony this morning? "Yeah?" I ask, cautiously.

"Well, he posted a confession all over social media last night. He admitted to cheating on you, to starting that fight in the club that night, to hurting you, and to giving Wolf a good reason to clock him—he confessed to everything." He waits for my reaction to continue. My thoughts are too busy trying to remember our conversation when I told him to give me a reason to trust him. *He actually went through with it.*

"Tony's five-year contract has been placed on suspension," Mitch says. "He can't record any songs, even under new representation. And his current representation thinks he needs a long break.

My jaw drops wide. Holy shit. "Wright will probably lose his shit over that one." Salvation Road was a huge moneymaker for Perform Live."

Mitch nods. "I'm pretty sure Wright *did* lose his shit when Soaring threatened to pull all future contracts with Perform Live."

"What?" I ask, breathlessly.

"The executives at Soaring are pissed that they had to hear about the truth from Tony after the fact, and not from Perform Live. You could have sued the label, Lyric. Soaring knows how much shit they could have been in for that type of behavior and for not doing anything about it."

Wow. Just thinking about Perform Live losing a handful of contracts is enough to set my thoughts down a long, windy path. My friends work for that company. I don't want anyone getting fired. Hopefully Wright will use this as an opportunity to do right from now on, instead of focusing on the bottom line while sacrificing what's right.

"Hey," I say, suddenly panicked. "Has anyone found Doug?"

Mitch and Wolf exchange looks as if there's a piece of the puzzle they haven't clued me in on. Wolf catches my eye first, so I wait for him to speak.

"He's okay," Wolf assures me. "Destiny called Doug to pick her up from some motel in Miami. I guess Crawley went apeshit on her too and dragged her out here. She says she didn't want any part in his plans to take you, although she also claims she didn't know what his plans were. After everything Destiny explained to him, Doug didn't want his phone or anything else to potentially lead Crawley to him, so he left his things on Tony's bus and picked Destiny up. She was high as a kite, and he took her to a hospital. They're transporting her to a detox facility today. From there she'll go to rehab."

I shake my head, confused. "So, Destiny wasn't in on Crawley's plot to take Wolf's money and leave the country?"

Mitch shrugs. "Apparently not. Who knows what we can believe, though. The point is, Destiny is getting serious help. This time, they're not letting her leave rehab until the doctors give her the all-clear."

"And what about my songbook?"

"Doug is bringing it by this afternoon. He wanted to stay with Destiny until she got transferred. I guess to make sure it actually happened."

I sigh and relax against the back of my chair. "I hope she does get help. Real help." I look at my dad, hoping that this is the end of all the craziness that's filled our world in such a short amount of time. Because while the crazy may have brought us all together, I just want to focus on the *together* part for a change.

I turn to Deloris next. She pats the top of my hand with her free one. "Stop giving me those sorry, puppy eyes." She nods at the empty plate in front of me. "Fill up and eat. You never know when you'll need your energy around here."

Everyone laughs as I do as she says, because as always, Deloris is right.

It's almost nine p.m. when Doug finally shows up, walking through the foyer and into the living room. He looks about five years older than he did last week, probably from the combined stress of Destiny and Tony.

I want to cry when I see my songbook tucked under the crook of his arm. It looks the same as I remember it, completely unharmed—unlike my poor wrists, which are bruised and raw from trying to free myself from a rope knot like fucking MacGyver. I roll my wrists subconsciously and sit back, allowing my dad to greet Doug first.

There's a long hug and a lot of back patting, their voices hushed for a few minutes. All the while, my hands are itching to steal my songbook back. Wolf must sense my anxiety because he stands from the couch first and holds out his hand, smiling down at me.

I take it, feeling Wolf's warmth in the simple touch—one that knows me all too well. I never thought I was the type of person who wanted anyone to know me inside and out. There's too much to lose when someone holds your heart—truly holds it.

But with Wolf, it's always been deeper than a simple attraction and great sex. It's a connection that started at fifteen years old, when each of our worlds were right at the edge of falling apart, yet neither of us knew it. We were kids, too wise for our own good. Kids who grew up way too fast in an industry designed to destroy innocence in one clean sweep. Somehow, we held on … and then we found our way back to each other.

When Doug is done speaking to my father, he pulls me toward him in a strong embrace.

"I have something for you," he teases, his voice thick with the same compassion a father has for his child.

Doug could never replace my father, but the fact that he's always embraced me like I'm his means more to me than anyone will ever know. He was there when I needed him … when my flesh and blood wasn't. Not because my father chose to stay away—that was completely my doing. But still, Doug was there when I needed him, never asking questions, never adding pressure. He's just another light in the bright, shining chandelier that's become my family.

"Thank you, Doug," I say, taking the book from his hands and holding it to my chest. "For everything. Thank you."

He cups my cheek and holds his forehead to mine. "No, Lyric. Thank *you*."

Once upon a time, Doug told me a story about himself that will forever stay close to my heart. The story of a proud gay man who has been with the same partner for twenty-plus years. He's always wanted kids, but for whatever reason, the man he loves never shared the same dream. Doug, being the selfless man he is, accepted this fate.

Deep down, I know there's something about our relationship that fulfils that dream for him. And I welcome that. It's enough, for me. And I know now that it's enough for him.

Epilogue

Lyric, nine months later

The man waiting for me when I exit the plane in Chicago is the exact opposite of what I expected. With dreadlocks so long they practically reach his ass and thick-rimmed glasses that hide far too much of his caramel eyes, I'd say this is Wolf's best disguise yet. But not even the brightly colored poncho can fool me when a huge grin lights up his face.

I'm one of the first passengers off of the plane, so there's plenty of room when I run the remaining distance to him and jump into his arms. Our bodies collide, our mouths crash together, and our arms squeeze each other tight.

I can feel it. Our energy sparking the air. Two dangerous souls finding a match in each other. It's clear our love is more intense than ever—so much so that after spending the week apart, a tear slips from my eye and my heart feels like it might explode in my chest.

"Babe, don't cry," he murmurs against my lips.

I bury my face in his neck and smile. "I've missed you so much." But he already knows this. He knows how emotional I've been this week. Abnormally so, but understandable given the situation.

It's been three months since the final leg of Wolf's European tour ended. I stayed on the payroll, but no longer as his road manager. Wolf, the band, and I agreed that it was best for me to hand that title over to someone else. Someone who wouldn't be screwing the lead singer every chance she got. Instead, I became Wolf's co-writer. Together, we wrote eight new songs for the band's next album. Wolf wrote the rest on his own.

Correction. Wolf didn't just write the rest of the songs. He wrote the hell out of them and then dropped the mic. I've never seen someone so dedicated to extracting their soul onto paper like that. It was like all the words were there, brewing, like prisoners waiting to be unleashed.

And the momentum hasn't stopped. Wolf has spent the last two months with his band in the studio working on the new album. Which is why, when I decided to visit Destiny at her rehab facility in Malibu, Wolf agreed to let me go alone.

Just over a week ago we received news from Davis that Crawley died in prison. He picked up an infection that he couldn't fight off, and that was the end. I can't help but think it was the gunshot wound to his chest that helped him reach his end faster, but I feel no guilt. No regret. Just … disappointment that a person could become so desperate to take something that wasn't his that he would hurt whoever stepped in his path.

After I heard the recent news, I planned a trip to see Destiny. I figured after nine months, it was time to face the woman that practically sold her soul to the Devil himself. At the very least, it was time for closure.

When I arrived at the rehab facility, paparazzi were everywhere, as if waiting for Destiny to be released so that they could pounce. Immediately after the "incident," as we call it, the media went crazy. Someone leaked the entire story to the press, beginning with the songs Destiny stole from me when I was seventeen. It's been insane, but at this point I'm getting used to the spotlight.

By the time I got to Malibu, she'd already heard the news of Crawley's death. She was somber about the whole thing, admitting that she trusted him for all the wrong reasons. And for the first time in my life, I saw something that resembled defeat in my mother's eyes. The game was over. The only thing she could do now was get better and find a way to move forward.

I dry my eyes with the back of my hand and look around in confusion when it dawns on me where Wolf and I are standing. "You were supposed to wait for me outside baggage claim. How did you get past security?"

Wolf grins and nods behind him at Rex. "I couldn't wait that long, so we bought tickets."

"To where?" I ask incredulously.

He shrugs. "I'm not sure." He pulls out the tickets from his back pocket, and I swipe them away.

"St. Louis?" I burst into laughter. "Really? You could have chosen to fly anywhere and you chose a city that's two hours away?"

Wolf shrugs, his face flushing. "Hush, woman. I asked for the cheapest flight and bought two tickets so Rex could keep the ladies away. It was supposed to be a romantic gesture."

I tug at a loc of his wig and tilt my head. "I'm pretty sure this getup worked just fine at keeping the ladies away. You didn't need Rex."

His eyes narrow dangerously, making me giggle. In an effort to soothe the blow to his ego, I wrap my arms around his neck and bite my lip. "Hmm. Were you hoping this romantic gesture would help you get lucky?"

There's a twinkle in his eyes as his palm slips down to grope my ass over my jeans. "As a matter of fact..."

We laugh and kiss until the plane begins to dump out the coach passengers, and our lip lock is rudely interrupted by a couple elbows.

"C'mon," Wolf says as he weaves his fingers through mine. "We've got somewhere we need to be. And I want to hear about your visit on the way."

He leads me through the airport to the exit where a limo is waiting for us. That's different. We never rent a limo unless the band is going out somewhere nice.

The driver holds our door open while we slip into the backseat and wait for Rex to collect my baggage. Wolf wastes no time removing his disguise and pulling me onto his lap so that I'm straddling him. He reaches for my hand, kissing each finger as he speaks.

"Was it hard to say goodbye?"

I spent every day of the past week with my mother at her rehab facility in Malibu. There were good moments and bad moments, and in the end, I came to the conclusion that Destiny will always be Destiny. With or without the drugs, she's still a cold and cynical woman, although somewhat subdued now.

She was kinder to me this week than she's ever been. Apologetic, even. But I don't think her resentment will ever go away. It's buried too deep. But I don't even think it's me she resents. I think she resents herself.

Hopefully her pain is something she can get to the root of and heal, but that's not for me to worry about. But I will wish her the best and hope that she finds happiness the way I have.

"After the week we spent together, goodbye was almost cathartic," I tell Wolf, leaning in until my body relaxes against his. "It felt good to walk away without animosity, knowing that I gave her my all this week. She seemed to accept it this time, not that she had much of a choice."

I lift my head and Wolf brings his nose to mine to gaze lovingly back at me. "She's lucky to have you, babe. But next time, I'm going with you. Even if I'm forced to drink Coronas on the beach while I wait for you outside the facility."

I laugh. "You're so sweet to take one for the team, but that won't be necessary. Destiny's getting out in two weeks, and then she's selling her house and moving to Malibu."

"She must really like it there."

"The change will be good, too. It's not like she has a music career to go back to, so she's gonna have to find some new hobbies."

It wasn't my intention for Destiny Lane's thievery to go public, but her betrayal made huge news—almost bigger news than the kidnapping. But even with everything out in the open, I refused to file charges and refused the rights back to the songs on *My Forever*. That part of my life is over and done with, and I don't need the royalty checks as a constant reminder of the suffering.

I'm happy with where I'm at, living with Wolf in a hotel in the Chicago Loop while we figure out our next step together. I've toyed with the idea of us finding a more permanent residence, something I keep hinting to Wolf about, but I won't pressure him. We both got into this relationship with an understanding that we're comfortable on the move.

But things have changed. I want us to have a place to call our own. One day I'll bring it up to him. When the timing feels right.

A loud thud catches my attention as Rex closes the trunk shut and walks around to the front passenger seat.

"So, where are you taking me, rock star?"

Wolf wiggles his eyebrows. "You'll see in forty minutes to an hour, depending on traffic."

I grin and lean in, brushing my lips against his while I grind against the hard bulge through his jeans. His eyes blaze with heat. "That's a long time," I say. "Maybe you should put the screen up."

Wolf shifts me off of him, and I wait until the tinted glass shields us from the front of the limo. Wolf is already unbuckling his belt while I toss off my slippers and peel off my leggings and underwear.

When I climb back onto his lap, Wolf's jeans are down just enough to pull out his thick cock.

"Damn, baby. Missed me?"

His fingers are unfastening my button-down blouse as he nods slowly. It's not until he has his face buried in my chest that he lets out a moan and then speaks. "Fuck yes, Lyric."

I lean back slightly, taking away his pillow and smiling slyly when he glares. "Patience. This is for you."

Wolf's eyes follow the movement of my hand as it traces a line from my stomach to my clit. With my middle finger, I begin to circle it slowly.

"I love the way you touch your pussy," he groans. "Look at how slick you are, babe."

"Only for you." I lift my hips and come back down just like I would on his length, up and down, as my finger slides between my folds until Wolf can't wait anymore. He growls then reaches for his cock, stroking it in time with my movements.

With a coy smile, I replace his hold with mine and plant myself around him, sinking deep and burying my face in his neck. "I've missed you," I breathe.

He chuckles and bucks his hips slightly. "You missed my cock, baby. And he missed your tight cunt, so fucking much. And I think I know what missed me."

In one swift motion, Wolf flips the cups of my bra, exposing my hard nipples and pushing my breasts up so they're on display. He takes one in his mouth, wasting no time in swirling his tongue around my nipple as he grips my waist and starts moving me.

Using the back of the seat as leverage, I roll my hips as I lift and sink, already spinning from Wolf's assault on my chest. He's relentless as he bites and sucks, giving me pleasure, pain, and relief so fast I'm not sure what comes first or last. I just want more.

When one of his hands moves to my ass, I gasp as he squeezes hard and then slides a finger down, applying pressure where no man has gone before. He adds to the intensity by rocking into me just as fast as I'm moving until I begin to feel my muscles clench in anticipation.

He's got a hand on my breast and a finger pressed against my ass, and he's thrusting so hard below me I think I might combust. Ours eyes connect and something tugs at my chest. He's watching me like he's waiting for me to explode, and he can't fucking wait.

"Come with me," I beg, knowing I'm close.

He shakes his head. "You know what I want this time?"

I take a deep breath, not sure if I can hold out long enough to get my answer. "Anything," I say, already feeling the quickening heat in my belly.

"Come all over my cock, baby. And then I want your mouth around me."

Jesus. It's not even the thought of the act that turns me on. It's the fact that Wolf is practically begging for it. That's all it takes for me to fall apart, pulling myself closer to him as I do, working his cock until my orgasm tears through me.

"Ready, beautiful? I've been thinking about your mouth all week."

Pulling myself from his length, I kiss him, and then slide to his side and bury my mouth in his lap, taking him in fully the first time and letting him hit the back of my throat. But then I slow my movements to teasing. I'm going to let him enjoy this.

Smiling, I push the tip of my tongue against the bottom of his shaft and drag it up slowly until I reach the tip, knowing I'm making him crazy with desire. He growls, and I know he's seconds away from taking control and feeding me his cock again, so I circle the base and start to slide down around him, keeping my mouth tight on his shaft.

His hands are in my hair, his voice turns to a low grunt, and then his hips begin to lift, pushing me deeper and deeper with each thrust. "You are so good to me, babe. *So. Good.*"

I move down so his length hits the back of my throat again. This time I swallow, tightening around him and causing something like a roar to leave his chest.

Every sound is such a turn-on, I'm rubbing my thighs together, already needing relief again. Spreading my legs, I reach my clit and massage it as my mouth works him harder.

Wolf tugs at his shirt, lifting it to get a better view of my handiwork. His exposed stomach muscles tighten and release, and it's so fucking hot. Proof that I'm bringing him to the brink so fast. His eyes squeeze together and his head draws back like he's in pain, but I know better. I take him deep again and again, faster and faster until he's warning me of his release too late. He's already spilling down the back of my throat in a warm, steady stream, and I take it all, licking my lips as I watch him come down from bliss when I'm done.

Wolf groans as he pulls out of my mouth and lifts me by my arms to sit beside him. He's breathing heavily, and the serious expression on his face makes me all kinds of hot. He scans my expression as he slides a hand down my waist to my clit. "My turn."

With a wicked grin, he slips down onto the floor and leans his head back on the seat.

"Sit on my face," he commands.

I shimmy above him, gripping the back of the seat like I did when I rode him, and now my wet opening is hovering above Wolf's mouth. I look down just in time to see him lick his lips before he uses his arms to tug me down, holding me to him while he fiercely laps against me.

My stomach clenches and I shift my hips, wanting desperately to ride his face like I just did his cock.

"Wolf," I beg.

He murmurs something that I can't comprehend, and I fall forward from the vibrations against my core. A finger plunges into me next, a guttural groan tearing through me in shock and pleasure.

Holy hell. What is this man doing to me?

It doesn't take much longer for the build to take over my body. He licks and sucks, pulling my clit into his mouth for the final draw. This time, I can feel the intensity building even stronger than the last. I'm detonating against his mouth, and then convulsing wildly around him as I muffle my screams into the back of the seat.

I barely recover by the time he's sitting and lifting me onto his lap again, kissing me hard on the mouth like it's our first and last time. And holy shit. Somehow, in the midst of our kiss, he gets hard again, and he's wedging his cock between my folds, thrusting hard and fast in steady rhythm.

I knew he missed me, but holy damn. It's like he's been saving all his orgasms for me this week, and I'm not complaining.

"Wolf," I say, trying to connect with him. He's completely lost in the feel of me, and as much as I love that, I need him right now. I need his eyes on mine. I need our intensity. "Slow down, babe. Come back to me," I whisper.

Our gazes lock, and something clicks in him, too. He slows his rhythm, still pushing deep inside me, but this time in a way that connects us on another level. Our favorite level.

This is us.

We make love, our favorite way. Slow, soft, and intense. Wolf's drive meeting my passion. Our mouths teasing each other's in between whispered words of warning, because when we come again, we want to come together.

And when it happens—when we're both at the edge and ready to fall together, we have all the confidence in the world we'll be there to catch each other ... forever.

"Where are you taking me?" I ask Wolf again.

He just smiles and lifts his chin to the front windshield.

Huh? I look up to where Wolf's eyes are focused as we're finally putting our clothes back on and gasp. "No way!"

We're pulling into the parking lot of the complex where I used to live with my father when I was a teenager. The only place I've ever been able to call home.

"Wow. It hasn't changed much at all."

The luxury condo building on North Burling Street still resembles a palace. The same gold-wrapped metal gates secure the perimeter, cascading ivy wrapping the bars. Wolf laughs at my reaction and tugs me out of the car as soon as we're parked. He leads me in the direction of the main courtyard, which is still landscaped with a fantasy-like garden filled with artfully sculpted shrubs, exotic plants, and a climbing ivy trellis.

My breath catches in my throat when I near the water fountain and see a familiar figure. Our old landlord, Henry, approaches us with a set of keys in his hand and a calm smile on his face. I look to Wolf, afraid to read too much into this. What is going on right now?

Wolf and Henry shake hands like old friends, and the next thing I know, Wolf is taking the set of keys like they're his. Like they're ours.

"So," Wolf starts with a grin, "Mitch and I did some house hunting while you were away, and he introduced me to Henry."

I let out a laugh. "You and my dad went house hunting together?"

Wolf shrugs. "I wanted to make sure he approved."

My heart settles in my throat as Wolf confirms my hopes. "Wolf," I breathe. "Did you buy a condo?"

His hand reaches out, keys dangling from his fingertips. "I bought *us* a condo, babe."

I'm too stunned to respond, so he takes a step forward, wrapping his arm around my waist and running a finger down my cheek. "I've never needed to settle down before. Never wanted to. When you were gone this week, I started thinking about you coming home to a hotel room, and I hated it. That's not a home."

And here I thought he was spending the week married to the studio. "Our hotel room is pretty nice," I tease.

Wolf is smiling despite his narrowed eyes of warning. "We can go back there any time you want." He places the set of keys in the palm of my hand. "I want to give you the world, Lyric Cassidy. This is only the beginning. Will you move in with me?"

I wrap my palm firmly around the keys and grin. "Yes, Wolf Chapman. I will move in with you."

With a laugh, Wolf leans away, arches his back, and howls his excitement. He picks me up and swivels me around before placing me back on my feet and taking my mouth in his.

When we pull away from our kiss, his face softens. "I love you so much."

I melt in his arms, letting him lift me again so I can wrap my legs around his waist. "I love you too," I murmur against his lips. "When do we move in?"

"It's ours this weekend. It's the exact same layout you had with your dad. He said you loved it. You're not mad, are you?"

I tilt my head, confusion washing over me.

"That I did this without asking you first. I figured it was kind of a given, and your dad was pretty certain. And I wanted to surprise you."

A smile blossoms on my face so fast. "You're cute." He looks like he's about to growl, so I laugh and shake my head. "No, I'm not mad. You did this for us."

He nods. "I did." He looks like he wants to say more, but he doesn't.

How did I get so lucky? Still smiling like a crazy person, I bite my lip and search his expression. "Maybe you should take me back to the hotel so I can thank you."

He chuckles and shakes his head. "As much as I love the fuck out of that idea, I'm not done with you yet. Come on, we've got dinner reservations. And we need to get there before sunset."

"A sunset dinner, too? Maybe I should go out of town more often," I say heartily, earning a slap on my ass.

"Not happening. This week was torture, and you know it."

I do know. Our nightly phone conversations were proof of how tortured Wolf really was. I've never had so much phone sex in my life. Now I get why Derrick and Terese couldn't take their hands off each other when they were together in person. And they haven't stopped taking their hands off each other since. Terese has become a permanent member of Wolf's entourage, more in love with Derrick than ever. The feeling is mutual. Rumor has it he's planning to propose.

Our driver gets us to the Aragon in just a few minutes, and I smile. "Rooftop dinner again?" I ask excitedly. I loved our first dinner on the rooftop. It was the night we realized we'd met before, and it explained so much about our connection.

After parking in the VIP spot reserved for us, we walk in through the back entrance of the theater. Wolf leads me toward the stairs at the back of the building, and I smile at the dark corner under the stairs. There's still a couch there, cloaked in shadows, but this one is newer. If I only knew on that night, when I felt like I was in so much agony, that the boy who coerced me onto the roof would become mine.

I sigh, but Wolf doesn't give me too much time to reminisce as he pulls me up the stairs and pushes the door open at the top, letting me exit first.

It's not unusual for us to come back to the rooftop where we first met to watch the sunset views or sneak a quickie against the wall like we did almost one year ago. But this time, the scene looks different. This time, we aren't alone.

I look around in confusion as I take in the smiling faces of our friends and family standing close by. The band, the crew, my father and Doug, Deloris, Terese...

A camera flashes, and then all eyes turn to focus on something beside me. I swivel in the direction they're all staring and see Wolf sinking down on one knee and staring up at me.

Holy shit. I gasp, tears filling my eyes as my father steps forward to hand Wolf a black velvet ring box. My hands fly to my mouth in surprise, causing our guests' laughter to rain down around us. My heart is officially lodged in my throat.

In that second, when our eyes connect, I become blind to everything except for the man who captured my heart and never let it go. He reaches out a hand to grip my waist and pull me closer. And then he takes a deep breath.

"Lyric Marie Cassidy," he starts, earning a loud cheer from our guests. "I love you with every breath that's mine." His eyes are so sincere, I can't stop the tears from falling. "Since the moment we met, right in this very spot, you've been it for me. I may not have realized it then, but you were everything I always wanted but never thought I deserved."

He swallows, and I'm already shaking because I have a feeling I know what's coming next. It's something he's told me before, and I know it's going to make me cry. "Falling in love with you is something my mother warned me about. It's the one thing I've been afraid of. The one thing I didn't believe would come true. I couldn't—"

When Wolf's voice cracks, I drop to my knees and hold his face in my palms. "It's okay, babe."

He smiles through his own tears and takes a deep breath. "Somehow she knew. She knew that you would come along and steal my heart like it was already yours. You blindsided me, Lyric, but the falling was effortless." His voice drops to a whisper so only I can hear his next words. "Thank you for giving me back a piece of myself I thought I lost a long time ago. She would have loved you, babe."

I kiss him, unable to help myself. And then I remember our audience. I look around us to see our friends and family bowing with tears, covering their faces to hide their emotions.

My beautiful man loved his mother more than life, and he carried on her dreams despite his own demons. He'll never understand his own beauty, but I'm more than happy to remind him of it every single day.

"Lyric Cassidy," he says finally, eyes red and brimming with emotion. "Will you be my forever?" We laugh lightly at the song reference before his expression grows serious again. "Will you marry me?"

My eyes shift to the ring box he's managed to open between us. The princess center stone practically winks at me from the box. I shake my head in amazement because Wolf blindsided me, too. He's giving me everything I swore I never wanted and more.

I slip my arms around his shoulders and nod emphatically. "Baby, I will marry the fuck out of you."

He pulls me in, smashing my lips to his, and we kiss. For how long, I'm not sure. Does it matter?

I just love this man. My heart is happy. My heart is full. And there's nothing else that can make a girl like me, one who hated the idea of a fairytale romance, feel more complete than I do right now.

And we'll live happily ever after. Until the very end. Whenever that may be.

Want More?

You do not want to miss what K.K. is working on next ;)
Sign up for new release alerts to never miss a thing!

SIGN UP HERE
smarturl.it/KK_MailList

Thank You

All the tears right now, you guys. All the tears. First of all, I am blown away by the unexpected LOVE for this story. I have never received so many messages, tags, shares—you name it—in my writing career as I did with Dangerous Hearts. You all made me so happy that I hit publish, and I couldn't wait to bring you more. So, thank you to all for enduring that short wait and cliffhanger. I don't make it a habit to torture my readers like that, but I truly believe it was the only way to tell this story.

Thank you AGAIN Roxie Madar and Jennifer Mirabelli for seeing this story in its original state and encouraging me to get it out there for others to enjoy. I am forever thankful for you both.

To my beta readers who came in at the emergency hour to give much needed feedback. Julie, Cyndi, and Amy THANK YOU! I appreciate the time you put into this one and all the feedback given to make Wolf and Lyric's story perfect.

Shauna Ward, once again, thank you for kicking my ass in the editing room. I needed that.

To my reader group, Forever Young. Thank you for spending your time with me, hanging out, having fun, sharing your stories, and supporting my work. I'm incredibly grateful for all of you and love that we continue to grow!

Foreword PR & Marketing, especially my publicist, Linda. Thank you, doll face! I love you and have so much respect for you and all that we've accomplished together. You truly make my heart (and calendar) full.

Nadège Richards with Vellum & Wing. I can't even tell you how much I adore your work. I'm honored to get to share one of your beautiful photos on my cover. Thank you for providing me with the perfect Lyric.

Sarah Hansen with Okay Creations. Always with the beautiful covers. You just can't help yourself. Thank you!

Thank you Mary Ruth (@TheReadingRuth), Bianca (@InBookEden), and Yvette Vega (@BooksandBandanas) for the stunning teasers, not just for this book, but for the duet! The level of creativity and talent that goes into making these beautiful pieces of art is out of this world. I'm so blessed to know you all!

Sammie Lynn. You, lifesaver, you. I love your 'eye' but I love you more.

Ashleigh, I'm kind of in love with you. Don't tell B. Let's make 2018 epic!

And to all the readers and bloggers with incredible passion for the written word. You spend your days (and long, late nights) reading and supporting authors like me. There are no words to describe my gratitude. I would not be able to do this without all of you.

Much Love,

K.K. Allen
XXOO

Let's Connect

Dear Reader, I hope you enjoyed Part Two of Lyric and Wolf's story! If you have a few minutes to spare, please consider leaving a review on Amazon and Goodreads. Reviews mean the world to an author. You can also connect with me on social media and sign up for my mail list to be sure and never miss a new release, event, or sale!

K.K.'s Website & Blog: www.KK-Allen.com
Facebook: www.Facebook.com/AuthorKKAllen
Goodreads: www.goodreads.com/KKAllen
Twitter: www.Twitter/KKAllenAuthor

JOIN K.K.'S INSIDERS GROUP, FOREVER YOUNG!

Enjoy special sneak peeks, participate in exclusive giveaways, enter to win ARCs, and chat it up with K.K. and special guests ;)

JOIN US HERE

www.facebook.com/groups/foreveryoungwithkk

Books

by K.K. Allen

Sweet & Inspirational Contemporary Romance
Up in the Treehouse
Under the Bleachers
Through the Lens (Coming in 2018)

Sweet & Sexy Contemporary Romance
Dangerous Hearts
Destined Hearts

Romantic Suspense
Untitled, Coming Soon

Young Adult Fantasy
The Summer Solstice Enchanted
The Equinox
The Descendants

Short Stories and Anthologies
Soaring
Echoes of Winter

I wanted to tell him all my secrets,
but he became one of them instead.

K.K. ALLEN

UP
IN
THE
TREE
G+C
HOUSE

Up in the Treehouse (Chloe and Gavin's Story)

I wanted to tell him all my secrets, but he became one of them instead.

Chloe Rivers never thought she would keep secrets from her best friend. Then again, she never imagined she would fall in love with him either. When she finally reveals her feelings, rejection shatters her, rendering her vulnerable and sending her straight into the destructive arms of the wrong guy.

Gavin Rhodes never saw the betrayal coming. It crushes him. Chloe has always been his forbidden fantasy—sweet, tempting, and beautiful. But when the opportunity finally presents itself, he makes the biggest mistake of all and denies her.

Now it's too late …

Four years after a devastating tragedy, Chloe and Gavin's world's collide and they find their lives entangling once again. Haunted by the past, they are forced to come to terms with all that has transpired to find the peace they deserve. Except they can't seem to get near each other without combatting an intense emotional connection that brings them right back to where it all started … their childhood treehouse.

Chloe still holds her secrets close, but this time she isn't the only one with something to hide. Can their deep-rooted connection survive the destruction of innocence?

Under the Bleachers (Monica & Zach's Story)

Under the Bleachers (Monica & Zach's Story)

One kiss can change everything.

Fun and flirty Monica Stevens lives for chocolate, fashion, and boys … in that order. And she doesn't take life too seriously, especially when it comes to dating. When a night of innocent banter with Seattle's hottest NFL quarterback turns passionate, she fears that everything she once managed to protect will soon be destroyed.

Seattle's most eligible bachelor, Zachary Ryan, is a workaholic by nature, an undercover entrepreneur, and passionate about the organizations he supports. He's also addicted to Monica, the curvy brunette with a sassy mouth—and not just because she tastes like strawberries and chocolate. She's as challenging as she is decadent, as witty as she is charming, and she's the perfect distraction from the daily grind.

While Monica comes to a crossroads in her life, Zachary becomes an unavoidable obstacle, forcing her to stop hiding under the bleachers and confront the demons of her past. But as their connection grows stronger, she knows it only brings them closer to their end.

It's time to let go.

To have a future, we must first deal with our pasts. But what if the two are connected?

A Young Adult Fantasy series, appropriate for all ages.

The Summer Solstice Series is a Contemporary Fantasy / Romance series inspired by magic, nature, and love. Rich with Greek mythology, romance, and friendship, the community of Apollo Beach is threatened by something dark ... someone deadly.

About the Author

K.K. Allen is an award-winning author and Interdisciplinary Arts and Sciences graduate from the University of Washington who writes Contemporary Romance and Fantasy stories about "Capturing the Edge of Romance." K.K. currently resides in central Florida, works full time as a Digital Producer for a leading online educational institution, and is the mother to a ridiculously handsome little dude who owns her heart.

K.K.'s multi-genre publishing journey began in June 2014 with the YA Contemporary Fantasy trilogy, *The Summer Solstice*. In 2016, K.K. published her first Contemporary Romance, *Up in the Treehouse*, which went onto win the Romantic Times 2016 Reviewers' Choice Award for Best New Adult Book of the Year. With K.K.'s love for inspirational and coming of age stories involving heartfelt narratives and honest characters, you can be assured to always be surprised by what K.K. releases next.

More works in progress will be announced soon. Stay tuned for more by connecting with K.K. in all the social media spaces.

www.KK-Allen.com

Made in the USA
San Bernardino, CA
26 July 2017